She stared at

Libby couldn't think of anything to say. She had opened the door expecting to find that her son's friend was a scrawny little kid with maybe a tooth or two missing, freckles across his nose and ragged-kneed jeans. She *hadn't* expected a man. A man closer to six feet than three. A man nearer forty than seven. A man wearing the green uniform of the United States Army.

She certainly hadn't expected a handsome man.

"Joe?" she asked, her voice quavering with disbelief.

He removed his cap. "Ma'am."

Groaning, she covered her eyes with one hand for a moment, then looked up at him. "I feel about as small as I expected you to be."

"I take it something got left out in Justin's explanation."

"Something," she agreed dryly.

Dear Reader,

When two people fall in love, the world is suddenly new and exciting, and it's that same excitement we bring to you in Silhouette Intimate Moments. These are stories with scope and grandeur. The characters lead lives we all dream of, and everything they do reflects the wonder of being in love.

Longer and more sensuous than most romances, Silhouette Intimate Moments novels take you away from everyday life and let you share the magic of love. Adventure, glamour, drama, even suspense—these are the passwords that let you into a world where love has a power beyond the ordinary, where the best authors in the field today create stories of love and commitment that will stay with you always.

In coming months, look for novels by your favorite authors: Kathleen Eagle, Marilyn Pappano, Emilie Richards, Kathleen Korbel and Justine Davis, to name only a few. And whenever—and wherever—you buy books, look for all the Silhouette Intimate Moments, love stories with that extra something, books written especially for you by today's top authors.

Leslie J. Wainger
Senior Editor and Editorial Coordinator

MARILYN PAPPANO

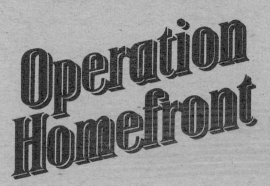

Operation Homefront

SILHOUETTE·INTIMATE·MOMENTS®

Published by Silhouette Books New York

America's Publisher of Contemporary Romance

SILHOUETTE BOOKS
300 East 42nd St., New York, N.Y. 10017

OPERATION HOMEFRONT

ISBN: 0-373-07424-7

First Silhouette Books printing March 1992

All the characters in this book have no existence outside the imagination of the author and have no relation whatsoever to anyone bearing the same name or names. They are not even distantly inspired by any individual known or unknown to the author, and all incidents are pure invention.

Printed in the U.S.A.

Books by Marilyn Pappano

MARILYN PAPPANO

has been writing for as long as she can remember, just for the fun of it, but a few years ago, she decided to take her lifelong hobby seriously. She was encouraging a friend to write a romance novel and ended up writing one herself. It was accepted, and she plans to continue as an author for a long time. When she's not involved in writing, she enjoys camping, quilting, sewing and, most of all, reading. Not surprisingly, her favorite books are romance novels.

Her husband is in the Navy, and in the course of her marriage, she has lived all over the U.S. Currently, she lives in North Carolina with her husband and son.

To the staff of Dwight D. Eisenhower Army Medical Center, the special agents of the Criminal Investigation Division Command, and the personnel of the U. S. Army Signal Center and Fort Gordon, Georgia. Thanks for welcoming our Navy family into your family.

Chapter 1

The shriek of a missile shattered the silence, followed an instant later by an ear-splitting siren. Tanks rumbled forward, crushing the flimsy, man-made obstacles meant to stop them, and bombs exploded all around, sending debris flying through the air.

Libby Harper glanced at her son, crawling across the living room floor on his belly behind an advancing army of toy soldiers and tanks, then turned her attention back to one of her most frequent pastimes lately: brooding. Today's mail, for once, had contained no bills, but only personal mail—letters from her older sister Faith in Delaware and her younger sister Renee, now living in Pennsylvania—but what should have cheered her up had depressed her instead.

Her sisters and their families were getting together for Thanksgiving in two more days. With nine kids between them, they would have a full house. Worse, the mail had also brought a postcard from her parents. They were somewhere in California, having a wonderful time, enjoying retired life and planning to spend the holiday with Aunt Mildred, her six kids and all of *their* families. Of the entire

Howell clan, it looked as if she and Justin would be the only ones spending the day alone. Again.

It just wasn't fair. When she'd decided this past June to move back to her hometown of North Augusta from Chicago, she'd had such high hopes. For the first time in his short life, Justin would be surrounded by family. He would have plenty of time to be spoiled by his grandparents and indulged by his aunts. He would have two uncles to fish and play football and do man things with, and he would finally get to know all nine of his cousins.

And *she* would be surrounded by family, too. She hadn't shared a single holiday with them in the thirteen years since she'd married Doug and left South Carolina. Her first Thanksgiving away, she had moped around all day. Her first Christmas without them, she had cried inconsolably. Gradually she had adjusted, especially after Justin was born, but she had always longed for those big Howell family celebrations.

So, when it had become apparent after the divorce that Doug had no intention of playing an active role in his son's life, she had decided to leave Chicago. There had been nothing to hold her there and fifteen very good reasons to return to North Augusta.

And now there were none.

Sighing, she slid down farther on the couch until her feet were propped on the other sofa arm. After she had moved hundreds of miles to be closer to her family, her family had deserted her. Oh, she knew Faith and Renee had had no choice; their husbands, both employed at the nuclear plant south of town, had been transferred. Naturally her sisters had had to follow, the same way *she* had followed Doug transfer after transfer. And her parents...well, they had planned this extended tour of the U.S. and Canada for years—had saved money for a motor home, had studied tourist brochures and pored over travel magazines and mapped out an itinerary that ensured they wouldn't miss a single attraction. She couldn't have asked them to postpone or cancel it just because she, like a frightened small child, had come running home to be with her family. Besides, they would be back.

Sometime in the spring.

She sighed again, the gloomiest, most morose sigh she could muster. The sound of it almost made her smile. She wasn't a brooding person by nature. In fact, her optimism, according to Doug, had been one of her least redeeming qualities. When someone tended to brood, as Doug did, the last thing he wanted was to live with someone who always looked for the silver lining.

Well, almost always.

It was Thanksgiving that was doing this to her, she decided. The family had been together for the Fourth. Labor Day wasn't that great a holiday, and Halloween hardly counted to anyone over the age of twelve. But Thanksgiving—and, next month, Christmas! Those were times to be surrounded by as many of the people you loved as possible. And as dearly as she loved Justin, he was too small to do much surrounding.

But he was certainly big enough to create an eardrum-threatening racket. "Hey," she called after a series of missile launches, "how about a cease-fire, soldier?"

He grinned at her, then solemnly intoned, "There will be no peace without victory."

"There will be prisoner of war camp for you—namely, your bedroom—if you don't turn it down," she warned just as solemnly. Turning onto her side, she surveyed the ravages war had wrought on her living room. The coffee table was on its side, and the wicker basket that belonged on it had been upended to form a bunker. Buildings, some made of blocks, others from books, were scattered around the room, and rulers formed bridges for the bombers to knock out.

Once, in the not-too-distant past, her home had been a peaceful place. Small and dangerously sharp-edged planes hadn't lined the runways created all over the floor. She'd been able to walk through a room without picking her way around battalions of soldiers, squadrons of tanks, or ammunition dumps filled with handmade missiles and an impressive array of plastic weapons. She'd been able to read or watch television or talk on the phone without being interrupted by heart-stopping explosions or sirens or battle cries. She'd been serenely ignorant of the fact that her sweet, seven-year-old son was capable of such destruction.

Now she lived in a war zone.

She supposed Justin's interest in things military was natural, considering that North Augusta was just across the state line from Augusta, Georgia, which was home to a large Army post. Many of his classmates at school had one or both parents in the Army, and several military families lived in their neighborhood.

But their proximity to Fort Gordon couldn't completely explain his newfound fascination, she knew. The first two months they'd lived here, Justin had been absorbed in typical little-boy things: fishing, baseball, video games and terrorizing his female cousins. The next six weeks his all-consuming passion had been trouble. Even now, she winced to think of all the calls from his principal, all the ominous notes from his teacher, all her talking and pleading and threatening.

Then had come war. Battles. The Army. He had dressed as a soldier for Halloween, begging for a pair of kid-size combat boots but finally settling for black high-top sneakers. He had begun watching the local news with her, focusing only on stories about the military—which, thanks to the current situation in East Africa, were plentiful—even though he rarely understood them. His career goals had changed from professional athlete and scientist in the off-season to soldier. He had even, just last week, brought home an embroidered patch, military in origin and given to him by a friend, and had pestered her to sew it onto the sleeve of his jean jacket. She had finally made time to do it, though she wasn't much handier with a needle and thread than he was, just so he would give her some peace.

But at least he wasn't beating up the kids at school anymore. He wasn't stealing homework or hiding lunch boxes or disrupting classes. He wasn't calling his teacher names that Libby herself barely knew, or spending more time in the principal's office than in class. For those small blessings, she could tolerate life in a combat zone.

For a while she had worried about his fondness for such violent play, but when she'd confided her fears to her best friend, Denise had laughed at her. Little boys had been playing war games since the beginning of time, she'd reminded Libby. That didn't mean Justin was likely to go out someday and launch a full-scale assault on an unsuspecting community. Maybe, she had suggested, it provided a safe outlet for his aggressive tendencies. After all, his behavior at school had started improving about the same time his interest in the military had developed. Maybe she'd been right, Libby admitted.

"Mom?"

"Hmm?"

"Are we having a big Thanksgiving dinner?"

"Let's see ... we're having turkey and dressing, candied yams, mashed potatoes and gravy, cranberry sauce and pumpkin, banana cream and pecan pies. I don't know. Does that sound big to you?"

"I like pecan pie."

"I know you do, sweetie."

After a brief silence, he added, "I bet my friend Joe does, too."

The name made her smile. *Joe.* It was so simple, so plain, so old-fashioned. In a world where most seven-year-olds had names such as Brandon, Christopher, Nicholas and, yes, Justin, it was refreshing to come across a little boy with a plain, simple name like Joe. "Is Joe a good friend of yours?"

Justin rolled onto his back on the floor, holding a camouflage-uniformed soldier high in the air above him. When he let go, the soldier fell and the tiny parachute on his back opened, letting him drift to a soft landing on Justin's stomach. "You bet," he replied. "He's my best friend in the whole world."

She watched as the soldier made another freefall. "You've never mentioned him before."

He didn't answer but instead supplied the steady *thump-thump* of a helicopter's blades as it flew in to pick up the paratrooper.

Libby tried again. "Tell me about Joe."

"Well, he's nice. And smart. And tall."

Justin liked tall kids, she thought with a hidden smile. She suspected it was because he was a few inches shorter than average height himself. Occasionally he fretted about whether he would ever catch up with his classmates, but Libby wasn't concerned. She and Doug had both been late bloomers, but she was now five feet nine, and Doug had topped out at six feet.

"So can he come?"

"Can he come where?"

"To dinner."

She blinked a couple of times. Carrying on a conversation with Justin while he was in battle required patience and a few good guesses. "You want to invite Joe to have Thanksgiving dinner with us?"

"Yeah. Can he?"

"Well, honey, I don't mind, but don't you think his parents would rather have him home with them for the holiday?"

Justin's giggle bubbled out, funny and soft and making her smile. "They won't mind. I want to ask him tomorrow, so can he come, Mom? Please?"

"It's okay with me." But, more than likely, she thought privately, Joe's parents wouldn't let him come. What kind of people would let their seven-year-old spend Thanksgiving with a total stranger? "But don't be disappointed if he can't."

"Joe never disappoints me," he announced with such conviction that she ached. How sad that the only person he could count on was another child. She and Doug had both let him down with the divorce, and Doug had done it again with his failure to show up for their scheduled visits. Then her parents' trip and his uncles' transfers—those had been major disappointments, too, and major contributors, she suspected, to his behavioral problems at school.

But he counted on seven-year-old Joe. She hoped the kid was up to the burden Justin had placed on him.

"Can I take my bath now?"

"Yes—but no metal toys in the tub. They're starting to leave rust stains."

He was kneeling beside a shoe box that had been converted into an airplane hangar. When she spoke, he turned and gave her a long-suffering look. "Carrier landings aren't easy, you know. Sometimes planes miss the deck and crash into the ocean."

"Not in *my* bathtub, they don't. Only plastic, kiddo."

Heaving a sigh, he replaced the handful of planes he'd picked out and chose plastic ones instead, then disappeared down the hallway.

Libby remained as she was, lying comfortably on her side, long after he was gone. She listened to the water running in the bathroom, then heard the sounds of battle resume. He was pretty talented with his sound effects—but then, what little boy wasn't good at making noise?

He was talented at a lot of things. He made good grades—now that he'd traded his goal of getting kicked out of school before third grade for the better one of becoming a soldier. And although his lack of height slowed him down, he was pretty good on the baseball diamond. He could listen for hours to his grandfather's stories about the "good ol' days" without showing the slightest hint of boredom, even when he'd heard some of them two or three times before. He adapted pretty easily to new environments, and he made new friends easily—fortunately, since Doug's job had moved them five times before Justin was five years old.

But not again. She had promised him when they'd left Chicago that this was the last time. North Augusta would be their home forever—or at least until he was grown up and could make the decision for himself. She would *never* move him again.

She had made other promises in her life. She had promised Grandmother Howell when she was seven years old that she would never leave her the way some of the other relatives had. In junior high, she had given her word to Aunt Luanne, the feminist, that she would get her college degree and never be dependent on a man for anything. She had told Billy Taggert in ninth grade that she would love him forever. Four years later she'd made the same vow to Doug at their wedding.

She hadn't kept any of those promises—though, God knew, she had tried with that last one. She had tried so hard that it had made the failure even harder to take. But she would keep this promise to Justin. She would give him a home, roots, the kind of security that she'd had growing up, the kind that could only come from stability.

Like his good friend Joe, *she* wouldn't disappoint him, either.

Libby took off work early Wednesday afternoon to pick Justin up at school. She still had some last-minute shopping to do for the holiday, and as her mother and grandmother had done for years before, she intended to get as much of the baking as possible out of the way tonight. Joe was coming, Justin had informed her excitedly last night, and pecan pie was one of *his* favorites, too, so her best pecan pie would be her priority tonight.

Slowly she inched forward in the long line of cars. Ordinarily Justin walked to the home of the older lady who watched him until Libby got home, but this morning she'd told him to wait for her near the front door. At this rate it would take forever to reach him, she thought, drumming her fingers on the steering wheel. Good thing that she was only in her usual hurry and not really rushed.

When she finally reached the circle driveway in front of the school, Justin was nowhere in sight. His teacher approached her, though, to explain that he would be out in a moment. "He's not in trouble, is he?" Libby asked apprehensively.

Miss Wilson laughed. "No, he's in the boys' room. He's really settled down, Mrs. Harper. We haven't had any problems with him lately."

"That's a relief to hear." Libby shaded her eyes as she looked up at the teacher. "Miss Wilson, Justin's been talking lately about his friend Joe. Do you know him?"

"Oh, everyone knows Joe. He's really special. He and Justin get along beautifully together. I think Joe's really had a calming influence on your son." The teacher suddenly frowned. "You aren't worried about their friendship, are you?"

"No, not at all. Just curious."

"Believe me, there's nothing to worry about with Joe. *Every* child should have a friend like him."

Interesting, Libby thought as the teacher excused herself and went to break up a scuffle. This paragon of childhood was growing more interesting with each day. He was, sight unseen, certainly the most intriguing of Justin's playmates to date.

She could hardly wait to meet him.

"Is it noon yet?"

Libby straightened from checking the turkey roasting in the oven and smiled patiently at Justin. "It's ten minutes closer than the last time you asked—and twenty minutes closer than the time before that. Did you tell Joe where we live?"

"I drew him a map. He said it was a good one." He rubbed his mouth, then his nose, transferring a streak of chocolate milk from one to the other. "And I gave him our phone number in case he needed it."

"That was good thinking, honey. It's still ten minutes until twelve, and I'm running a little behind with dinner, so it'll be all right if your little friend is late."

"He's not little, Mom. I told you, he's tall. Taller than you."

When she'd listed his talents the other night, she wondered, had she remembered to mention his gift for exaggeration? Then again, maybe Joe really *was* tall. She'd seen a few of the older students at his school. When she was their age, *she* had certainly never been that tall, that well developed or that sophisticated.

"Rinse your glass out, then go wash your face and hands. And comb your hair, will you? It's standing on end again."

While he did as she'd asked, Libby began gathering the ingredients for the dressing. The recipe had been passed down through so many generations of Howell women that no one knew anymore with which one it had originated. Someday she would give it to Justin's wife—though, hopefully, not for a long, long time. Not until he was old enough and wise enough to make a marriage that would last forever, the way her grandparents' marriage had. The way her parents' had. The way *hers* was supposed to.

She put the brakes on that line of thought. This was too important a day for her to let bitterness or resentment toward Doug and their failed marriage intrude. She could resent her ex-husband anytime, but she had only today to enjoy a Thanksgiving dinner with two little boys.

As she began measuring the spices, she heard the muted sound of a car door outside. Joe was a few minutes early, she noticed with a glance at the clock, but that was all right. His parents were probably dropping him off on the way to their own holiday meal.

She was halfway down the hall before the knock sounded. Since Justin didn't come racing out of the bathroom to greet his friend, she could only assume that the running water had drowned out the knock. That was all right, too. She would like a few peaceful moments with Joe's folks before the kids got together.

Nudging a jeep out of the way with her foot, she opened the door, prepared to give the child a warm welcome. But the welcome died unspoken, and her smile slowly faded as everything she'd heard about Justin's new friend in the past few days echoed through her mind.

Joe's my best friend in the whole world.
He's nice. And smart. And tall.

Joe never disappoints me.

Everyone knows Joe. I think he's really had a calming influence on your son.

There's nothing to worry about with Joe.

Dumbly she stared at the man waiting on her porch. She simply couldn't think of anything to say. She had opened the door expecting to find a scrawny little kid with maybe a tooth or two missing, freckles across his nose and ragged-kneed jeans. She *hadn't* expected a man. A man closer to six feet than three. A man nearer forty than seven. A man wearing—she silently groaned—the green uniform of the United States Army.

She certainly hadn't expected a handsome man.

"Joe?" she asked, her voice quavering with disbelief.

He removed his cap and held it, folded flat, in both hands. "Ma'am."

There was a slight questioning note to his respectful greeting and, underlying that, a soft, slurred Southern accent. Not a South Carolina or Georgia drawl; even after living away for so many years, she could still recognize them in an instant. No, the man wasn't from this area—but how many of the thousands of soldiers assigned to Fort Gordon were?

Groaning aloud, she covered her eyes with one hand for a moment, then looked up at him. "I feel about as small as I expected you to be."

The look he wore was solemn. "I take it something got left out in Justin's explanation."

She could feel her cheeks burning, could feel the chill air cooling them. "Something," she agreed dryly, extending her hand to him. "I'm Libby Harper, Justin's—"

Before she could finish, Justin came rushing down the hall. He slid underneath her outstretched arm, stopping only inches from crashing into the soldier. He had to tilt his head back to see the man's face, and he did so with a delighted grin. "Joe! I knew you would come! Mom said maybe you couldn't, but I told her you *always* do what you say. Dinner's not ready yet, so come see my room. I've got all kinds of neat things.''

Libby watched the man—Joe, she corrected herself, still having trouble reconciling her expectations with reality—fondly muss her son's hair. "You go ahead. I'll be there in a minute."

"Yes, sir." Justin executed a snappy salute, then squeezed past his mother and returned to his room—no doubt to set out every single war toy he had for inspection, she suspected.

Then she gave a rueful shake of her head. "I'm sorry. I just assumed you were one of Justin's friends from school."

"I am. My unit sort of adopted his school. We go there once a week and spend time with the kids." He offered his hand for the formality that Justin had interrupted. "I'm Joe Mathison."

"And I'm Libby." She placed her hand in his. He had a firm grip, but not bruising, and his palm was warm and callused. How long had it been, she wondered, since she'd met a man who worked with his hands? Not once in her entire twelve-year marriage, that was sure. Doug's friends and associates had had smoother, softer skin than her own, a fact that she'd found disconcerting after growing up the daughter of a construction foreman and the granddaughter of a farmer.

He glanced past her down the broad hallway, then returned his gaze. His eyes were blue, she noticed, as blue as any big-screen actor's. As blue as Justin's. "I didn't come here expecting to be fed, Mrs. Harper," he said quietly, as if he didn't want to risk Justin overhearing. "But it seemed to mean a lot to Justin when he asked, and I didn't want to let him down. If it's all right with you, I thought I'd just spend a little time with him, and then I'll be going."

She stepped back so that he could enter. After closing the door behind them, she gestured toward his uniform. "You must have plans." Maybe she had been gone a long time, but she remembered that the combination of dark green coat and trousers, light green shirt and tie wasn't an everyday uniform.

"Justin asked me to wear this. When we go the school, we're usually wearing BDUs—the battle dress uniform." At her blank look, he explained further. "The camouflage uniform. But Justin wanted to see my ribbons and badges, so he asked me to wear the Class A's. As for plans...well, the chow hall puts on Thanksgiving dinner for everyone who...who's interested."

Everyone who had no place else to go, Libby silently finished for him. Everyone who was too far from home, who had no family here to share the holiday with. She had been through that herself, and the understanding of just how lonely it could be prompted her to offer her own invitation. "We'd like you to join us. There's plenty of food, and the table's already set for three." She smiled awkwardly. "I really was expecting you to stay."

"You were expecting a seven-year-old."

"I was expecting Justin's best friend in the whole world. Please..."

He seemed to be thinking it over, but she wasn't sure. He was quiet for so long, and his expression gave no hint of what was going through his mind. But, with a sinking feeling, she was afraid she knew. He hadn't really wanted to come here, hadn't wanted to waste any of his precious time on her son, but he hadn't known how to refuse the invitation. Now it seemed likely that the last person in the world her son counted on was going to disappoint him. She sighed softly. "Look, Mr. Mathison, my son is a little boy who hasn't put much faith in anyone lately, with the exception of you. If you didn't want to spend this afternoon with him, why didn't you say so? Why did you let him believe—"

His eyes turned steely. "If I didn't want to be here, Mrs. Harper, I never would have accepted Justin's invitation. I don't play games with kids. I don't lie to them." He paused long enough for that to sink in, then continued. "Yes, I'd like to stay for dinner. And it's not 'mister.' It's first sergeant."

He walked away from her then and straight into Justin's room. Watching, Libby silently mimicked his last words. She didn't care if she had offended him. Justin could be Joe Mathison's best buddy, or he could simply be a passing fancy. But he was *her* son, and looking out for him, protecting him, preventing him from being hurt—those were *her* responsibilities.

She returned to the kitchen and for a moment simply stood there before remembering the unfinished dressing on the counter. As soon as it was mixed and in the oven, she would be through for a while. Just before dinner, she would reheat the light, yeasty rolls she'd picked up at the local steakhouse last night, mash the potatoes and make the gravy and carve the turkey. Then she would put all the serving dishes on the table, pour their drinks, call Justin and his friend, and sit down to eat dinner with a virtual stranger whom she had just insulted in her front hallway.

And she had thought company—any company—had to be better than a holiday dinner alone.

Joe shrugged out of his coat and laid it across the foot of the bed. It had taken twenty-five minutes for Justin to show him all his soldiers, planes, tanks and weapons; now the boy was sprawled across his bed, drawing a picture for him on a thick pad of paper.

"I wasn't sure you would really come," Justin admitted when he paused to select a different marker.

Joe took a seat on the floor so that he and Justin were on the same level. "I told you I would," he gently chided.

"I know." Justin rubbed his nose, a habit that Joe had recognized the first time he'd seen it as arising from nervousness. "But grown-ups say they'll do things, and then they don't."

Like Doug Harper, Joe thought darkly. Justin rarely mentioned his father, but he'd revealed enough to make Joe despise the man. What kind of father ignored his own son as thoroughly as Harper did? What kind of father forgot his child's birthday and neglected to send him even a card at Christmas? What kind of father could tell his little boy, "I'll pick you up at ten o'clock Saturday morning," then never show?

"Some grown-ups are like that," he admitted. "But I'm not. I've never lied to you, Justin, and I never will."

That earned him a smile, bright and innocent. As if Justin didn't know that people could sound one-hundred percent sincere while telling outrageous lies. As if he wasn't aware that people who liked him, people who loved him, could deliberately hurt him. As if he hadn't seen firsthand proof that fathers could divorce their children as completely as they divorced their wives.

It was the lack of such innocence—the sense that this kid had seen too much, experienced too much, in his short life— that had drawn Joe to Justin on his first visits to the school. He had never before met a child so sullen, so angry, so bitterly unhappy. He had never before met a child so much in need of understanding and personal one-on-one attention, the kind a teacher with thirty other students had trouble giving. So, while Joe had spent some time with all the kids in the class, he had singled out Justin. He had tried, visit after visit, to talk to him, to draw him out, to be the friend the kid had needed.

It hadn't been easy. In the beginning, Justin had ignored him or had responded to his questions only grudgingly. One time, angry and in trouble with the teacher and all his classmates yet again, he had sworn at Joe with words that Joe himself rarely heard. Somehow Joe had managed to hide his surprise, to avoid giving Justin the reaction he was hoping for.

Then, gradually, Justin had begun opening up, and one day he had told Joe everything. "My father divorced us," he had calmly said; then all the details, all the bad things, had come spilling out. His mother would endure all sorts of embarrassment if she knew everything he knew about her, Joe thought with a grin as he watched Justin work.

When the invitation to have dinner with them had come, Joe hadn't been sure he would like Libby Harper. He had blamed her, perhaps unfairly, for some part of her son's unhappiness. Maybe she hadn't spent enough time with her son or given him enough attention to balance his father's absence. Maybe she was too involved in her own life and her own problems to deal with her son's. Maybe a seven-year-old's troubles didn't rank high enough in her list of priorities.

And maybe, never having had a child of his own, he didn't really understand what he was talking about. Children were complex little creatures. One single person hadn't caused Justin's unhappiness; one single person couldn't bear the blame for it.

But he still wasn't sure he was going to like Libby.

Just as he hadn't been what she had expected, she had been a surprise, too. He supposed he had expected someone more like Justin—small, energetic, fair-haired—but Libby bore less resemblance to her son than *he* did. She was tall, taller than most women he met, and her coloring was dark, from the rich brown of her hair to the cocoa shadows of her eyes to the olive tone of her skin.

She did have one thing in common with her son, though. She didn't seem to put much faith in people. Justin's wariness came from the divorce, from his father's neglect and his family's abandonment. Those things must have affected his mother, too, and in much the same way.

The stillness in the room was broken by the rumble of Justin's stomach. He laid the pad and markers aside, then rolled off the bed to sit in front of Joe. "I'm hungry."

"I heard. Want to see if your mom needs any help?"

"Cooking is girls' work."

"Who told you that?"

"Robert Calhoun. He sits across from me at school."

"Well, Robert's wrong. What's he going to do when he's grown up and not living at home anymore? How's he going to eat?"

"He'll get him a wife to cook and clean."

Joe stood up and offered a hand to Justin, hauling him off the floor. "Not with an attitude like that, partner. Come on, let's see what's going on in the kitchen."

He didn't need directions to find his way. All he had to do was follow the aromas to the room at the end of the hall. Last Thanksgiving he'd taken leave and gone home to Kentucky to spend the holiday with his family. If he closed his eyes and ignored the quiet in the house and breathed deeply, he could believe he was there again.

But he'd never seen anyone quite like Libby Harper in his mother's kitchen. There'd been his mother and grandmother, his sisters-in-law and an assortment of aunts, female cousins and nieces. For a brief time—very brief—there'd been his own wife, until she'd decided that marriage to a soldier was never going to give her what she wanted. But Libby was different from all of them in a way he hadn't quite figured out yet. But he would. In time.

"We came to help," Justin announced.

"You did, huh?" She dried her hands and took three glasses from the cabinet, setting them on the counter. "You can put ice in these, then ask First Sergeant Mathison what he'd like to drink. But wash your hands first, okay?"

Joe leaned against the doorjamb, his arms folded over his chest. She hadn't looked in his direction yet, but she'd put enough of a twist on his name to let him know that the incident in the hallway wasn't completely forgotten, though she'd avoided revealing anything to Justin, who went racing past him to the bathroom. Joe let the silence in the room deepen before he quietly broke it. "My name is Joe."

For a moment she stood still, her back to him. Then she turned and slowly met his eyes. "I don't mean to seem ungracious—really, I don't. I guess I overreacted when you seemed so reluctant to stay and have dinner with Justin. He's been through a lot in the past year and a half and—"

"I know. To be honest, it wasn't Justin I was reluctant to have dinner with. It was you. An invitation to Thanksgiving dinner from a complete stranger feels too much like pity." He paused, glancing down the hall to check Justin's progress. The water was still running in the bathroom. "I like your son, Libby. He's a bright, funny, charming kid...and he's been abandoned by virtually everyone he loves but you."

"My family didn't abandon him," she protested hotly.

"Maybe not willingly, but the result's the same—they're gone. He's no longer a part of their lives. He needs someone to replace them."

"And you chose to be that someone." There was skepticism in her voice, doubt that he could be trusted.

"We chose each other. You have to believe me. I would never do anything to hurt him."

She parroted his own words to him. "Maybe not willingly, but the result would be the same."

He studied her for a long moment, then shook his head in dismay. "You're even less trusting than Justin was in the beginning."

"He's my *son.*"

They stood there a moment, separated by half the kitchen, their gazes locked. Then Justin returned, and Libby turned away. She felt... She didn't even know the right word to describe the turmoil inside her. Shaken? Disturbed? Concerned?

Confused. That was as good as any. Justin clearly adored this man, and his teacher had seemed truly impressed by him—although, now that she'd met him, Libby had to wonder what had impressed the single young Miss Wilson the most about Joe Mathison: his easy rapport with kids, his apparent respect for them, or his broad shoulders, clear blue eyes and ringless left hand?

And that thought confused her even more. The issue here was Justin, not his friend's physical attractiveness. Which, of course, he had no shortage of, if a woman liked big, strong men with hair the lightest shade of brown possible before it turned blond. Men with Paul Newman eyes and Southern drawls. Men in uniform.

As she bit back a frustrated groan, the buzzer on the oven behind her went off. Grateful for something to do, she grabbed the thick mitts from the counter and bent to remove a pan of steaming, fragrant dressing. The rolls went in next; then she got started on the gravy.

"Can I help?"

He had finally left his place in the doorway to help Justin fix their drinks and carry them into the dining room. Now he was standing just off to her right, close enough for her to catch a glimpse of light green from the corner of her eye. He could help by going into another room and waiting politely, the way a proper guest should, she thought with a scowl.

Then she remembered what he'd said about not wanting to have dinner with her: an invitation to dinner from a total stranger felt too much like pity. She could understand that. "Are you any good at carving a turkey?"

"I've done it a time or two."

She gestured toward the bird and utensils waiting on the opposite counter. "It's all yours." While he rolled his sleeves up and set to work, she measured flour and seasonings, drippings and broth, then poured and stirred and strained. They finished about the same time and carried the dishes into the dining room, where Justin waited, gleefully seated at the head of the table. When everything was on the table and she was seated across from Joe, her head bowed for Justin's prayer, Libby almost smiled.

Maybe Thanksgiving dinner with a stranger wouldn't be so bad after all.

Chapter 2

"Thank you for coming over. You made Justin's day."

"Thanks for inviting me." Joe stopped at the top of the steps, shrugged into his jacket and buttoned it before looking at Libby. She was watching Justin, and he directed his gaze that way, too. The boy was on his knees in the driver's seat of Joe's car, his engine and brake sounds clearly audible through the open window. The sight brought back memories of times when *he* was a kid and had played at driving, too, only for him it had been his father's old tractor instead of a car. They were good memories.

He put his cap on, then faced Libby. "I'd like to see him again."

"Why?" She shifted her gaze to him. It was steady, measuring and more than a little suspicious. "Why do you want to spend your time off with a kid you owe nothing to?"

"Because I like him," he answered honestly. "He's a special kid. And he needs me." He waited for her to argue the last point with him, but when several moments passed without any response, he asked, "How about Saturday? We

could take a picnic lunch to the lake and do some fishing."
When she hesitated, he quickly added, "Of course, you're
invited, too."

After another long moment, she nodded. "I'll take care
of the lunch."

He nodded, too. "I'll pick you up around ten."

"Hey, Joe." Justin stuck his head out the window. "Can
I have a ride in your car?"

With one last look at Libby, he went down the steps. "Not
tonight, partner. But Saturday morning you and your mom
and I are going to the lake, so you can ride in it then, okay?"

"To fish?" Justin climbed through the window and into
Joe's arms. "I haven't been fishing since Uncle Rich moved
away. We caught a fish once that was *this* long." He demonstrated with his hands spread wide, then sheepishly narrowed the gap to about eight inches. "Well, about this long.
But I like to fish. I like it more than just about anything."

"Then get your gear together, okay, and we'll see how
many fish we catch Saturday." He set Justin down, then
crouched in front of him, straightening his shirt. "Thanks
for letting me come over today."

"I'm glad you came," Justin replied gravely. "It was
more fun than being alone."

"Yeah, it was." Joe started to stand, but Justin caught
him in a sudden hug. The fierceness of it filled him with a
warm rush of emotion.

Just as suddenly the boy released him. "See you Saturday, Joe!" he called as he raced across the yard and onto the
porch to join his mother.

"See you." Joe got into his car and backed into the street.

He'd been wrong earlier, he thought as he drove away,
when he'd thought he wasn't going to like Justin's mother.
He *did* like Libby—a lot. He'd learned quite a bit about her
in the seven hours he'd spent with them. He knew that her
son was the single most important thing in her life. He knew
that, just as Doug Harper had caused Justin a great deal of
pain and unhappiness, so had he hurt Libby. He knew that

she would be as slow as Justin had been to give her trust again.

And he knew that, just as Justin had gradually come to trust him, so would Libby. It would be worth every bit of effort he spent on it.

Traffic was light on the interstate as he crossed the Savannah River into Georgia. He had lived in Augusta for over two years now, and he liked it as well as he'd liked any assignment. The people were friendly, though terrible drivers, and the city was only a few hours from the beaches of Charleston, the mountains of North Carolina and the big city bustle of Atlanta. Even better, he was only a day's drive from the family farm in Kentucky—a very long day's drive.

But, in another year, his time here would be up and he would go someplace else. In twenty-two years in the Army, there had always been one more "someplace else." The life suited him—the moves, the new places, the new people. He had joined the Army so long ago to see someplace besides Kentucky, and he'd certainly done that: Georgia, Alabama, Oklahoma, New Jersey, California, Texas, Germany, Korea, Vietnam.

There had been a time when he'd thought he would do his twenty years and a day, then retire to Kentucky, work on the farm and live on his military pension. But twenty had come and gone. Retirement hadn't held much appeal, not when he was alone and had no family of his own to settle down with. Besides, he'd been only thirty-eight—too young to get himself tagged as a retiree. So here he was, still on active duty.

He left the interstate for the expressway, then exited and followed winding streets to the apartment complex where he lived. Ever since Theresa had divorced him fourteen years ago, he'd chosen to live in the barracks on post, but at Fort Gordon those rooms were reserved for the lower-paid junior enlisted. Senior noncommissioned officers were instead given a quarters allowance and sent out to find housing in town.

Personally, he preferred the convenience of barracks life. The barracks were located within minutes of everything he needed—his job, the PX and the commissary; medical, dental and legal; the post office and gas station; the laundromat and movie theater; the restaurants, the video store, even the bowling alley. He was senior enough in rank to earn a few privileges, such as a private room. Plus, if he got shipped out unexpectedly, it was a simple matter of packing what he needed and going. No leases, no notices, no deposits to worry about.

Simple. Since Theresa, he'd kept his life simple. Work, family, friends—those had been his priorities. Women had placed a distant fourth, although there had been enough of them. Children, beyond his own nieces and nephews, hadn't appeared on that list at all.

Until Justin.

He couldn't adequately explain the bond he felt with the kid. It wasn't just Justin's need for a friend; there was also his own need to be that friend. As he'd told Libby, he *liked* Justin—liked talking and listening to him, liked playing with him. He liked knowing when he walked into that classroom every Tuesday that Justin would be waiting for him. He'd especially liked spending today with him, away from the school and the limits it imposed. If he'd ever had a son, or if he ever got that lucky in the future, he would want him to be just like Justin.

Of course, a mother like Libby for that son wouldn't be too bad, either, he thought with a grin as he parked his car, then unlocked his front door. She was pretty, though a little overprotective of her son and definitely prickly. But then, if everything Justin had said about their lives in Chicago was accurate, she was entitled to that.

He wished he could have asked her today about some of the things Justin had told him—like whether her ex-husband had always disliked their son. Whether Justin was in any way responsible for their divorce. Whether Harper really had left her for another woman. Whether she was over the guy yet.

But, of course, those weren't questions you could ask a virtual stranger, and in spite of the seven hours they'd spent together today, that was what they were. Strangers.

But not for long.

Saturday was a beautiful day, perfect for a walk in the woods, scuffling dead leaves beneath her feet—and not bad at all, Libby decided, for sitting on a bank above the lake and watching Justin and Joe sort through their tackle boxes for just the right lure. The sun was bright and warm and took the edge off the breeze blowing across the water, and the air held that special scent that she'd always associated with autumn and woods and the coming winter.

Although she had initially been hesitant to accept Joe's invitation for today, she was glad she had. She hadn't seen Justin this excited about anything in a long time. All day yesterday he'd played with the tackle box his grandfather and uncles had put together for him last summer, rearranging its contents in the numerous small compartments, making sure he had everything he needed. When she'd finally chased him out of the house so she could clean, he had gone only as far as the front yard, where he'd practiced casting and reeling in the big ones.

And even though she hadn't really expected to have a good time—she was no fan of fish or fishing—she'd enjoyed herself so far. The drive up here to the lake had been pretty and peaceful, and the lake itself had brought back a lot of memories—of her grandparents and the farm they'd worked not far from here; of long, hot summer days when she'd come here with all her teenage friends to beat the heat; of camping trips and learning to swim and trying to learn to ski.

She rolled onto her side and watched as Justin sent a sparkling silver lure flying through the air and into the water with a plop. She was too far away to catch much of the conversation, but she knew her son was having a good time. She would owe Joe Mathison a sincere thank-you when he took them home later today for giving her son two special days to remember.

After a moment, her gaze shifted to Joe. He wore faded jeans and a T-shirt a shade darker than his eyes, but the civilian clothes didn't disguise the fact that this man was a soldier. It was more than the regulation short haircut and the erect posture. There was an air of authority about him, one that he wore comfortably.

Why wasn't he married? Why wasn't he raising his own little army of sons to play soldier and go fishing with? He must be divorced—she reached that decision after little deliberation. After all, it was rare that a man as handsome as he was could escape marriage entirely. And maybe he did have sons of his own who lived with their mother in another state so that he rarely saw them. Maybe that was why he was so interested in *her* son. Maybe that was what he'd meant when he'd said that he and Justin had chosen each other—that Justin had needed a replacement father as much as he had needed a replacement son.

She gave herself a mental shake. Why was she creating a fantasy background for her son's friend when she could lie here on the quilt and, for the first time in ages, do absolutely nothing?

That was what she was doing—nothing but lying on her back with her eyes closed against the bright sun—when a shadow fell over her face. She knew it was a person because there was nothing else around to cast so solid a shadow, and she knew it was Joe who stood there. If it had been Justin, he already would have jumped on her stomach and asked for a soda or a cookie or to take his shoes off and go wading or *something*.

Goose bumps appeared along her bare arms. She told herself it was because of his shadow blocking the sun, not because of *him*. She told herself to open her eyes and casually sit up, but her movements were jerky and awkward and anything but casual.

He was closer than she'd expected. She had thought he was standing beside the quilt, but instead he was crouching beside her. Sitting up put her eye-to-eye with him, closer than she'd been to any man in a long time. She scooted back, and when she did, he sat down, not as close, but still *too* close.

Without looking away from her, Joe drew two cans of soda from the ice chest and offered her one. When she hesitated, he set it on the quilt between them, then watched her slowly pick it up. He wondered if it was him in particular that made her nervous, or men in general. He wondered what it would take to make her relax with him. He wondered what it would take to make her trust him.

He hadn't meant to disturb her. In fact, when he'd first come over here to get a cold drink, he had thought she was asleep, and that was why he'd taken advantage of the opportunity to look at her. Just look—that was all he'd wanted to do. To admire the thick, rich fall of her hair across the faded colors of the quilt. To study her face with her eyes closed, hiding her weariness, her distrust, making her look ten years younger. To appreciate, for just a moment, the long, slender lines of her body.

Then those long, slender lines had tensed, and he'd known that she wasn't sleeping at all. A shiver had passed through her, leaving tiny bumps on her arms and drawing her nipples into tight points beneath her cotton shirt. He would have walked away then—*should* have walked away then—but she'd opened her eyes, and he hadn't been able to leave.

"How's the fishing?" Her voice sounded husky, and her accent was stronger than he'd ever heard it. Because she'd been disturbed when she was nearly asleep? he wondered. Or because *he* was the one who'd done the disturbing?

"He's had a few nibbles, but no bites. It takes patience. It's good for Justin to learn that now. Everything important requires patience." Fishing, hurt little boys, their wary mothers...

She popped the top on the soda and took a long drink, then turned her gaze on Justin. "Whenever you guys get hungry, let me know."

"I think we can wait a while longer."

She nodded and continued to watch her son, and Joe continued to watch *her*. When she suddenly looked at him, he caught a glimpse of confusion in her eyes before she hid them behind a pair of sunglasses. "Thank you," she said quietly, "for coming over Thursday and for spending today with Justin. This has really meant a lot to him."

He hadn't wanted her pity Thursday, and he didn't want her gratitude today. But it was better than her enmity. It was a step toward what he did want from her: a chance. A chance to spend time with Justin, to spend time with *her*. A chance to find out exactly what it was he already felt for one and was well on his way to feeling for the other.

"I've enjoyed it," he said, finally opening his own soft drink. "It's been a long time since I've spent much time with a kid."

"Do you have children of your own?"

He shook his head. "The marriage didn't last long enough. But I have about eighteen nieces and nephews back home in Kentucky. I see them when I can."

Her smile was faint. "My older sister has five kids, and the younger one has four. I was supposed to have about that many, too."

"Why didn't you?"

If she resented his blunt question, she didn't let it show. She didn't let anything show. She just continued to stare out across the lake, keeping Justin in her line of sight. After a moment, she sighed. "Some people aren't meant to be parents."

Meaning Harper, Joe acknowledged grimly. The man must have had some redeeming qualities—after all, Libby *had* married him—but damned if he could figure out what they could possibly be. Maybe things had been all right between them until Justin was born. Maybe he'd been a good provider—although Justin had asked Joe once at school what child support was; he'd overheard his mother and father arguing because it was late *again*. Maybe he'd been a decent man who simply never should have become a father—but the time to make that decision was before the kid was conceived, not after he was born. By that time, a man lost the right to walk away if he decided he didn't like the responsibilities. He *had* to give it his best shot.

He finished his soda, rose to his knees and set the empty can on top of the ice chest. "Well, there's plenty of time. You're still young."

Her laugh caught him off guard. It was short and half-funny, half-bitter. "No one's called me young in a long time. To Justin thirty-two is so old that he can't even comprehend it. And to Doug—" Her cheeks turned rosy as she abruptly cut off the flow of words. "Never mind."

Giving her a polite smile, he got to his feet and returned to sit beside Justin. But while they traded lures for live bait, cast their lines and exchanged fish stories, his mind was on Libby's unfinished statement. What about Doug? What about her age had bothered her ex-husband? According to Justin, his father had left them for another woman. A *younger* woman? Younger than *thirty-two?* What did the man want—a child bride?

After another half hour of fishing, they set the poles aside and joined Libby on the quilt for lunch. She'd made turkey sandwiches and potato salad and deviled eggs, and for dessert she'd brought thick slices of pumpkin and pecan pies, along with a plastic bag of odd-shaped cookies.

"Justin made the cookies himself," she confided in a soft voice when her son wandered off, sandwich in one hand and a stick in the other. "He said that when he grows up and moves away from home, he needs to know how to cook something, and chocolate-chip cookies sounded good."

"Why not?" Joe agreed. "A man could live on chocolate chip cookies—for a while, at least. My mother used to have cookies warm from the oven practically every day when we got home from school. She was convinced we needed a big snack before we got started on our chores."

"What chores?"

"Milking the cows, feeding the animals, helping Dad in the fields—whatever needed to be done. We lived on a farm."

Libby's smile was warm and unexpected. It brightened her entire face. "My grandparents farmed here near Clarks Hill. I always loved spending the night with them and helping out—with everything except gathering eggs. I hated the chickens. I always had marks on my hands and legs where they were constantly pecking at me."

"Where is Clarks Hill?"

"Here." She nodded toward the lake. "This is Clarks Hill Lake."

"This is Thurmond Lake."

Her smile faltered then faded, making him wish that he hadn't spoken. "That's right. Mom told me they changed the name a while back, but I forgot. It'll probably sink in in twenty years or so." She fished a long pickle spear from a jar and took a bite. "Do your parents still have their place?"

"Yeah, but now they share it with my older brother and one of the younger ones. They're in their sixties, so it's too much for them alone."

"And you'd had your fill of farming by the time you finished high school, so you joined the Army and went off to see the world."

Joe grinned. "The first part's wrong—I didn't mind farming—but the second one's right. How did you know?"

"I think everyone who lives in a small town has a secret desire to be someplace else, at least for a while." She broke off to warn Justin away from the water's edge. Then, instead of continuing, she began clearing away the remains of their lunch.

He moved to help her; then, when the food was back in the ice chest and the trash in a plastic bag, he prompted her to continue. "You've seen enough of the world already?"

"About five moves ago," she agreed with a sigh. "I was nineteen when I got married. Doug had just been transferred to Ohio, so we went straight from our honeymoon to his new job. I loved it—being in a strange place, making new friends, finding my way around. Then, just when I was starting to feel at home there, he got sent to Colorado. Then Arizona. Kansas. Louisiana. Eventually we wound up in Chicago. Somewhere along the way, I quit loving it. Instead of being excited about living in a new place, I became apprehensive. I dreaded making new friends, because I knew that soon another transfer would come through and I'd have to leave them behind. When Justin started school, I hated the idea of having to uproot him every year or two at the company's whim and stick him in a new school with new teachers and new kids.''

"Military kids move pretty often," he pointed out, keeping his tone even and impersonal, "and they're none the worse for it. They adapt. Justin adapted to this last move."

"Because it *was* the last," she said, giving a different meaning to his words. "He knew that I would never take him away from here. Look, I realize that the way Doug and I lived isn't much different from the way you live, and I'm not criticizing that. For people who enjoy having no roots, that's fine. But it's not for me, and it's not for my son. He needs stability, the kind that staying in one place can bring."

She fell silent again, as if in thought, but he waited patiently. He wanted—needed—to hear whatever else she might say. Finally she went on. "If someone asks me where I'm from, I have no doubts. I'm from South Carolina. You're from Kentucky. There's something special about knowing where you come from, where you belong. There's something special about *home*. But Justin doesn't know where he's from. He was born in Louisiana, but he's not from there. He has no ties there. He has no ties to any particular place. I want to change that. I *have* changed that."

That was about as clear as a warning could get, Joe thought grimly. The wise thing to do now would be finish out the day, take them home, tell Libby goodbye and continue his friendship with Justin in the way it had started: at school. A few hours every Tuesday. Surrounded by all the other soldiers in the unit and all the other kids in the class.

But these two days they'd spent together might have made going back to the way things had been impossible. Justin wouldn't understand why there could be no more shared dinners, no more fishing trips. If it had been okay twice, why not again? And Joe wasn't sure he wanted to go back to the old way, either. He had a lot of empty hours in his life, and he couldn't think of anyone he'd rather spend them with than Justin. There was so much they could do with each other—so much they could do *for* each other.

Except for the complication of Justin's mother.

It wasn't that he was planning to fall in love with her or anything. But only a fool would attempt to begin even a casual romance that had no chance of succeeding—and neither he nor Libby was the casual type. It was a simple fact of life: in six months he would be transferred away from Augusta. Until he retired, he would receive permanent change of station orders on a regular schedule.

And it was a fact of life, although not so simple, that a man with a future like that didn't stand a chance with a woman like Libby.

If only she wasn't Justin's mother...

If only she wasn't nice, interesting and intelligent in her own right...

If only she wasn't so damned pretty...

Maybe he was a fool, he decided—no, no maybes about it. He was *definitely* a fool—but he was going to disregard her warning. He was going to pretend that there was nothing incompatible between them—not her desire for roots or his obligation to move. There was an attraction here that he fully intended to pursue. If it turned out to be nothing substantial, at least he could say he'd tried. At least he wouldn't be wondering somewhere down the line if he'd given up too easily, if he'd let someone special slip away.

And if this attraction developed into something more... Well, barring emergencies, he had six months left here. Six months could bring changes in a person's outlook. Six months and the right incentive could work miracles.

And he believed in miracles.

By late afternoon, Justin and Joe had caught nearly a dozen fish between them, but there wasn't a single one on the stringer, Libby noticed gratefully. Justin had wanted to take them home for dinner—for *her* dinner, not his, he'd made it clear, which she would have been duty-bound as his mother to eat, even though she detested the taste of fish—but Joe, after catching the look on her face, had persuaded him to return each catch to the lake. Leave them here, he'd told Justin, so they'll be bigger and fatter the next time we catch them.

Would there be a next time? she wondered as she shook dirt and leaves from the quilt, then folded it. She was beginning to believe that there would. Joe always did what he said he would, according to Justin, and he had certainly behaved beautifully today. Not once had he lost his patience or his temper, not even when her son had knocked his open tackle box over in the mud only minutes after being told to watch out for it. Without even a flash of annoyance, Joe had laid his fishing rod aside and gotten down in the mud with him, helping him pick up and clean off every piece of equipment, then picking up and cleaning off Justin.

It was a shame that a man with that much patience and that much affection for children didn't have any of his own, she thought—and a shame, too, that he lived the kind of life he did. If not for his job, he could offer a child, and that child's mother, everything: love, understanding, guidance, patience, gentleness, respect. But without stability, without the security of knowing where you would be three years or even three months from now, without roots, all those other things weren't enough. Under the stress of constantly moving, constantly starting out all over again, love could die, patience could shatter, respect could disappear.

Then you'd be left with nothing...the way Doug had left her with nothing.

That would never happen to her again. And she would never let it happen to Justin, either.

Joe and Justin were already on their way to the car with their fishing gear when Libby finished gathering everything. She laid the quilt across the top of the ice chest, tied the trash bag shut, then picked it all up. Even though they'd eaten most of the food and drunk all of the soda and she'd drained the water from the melted ice, the load was still heavy and the footing uneven. She hadn't gone far when Joe appeared in front of her, taking the chest from her and carrying it easily.

"I could have managed."

"I'm sure you could have."

He didn't say anything else, but she silently finished his statement for him: there was no reason to, not when he could carry it for her. She hadn't always been so touchy about things, but for most of the last eighteen months—and especially since her brothers-in-law had both moved away—she'd had no one to count on but herself. She had prided herself on becoming more independent since the divorce, but had she become so independent that she couldn't graciously accept help when it was offered?

"Justin looks tired," she remarked after detouring to drop the trash bag into a garbage can.

"He'll probably be asleep before we get home. Do you want to put the quilt in the back seat for him?"

Her fingers brushed the warm skin of his arms when she took the quilt off the ice chest. As contact went, it wasn't much, but it made the tips of her fingers tingle pleasantly and made her feel warm inside with an intensity that was all out of proportion to the catalyst.

Not that tingling fingertips and warmth meant anything, of course, she told herself with a faintly reproachful smile. Casual contact with any man could probably generate the same sensations. It was a perfectly normal response, especially for a woman who hadn't been this close to a man who wasn't family in eighteen months. It didn't mean a thing.

While he stowed the chest and gear in the trunk, Libby knelt on the front seat and got Justin settled in the back. His big blue eyes were drooping when he leaned forward to give

her a kiss. "I had a good time, Mom," he said with a yawn.
"I caught five fish all by myself."

"I know you did. You're a good fisherman, kiddo."

"That's 'cause Joe helped me. Maybe next time we catch
those fish, they'll be big enough so you can eat them."

She smiled sweetly until she got turned around in her seat.
And maybe, in the meantime, they would sprout wings and
fly away, she hoped.

She was fastening her seat belt when Joe slid into the seat
beside her. He was so tall and broad shouldered that, even
though he was lean, he seemed to fill the small car. "I like
your car," she remarked, rubbing her fingers across the
dashboard.

"It's almost as old as you are," he said wryly as he
cranked the window down a few inches.

"It's a classic. I wanted a 'sixty-five Mustang so badly
when I was a teenager. My best friend got one for her six-
teenth birthday—she was an only child, so her parents could
afford it. It was pretty battered, and it had been painted the
most awful shade of lavender, but she loved it." She glanced
around. "You've taken much better care of yours."

"It was pretty battered when I bought it. Some friends
helped me restore it."

She fell silent as he backed out of the parking space. She
was tired, she realized as she settled comfortably in the
seat—not the bone-deep tiredness that she felt most Saturdays after a week of long workdays, cooking, cleaning,
running errands and being a mother, but a pleasant weariness that made her feel sleepily, warmly satisfied. Good
food, good weather, a good day—and good company, she
admitted. She couldn't say he was easy to be around—the
unsettled way he made her feel ruled that out—but in some
way that directly contradicted her own uneasiness, she had
enjoyed his company.

When the sun set, darkness came quickly. The dim glow
of the dash lights faintly illuminated Joe's face, and Libby
took advantage of the shadows on her own side of the car to
covertly study him. He seemed comfortable behind the

wheel, as relaxed and easygoing there as anywhere else, she assumed. As a driver, Doug had been just the opposite. He had seemed to absorb some of the power from the engines of the expensive European cars he'd begun buying as soon as they could afford them, constantly driving too fast, braking too slowly, beeping the horn and swearing at the other drivers on the road. Riding with him had always left her frazzled and gritting her teeth. But Joe...

When she realized that she was comparing the man beside her to her ex-husband—and favorably—she deliberately put an end to her thoughts. A woman could compare current husbands to former ones, new lovers to old, but to judge Joe against Doug was like comparing apples and oranges. She'd been married to one, had loved him dearly, had known him intimately for nearly half of her life, while the other was a stranger. A friend of her son's. A man whose only reason for being in her life was her son.

Of course, the sly side of her nature pointed out, Doug lost out there, too. Joe, who had no children whatsoever, showed far better father potential than Doug, who had a child but had never been a father.

Annoyed with herself, she turned to stare out the side window at the dark woods. They weren't far from North Augusta and the bright lights of Augusta, but out here she could believe they were miles away from anywhere. With each passing mile the sky grew lighter, though, and all too soon the harsh lights of street lamps were flashing through the car at regular intervals. Now she could see Joe's profile all too well, and the shadows that had given her refuge were too weak to hide anything.

As Joe had predicted, Justin was asleep, snoring softly in the back seat. She wondered what the chances were that he would sleep through the night and decided they were pretty good, since his regular bedtime was little more than an hour away. She would have what every mother craved: a quiet evening alone, with no housework to do and no demands for attention.

Why didn't the prospect sound more appealing?

When Joe parked in the driveway, he shut off the engine and glanced in back. "Go ahead and unlock the door," he suggested. "I'll get Justin."

She didn't object or point out that she was perfectly capable of carrying her son inside—which, of course, she was. She simply accepted his offer and did as she'd been told, switching on lights as she went, on the porch, in the hall and finally in Justin's room. She was folding back the covers on his bed when Joe appeared in the doorway. He hardly seemed to feel his burden as he gently lowered Justin onto the mattress. Of course, Libby thought, watching from the opposite side, what were fifty extra pounds to a man as big and strong as he was?

"Do you want to try to undress him?"

"No. Let's just take his shoes off." She unknotted the wet laces and removed the left shoe and sock while Joe did the same on the right. Then she drew the blankets over her son, turned out the lamp, followed Joe from the room and closed the door behind her.

For a moment they both simply stood there. It was the first time since they'd met, Libby realized, that she'd been truly alone with him. Granted, Justin had occasionally wandered off at other times, but she'd always been able to see or hear him, and she had known that he could come popping back at any instant. That wasn't the case tonight. He was so deeply asleep that, even when they had tugged his shoes off, they hadn't disturbed his slow breathing.

She took a deep breath and immediately wished she hadn't. After all day outside with the woods and the lake and the wind, the scent of Joe's after-shave had grown faint and elusive, but here in the hallway, where no other fragrances competed with it, she could smell it. It smelled incredibly good.

Incredibly sexy.

Wrong. "Sexy" wasn't a word she was supposed to think of in reference to seven-year-old Justin's best friend in the whole world. But then, Justin's best friend wasn't supposed to be an attractive, forty-something-year-old man, either, and he wasn't supposed to be looking at her right now as if she were anything but his best friend's mother.

She took another deep breath—through her mouth this time—and let it out in a sigh. "Justin had a nice time. Thank you."

"Maybe we can do it again sometime."

"He would like that."

"And what about you, Libby?"

His question made her uneasy. "What about me?"

"What would *you* like?"

She held his gaze for a long time. It was possible, she knew from past experience, to get lost in ordinary blue eyes—both Doug and Billy Taggert from the ninth grade had been proof of that. Eyes *this* blue could make her forget her own name... her common sense... her better judgment. Eyes this blue could darn near make her forget that she was happy alone with Justin. That she didn't need or want a man in her life. That although she was long since over her love for Doug, she hadn't begun to forget the heartache.

She deliberately shifted her gaze away and considered his question. What would she like? She would like to believe that he was everything he appeared to be. She would like a guarantee that he wouldn't get bored with the role he'd taken on, that the novelty of playing hero to a lonely little boy wouldn't wear off too soon. She would like to know that he truly, honestly cared for that little boy. She would especially like to know that when the day came, as it inevitably would, when he got transferred away, Justin wouldn't miss him too much.

She would like to believe that *she* wouldn't miss him at all.

When she replied, though, it was the most innocuous answer she could think of. "I'd like to sleep late tomorrow morning instead of having an overly energetic child wake me at seven o'clock to fix his breakfast."

That wasn't what he'd meant by his question, and he suspected—damn, he *hoped*—she knew it. But he didn't press the issue. He didn't ask if *she'd* had a good time. He didn't ask if *she* would like to do it again. "Maybe you'll get lucky and he'll sleep in."

"Maybe. But I doubt it."

She started back down the hall—his cue to say good-night and leave—and he politely followed her, stepping around her when they reached the door. "Let me get your ice chest."

That extended his stay by only a few minutes more. Unable to delay any longer, he found himself once more at the front door with her. "Will you and Justin have lunch with me tomorrow?"

She was silent for a long time. Today, when they'd talked, he hadn't been able to read anything in her expression, but now he could clearly see her negative response forming. He even had a pretty good idea of what arguments she would use if he allowed it to get that far: they'd taken up enough of his time; Justin had already spent too much time with him; he needed a break. "Just lunch," he said, forestalling her reply. "You have to eat, and it will give me a chance to repay your hospitality."

Her silence lasted a moment longer; then she nodded. "All right."

"I'll pick you up at noon."

She nodded again.

"Good night, Libby."

He was halfway down the steps when the screen door closed with a quiet thump, followed by an even quieter farewell.

"Good night."

Last night Joe had thought he knew all the arguments Libby would use to avoid spending today with him. When he arrived at her house Sunday a few minutes before twelve, he suspected that he should have used those arguments to convince himself against inviting her in the first place. They *had* taken up a lot of his time; they *had* already spent too much time together; he *did* need a break. Whenever he could take one look at a woman and feel the way he felt right now—warm and contented, just a little bit nervous and a little bit . . . needy—he'd done too much of something.

Or not enough, his little voice suggested.

She was even prettier today than the other times he'd seen her. Dressed in jeans and a white cotton shirt, with a bright turquoise scarf woven around her waist and a wide matching clamp securing her hair, she looked young and innocent, as if she hadn't suffered the disillusionment of a marriage turned bad, an unfriendly divorce, separation from her family when she'd needed them most and problems with her son. She looked carefree.

She looked like his future.

He had just circled around his car when she stepped onto the porch. Before he'd finished looking at her, before he'd had a chance to offer a greeting, Justin came racing outside, swerving around his mother and taking the steps in one big leap. When the force of his momentum threatened to topple him over, Joe reached down and caught him, steadying him until he'd regained his balance.

"Look what I found under my bed," Justin said excitedly, holding up a toy plane. "I thought I'd lost it. It's a Harrier jet. It can land and take off just like a helicopter."

"I saw one of those at an air show once. It was pretty neat."

Justin flew the plane around in a circle. "What kind of air show?"

"It was the Blue Angels. Have you heard of them?"

"Sure. They do all the neat tricks with their jets. Can we go see them?"

"Next time they're in Charleston or Beaufort, okay?" He mussed Justin's hair, then turned his attention back to Libby. She was leaning one shoulder against the post at the top of the steps, her hands in her pockets. "Are you ready to go?"

"Let me lock up." But for a moment she remained where she was, simply watching them. Then suddenly she went back inside the house, letting the screen door bang behind her. Another long moment passed before she returned with her purse and keys in hand.

Joe got Justin settled into the back seat while she locked the door; then he watched her over the top of the car. "Where would you like to go?" he asked as she approached.

"That's up to you and Justin. I'm easy to please."

He grinned and shook his head. "I don't think so."

Libby wished he wouldn't grin like that. It was too appealing, making him look too much like a mischievous little boy when he was anything but. Anything but a little boy, she amended as she got into the car beside him. She didn't yet know what degrees of mischief he was capable of.

He and Justin discussed food as they drove through North Augusta and across the Savannah River, settling at last on a hamburger restaurant on Washington Road. Although the food was good, it wasn't one of Libby's favorite places. Justin spent every minute that he wasn't actually eating at the video games, leaving her alone at the table until her patience or his quarters finally ran out. In the eighteen months since the divorce, she had never grown comfortable sitting alone in a restaurant.

But she wouldn't be alone today. Unless he deserted her for the video games along with Justin, Joe would be with her.

Every restaurant in town got busy when church services ended, but they were early enough to avoid the rush. They placed their order at the counter and got their drinks; then, in a huge room filled with tables, Justin chose one of the half-dozen booths that lined the windows. Libby slid across the bench, intending for her son to sit beside her, but instead he claimed the opposite bench. "You sit with Mom," he told Joe, "and I'll have a whole side to myself."

The bench was perfectly comfortable for two adults, so why did it suddenly seem inches too small when Joe sat down beside her?

"Does your mom let you play the video games?"

Justin's smile brightened. "Yeah. But only for six quarters, and three of them are part of my allowance."

Joe shifted on the seat, stretching his long legs out and digging deep in his jeans pocket. He brought out a handful of change and offered it to Justin, who picked out the quarters—only six, Libby noticed, even though he looked longingly at the seventh and last one.

"Thanks, Joe. I'll be in the game room."

"Don't—" Justin was already gone before Libby could finish "—run."

Joe returned the change to his pocket, then turned slightly in the seat to face her as he placed his arm along the back of the cushion. The position placed his knee against her thigh, and his arm naturally slid down until it rested as much against her shoulders as it did on the cushion.

Her first thought was to move away, but there was nowhere to go. She was trapped by the wall on one side and Joe on the other.

Her second thought was that being trapped wasn't so bad. She found a certain schoolgirl pleasure, she decided, in sitting so close to a big, strong, handsome man. There was a certain comfort in the warmth that spread slowly, lazily, through her. A certain rightness, after so many long months alone, to no longer be alone—for these few moments, at least.

"How much time did I buy us?"

"He's pretty good. Depending on which games he plays, six quarters can last a long time. But if you wanted to get rid of him—"

"Come on, Libby, you know better than that," he chided. "The kid hardly ever plays his video games at home anymore. What does it hurt to let him play here? You let him yourself."

Grudgingly she glanced at him. "Can I ask a favor of you?"

He grinned charmingly. "Anything."

"Please don't make promises to Justin—like taking him to the next air show."

His grin slowly faded, and a somber look filled his eyes. "Why not?"

Libby sighed, lacing her fingers together on the tabletop. "He won't forget about it. Five minutes after I tell him to clean his room or do his homework, he may not remember hearing it, but he doesn't forget important things, not after five minutes or five months.''

"Neither do I. The next air show will be in March or April. Barring orders to Africa, I *will* be here then, and I *will* take him to see the Blue Angels. That's a promise, Libby.''

She didn't know what made her respond so sarcastically—because he expected her to trust him when she hardly knew him? Or because she *wanted* to trust him? She *wanted* to believe him. Whatever, her tone was unnecessarily sharp when she answered. "Pardon me for being skeptical, but I've seen other people make promises to Justin, and I've seen them break his heart. His father promised him a trip to Disney World last summer. His grandfather promised to take him deep-sea fishing. His uncle promised to take him white-water rafting.''

She broke off for a moment, remembering the depth of Justin's pain at each disappointment, no matter how minor it had seemed to *her*. Then she looked at him again. "He hasn't learned to be skeptical yet. He *believes* what people tell him. He especially believes in *you*. Maybe you deserve his trust. Maybe you're different from my family, who intended to keep their promises but couldn't, or from his father, who made them with no intention of keeping them.''

"I *am* different.''

"Maybe. But the point is, *I* don't know that.'' She sighed softly. "I'm not saying that you can't take him to the air show next spring. I'm just asking that you don't get his hopes up. Don't set him up only to let him down. Don't disappoint him.''

Joe was silent for a long time, his expression difficult to read. Then he quietly said, "Eventually, Libby, you're going to learn something about me that Justin has already figured out. I don't treat my friendships lightly. I don't say things that I don't mean. I don't get involved unless I plan to stay involved. And Libby?'' He leaned closer, intimidatingly so. "I *always* keep my promises.''

Chapter 3

Libby didn't want to debate his trustworthiness, not now, not when she knew so little about him. It was too easy to misjudge a stranger. If everything he said was true, he was *exactly* what Justin needed in his life. Until she knew for sure, she couldn't jeopardize their friendship with her doubts.

Instead she focused on something he'd said earlier: *Barring orders to Africa* ...

Africa. In the past few days, she had practically forgotten the problems—and the three hundred thousand American troops—in the newly-formed nation calling itself the Eastern African Republic. Shortly after its government was in place and its pro-Western alliances formed, the small country had been invaded by neighbors to the north and to the west, eager to reclaim the oil-rich land that had once belonged to them and to punish their former countrymen for daring to secede. The republic's western allies had immediately stepped in, winning the United Nations' condemnation of the invasion and sending in troops. Naturally, the majority of those troops were American.

Odd, that when she hadn't known a single soul who would be affected by the buildup, she had followed the situation pretty closely; yet, since meeting a man who, if there was a war, would very likely go, she'd let it slip unnoticed to the back of her mind.

She wondered how it would feel to know that Joe was over there, to know he was fighting a war that he might not survive. Unnerving. Frightening.

And she wouldn't think about the possibility, either. She pushed the subject right back into its forgotten corner and returned to a safer topic of conversation. "Justin could get used to having you around," she said, a reproving note slipping into her voice. "You indulge him too much."

"Kids deserve to be indulged once in a while." Then he asked her a question that he'd asked last night, and just as it had then, it caught her by surprise. "What about you, Libby?"

Biting the tip of her tongue, she didn't answer.

"Could *you* get used to having me around?"

Could she? she wondered, fiddling with the cup in front of her. Could she get used to having a man in their lives, even if he was Justin's friend and not hers? Could she get used to that grin and those blue eyes and that deep, masculine voice? Could she get used to butterflies in her stomach and occasional interested-male looks and a wickedly errant thought or two?

He laid his hand over hers to stop its nervous action and, just like last night, her fingertips started tingling again. The warmth from his hand spread up her arm with a discomfort—the most weirdly *pleasant* discomfort—that made her want to squirm away.

But she sat still, silently, sternly admonishing herself to gain control over her wayward thoughts. When she had accomplished that, she finally looked at him. "Isn't one adoring fan in the Harper family enough?"

"Two would be better." With an easy laugh, he removed his hand and resettled himself in the seat, leaving some distance between them this time. "But you're not the adoring type, are you?"

He was wrong there. She had adored Billy Taggert—until he'd broken her heart. Simple friendship with Doug had turned into adoration, then love, and that had led to a broken heart, too. If she gave Joe Mathison half a chance, he could easily make her a three-time loser in the game of love. *Or an all-around winner,* something—maybe her heart—silently whispered to her.

"No, I'm not," she pleasantly, agreeably lied. "What little capacity I have for adoration is reserved for Justin."

"Adoration's like love. As the old saying goes, the more you give, the more you have to give. You never run out."

Like Doug, she thought grimly. That adage had certainly held true for him. The more of himself he'd given, the more he'd had to give. The only problem had been that he was sharing himself with everyone: his secretary, the woman in the office next to his, their widowed neighbor, the flight attendant he'd met on a business trip, his boss's assistant, the service representative for one of their accounts... And those were just the ones she knew about. The list could be endless.

She realized that Joe was waiting for some response from her, and she gave it without looking at him. "So I've heard. But I don't care for overly generous people. There's a limit to how much you can give—to how much you *should* give."

"What do you mean?"

But the loudspeaker interrupted, broadcasting their ticket number across the dining room and saving Libby from having to answer. She flashed him a deceptively sweet smile. "You get the trays, I'll get Justin, and we'll meet you at the tomatoes."

He wouldn't say he was making progress with Libby—Joe was too honest with himself for that—but at least he was enjoying trying. When she chose, she could charm his socks right off—and the rest of his clothes, he admitted, if she had any interest in trying. When they returned to the table with their lunch, he watched her turn it on for Justin and thought it no surprise that the boy absolutely adored her.

Yet when she wasn't captivating both him and Justin, when she was quiet or uneasy or protective or wary, he found those sides of her even more interesting, more appealing. She was a complex woman, and he would give a great deal to unlock all her secrets.

He would give even more for some small part of that adoration she hoarded so closely.

After lunch they stopped by the restaurant's bakery to buy a dozen chocolate-chip cookies, then went outside to the Mustang. He and Libby had never gotten around to discussing what to do after lunch, he thought as he unlocked the door. She had agreed only to the meal, but he had no intention of taking them home now.

"Want to go down to the Riverwalk?" he asked casually, deliberately, so Justin could hear. The little boy's response was an immediate, enthusiastic yes, one that his mother had little choice but to agree with. But that didn't mean she was happy about it. He got that message in the look she gave him over the roof of the car before she got inside. There was another old saying that she needed to learn if she hadn't already: all's fair in love and war. And while this wasn't love—yet—it certainly wasn't war.

The Riverwalk was a park built on the bank of the Savannah River, most of it located between the water's edge and the levee that protected the downtown area from occasional high waters. They left the car in a nearby lot, then walked past the shops and the fountain and through the breach into the main part of the park. There, even though it was late fall, the flower beds and planters still held bright-blooming pansies that created a pleasing contrast against the muddy river beyond.

Just inside the breach they paused. To the left was the amphitheater, to the right the playground, and straight ahead was the shaved-ice stand. Justin headed right for the yellow umbrella, never doubting, Joe thought with a grin, that they would follow.

He bought Justin a lemon-lime ice and got coconut cream for himself. Libby simply shook her head and went to wait at the railing that overlooked the river. When they joined her there a few minutes later, she was staring solemnly at the woods on the other side. "Don't you like ices?" he asked, leaning on the rail beside her.

She gave him a long, measuring look. "Not as much as I like those chocolate-chip cookies we left in the car. If I'm going to put on five pounds, I'm going to do it with something I really love."

Those last few words opened the door for a wide range of questions, but before he could ask even one, Justin wiggled in between them. "Look at that jet ski, Joe. Have you ever done that before?"

He turned his attention to the skier on the river. He was a young man, black haired and dressed in a knee-length wet suit, and he was putting on a show for all the people on shore—especially the teenage girls, Joe noticed, lined up at the rail a few yards away. "No, I never have," he replied. "I can't honestly say I'd want to get wet in the Savannah. It's not the cleanest water I've ever seen."

"Before Uncle Travis moved away, he took me fishing in the river once, and Mom said she wouldn't eat any fish that had lived in that water." Justin sneaked a look at his mother, then leaned closer to Joe. "We won't tell her that the lake yesterday is sort of part of the river, too, okay?"

Knowing that Libby had overheard—and knowing, too, that she wasn't going to willingly eat fish no matter where they'd come from—Joe grinned. "It'll be our secret, okay?"

"Okay. Can we go to the playground now?"

They took a leisurely walk to the far end of the park, finishing their ices along the way. There Justin left them and went through the gate to play. Within five minutes, Joe noticed, he was old friends with two little boys and a pigtailed girl. Quite a change from the kid he'd first met who had disliked—and been disliked by—practically everyone in his class.

Satisfied that everything was all right with Justin, he focused on the boy's mother. She was sitting a few feet away on a backless bench near the water. He started to sit beside her, then changed his mind and swung his leg over the bench so he could face her. "He's a good kid."

"Most of the time—at home, at least. At the beginning of the school year, though, his teacher and the principal told quite a different story."

"I know. He was pretty unhappy."

She sighed softly. "I didn't know what to do with him. He hardly ever misbehaved at home, but he was so bad at school. I talked to him for hours, reasoned with him, pleaded with him, and he would promise to behave, but the next day..." She shook her head in dismay. "I was starting to consider counseling. He'd been through a lot with the divorce, and he was having such trouble adjusting at school. I thought a psychologist could help. Then, out of the blue, he started getting better. I understand you had a lot to do with it. I appreciate it."

He shrugged modestly. "Like I said, he's a good kid. I like him. I like spending time with him."

"I wish his father did."

For a moment he remained silent, watching Justin run and slide. He was so active that by the time they left, Joe knew the fine white sand that filled the playground would be in his hair, his clothes and his shoes, and the majority of it would wind up in *his* car. But he didn't mind. The car was just a car. Competing against a little boy's fun, it came in a distant second.

Then he looked at Libby once more. "Was your husband—"

"Ex-husband," she corrected.

"—as bad a husband as he was a father?"

She gave him a quick glance—he was beginning to think she wasn't comfortable meeting his gaze—then looked past him to the railroad bridge practically overhead. "Are you always so nosy?"

He smiled and treated the question lightly. "Always."

Her expression was as somber and grim as he'd ever seen. "Why do you want to know?"

"It's just one of the questions about you that I'd like to have answered."

"Why?"

He shrugged. "Maybe I'd like to be *your* friend, too, Libby, and not just Justin's. I can be a good one."

"I have a good friend. Her name is Denise, and we've been best friends all our lives. She lives three blocks away from me and knows everything there is to know about me."

"Maybe I should be trying to get close to her," he said irritably, feeling his patience start to slip. "I bet she'd tell me about you."

She gave him a disagreeable look. "Best friends don't betray your secrets to strangers."

"To quit being a stranger, Libby, I have to get to know you. That's kind of hard when you won't talk to me."

"It's kind of hard to talk when you only want to talk about my ex-husband and my marriage," she countered. "You want to ask me about my job, go ahead. I'll give you all the details. You want to know about the places I've lived or the people I've known or the way I grew up, I can tell you about those, too. But I won't discuss my ex-husband with you. I only discuss things that personal with my friends, and *you* aren't my friend."

After a moment's silence, he tried again. "Maybe I'd like to be more than a friend."

"I'm sure you can find plenty of women who would like to be 'more' than your friend," she said flatly, leaving no doubt exactly how she interpreted that phrase. "But I don't need that, either."

He moved closer, close enough that she couldn't avoid his gaze without getting up—close enough that she couldn't do that, either. "What about a lover, Libby?" he asked in a soft, angry voice. "Or don't you need one of those, either?"

He expected anger to match his own. What he got was a brilliant smile that couldn't hide the fear in her eyes. "If I learned one thing from my divorce, it's that I don't *need* anyone or anything in my life except my son. I don't need to depend on a man to support me. I don't need sexual gratification enough to depend on a man for that, either. I don't need a man to make me feel worthy.'' She paused, and the smile became more brittle, while the fear became something else. ''If it weren't for Justin, I wouldn't even be here to have this conversation with you, because I don't need anything you have to offer. Only your friendship for him.''

He reminded himself that he'd only known her a few days, that this was only the third day he'd spent with her, that it was ridiculous to think that she could say or do anything that could hurt his feelings. But emotions were simply that. Feelings. They didn't have much to do with thinking, with rationale and logic. Emotions couldn't know that she wasn't supposed to have the power to hurt him, that she was just a casual acquaintance capable of inflicting only casual discomfort, not pain.

After a long, tense moment, he slid back, but he never took his eyes from hers. ''Maybe we'd better go now,'' he said dully. ''I have to get ready for a date this evening.''

There was a flicker of something in her eyes, but she turned away before he could identify it. Probably relief—the same relief that he ought to be feeling at the thought of a simple, uncomplicated evening with a sweet, uncomplicated woman.

But as he watched her walk to the low fence that surrounded the playground and listened to her call Justin's name, her tone firm and tightly controlled, he felt no relief. Only sadness.

Libby lay in bed that night, unable to sleep and unable to stop thinking about the unpleasant way the afternoon with Joe had ended. Although she had acted as if his questions had offended her, they really hadn't. They had *scared* her. Beyond belief.

It was one thing to enjoy spending time with a man when her seven-year-old son was always right there to interrupt.

To enjoy the brief physical contact they'd shared. To tease herself about tingling fingertips, body heat, butterflies and pleasure.

But it was another thing altogether to think about being more than friends. About being lovers. About being close. About caring again. Trusting again. Maybe even loving again.

And it was yet another to lie, and in that final little speech she'd made, she'd told several of them. She *did* need someone besides Justin. As much as she loved him, he couldn't begin to fill all the empty places in her life. He was just a little boy.

And she needed physical intimacy, too. For so many months she had turned off that part of herself. There'd been more important matters—dealing with the divorce, finding a job, first in Chicago and then here, taking care of Justin, adjusting to all the changes in her life. She'd been too busy to care about what she was missing.

And the biggest lie of all: I don't need anything you have to offer. She was afraid of needing, afraid of even wanting again. And the fact that Joe was the first man she'd met since Doug who could make her even think of wanting or needing scared her, too.

Swearing softly, she rolled onto her side and checked the alarm clock on the dresser. It was nearly midnight. She wondered if he was home from his date yet, or if he was spending the night with her. She wondered if the woman he'd taken out was one of those women she had referred to, the ones who would gladly be more than friends with him. She wondered if he'd spared even a moment's thought for her, while she'd been able to think of nothing but him.

She hoped he had a miserably unlucky night.

"Do you want to come in?"

Joe glanced at the woman beside him and smiled faintly. "I can't. I've got to get up in about five hours."

She smiled, too, a predatory gesture. "If you stay here, you'll get to bed quicker than if you drive all the way back to your apartment."

He didn't doubt that, but getting to bed had absolutely nothing to do with getting to sleep, especially when Candace was in the same bed. He'd been turning down her less-than-subtle advances all evening. A simple, uncomplicated date? Boy, had he been wrong. This had no more been simple or uncomplicated than today with Libby had been "just lunch."

He'd known Candace three months and had gone out with her three or four times over the past six weeks. He'd thought he had learned a lot about her in that time, but he hadn't been prepared for tonight. Sweet had given way to aggressive, uncomplicated to demanding. Driving her home had been a chore, since she hadn't been at all shy about reaching for what she wanted. Maybe the other men she saw found such a blatant approach exciting, but he was old-fashioned enough to disapprove.

Or maybe he had simply been thinking too much about another woman to allow this one to arouse him. A woman who would never be bold or forward. A woman who wouldn't dream of touching him the way Candace had. A woman who neither wanted nor needed anything he could give her.

How did he get so lucky, he wondered cynically as he shut off the engine, as to spend the afternoon with a woman he wanted but couldn't have and the evening with a woman he could have but didn't want?

"Come on, Candace. I'll walk you to the door."

There she twined her arms around his neck and kissed him. For a moment he let her, simply to see what he felt. Nothing but a vague distaste. He gently, firmly, pushed her away, said good-night and started back to his car. Before he'd gone too far, he heard her softly muttered curses.

He wouldn't be seeing her again. Even if he forgot how uncomfortable this evening had been and asked her out once more, he seriously doubted that she would accept. She didn't like rejection, and she wouldn't risk it again when there were plenty of men who would be more than happy to spend the night with her.

The familiarity of those words made him pause in the act of starting the car. Libby had made a similar statement about him this afternoon. Was that how she saw him—as simply a male version of Candace? This afternoon he'd been annoyed; now he felt insulted. The situations were hardly the same. He hadn't tried to seduce Libby—although he couldn't deny the thought had been in his mind. He didn't view sex as casually as Candace did. He had never been to bed with a woman he didn't care a great deal for, not even when he was an inexperienced seventeen-year-old back in Kentucky.

All he was guilty of with Libby was impatience. He had taken the time and care necessary to win Justin's trust, but he'd been overeager with her. He had rushed her, had pushed too hard, and he had seriously jeopardized his chances with her.

Then, as he pulled away from the curb, he laughed bitterly. Chances? _What_ chances? She didn't want anything from him, not even friendship. She was tolerating him for Justin's sake. If he was lucky, she might continue to tolerate him for Justin's sake. And if he wasn't lucky? The next few months might be difficult indeed.

The phone was ringing when Libby walked in the door after work Monday evening. She picked it up as Justin squeezed past her on his way to his room. She didn't know who she'd expected it to be—Denise, maybe, or even Joe. He didn't strike her as the sort of man who would walk away from a child who counted on him simply because of a disagreement with the kid's foolish mother.

But she hadn't expected to hear her ex-husband's voice on the other end. She set her purse on the hall table, then stretched the cord so she could move the phone from the hallway into the living room. "Hello, Doug," she said, her voice cautious.

He was in a nasty mood. After living with the man for twelve years, she could recognize it in an instant. That meant no fatherly chat with Justin and probably not even a message for him. He could barely tolerate their son when he was in a good mood; when he was like this, it was best to take care of business and break the connection—quickly.

"I wanted to tell you that the check should be in the mail. I gave it to your damned attorney Friday."

"Thank you, Doug. I don't suppose you went ahead and added December's support payment to it." After all, November's payment was twenty-seven days late; it was already time for December's anyway.

"As a matter of fact, I did. Your lawyer suggested it." He muttered something to someone in the background—his little girlfriend? Libby wondered—then turned his attention to her again. "Why the hell didn't you call *me*, Libby? Why did you go to your attorney instead?"

"The first half dozen times you were late, I *did* call you," she patiently reminded him. "And every time but one, I ended up having to call my lawyer anyway. Doing it this way saves me one long-distance phone call."

"I should have known you'd be counting," he said scornfully. "I bet you know exactly how many payments have been late and by how many days. You always were greedy."

Libby wrapped the phone cord tightly around her right hand. "I know how many visits you've missed, too," she responded sarcastically. "I know how many holidays you've forgotten, and how many birthdays."

"Don't start with that. You're the one who decided to move back to South Carolina."

"Doug, we stayed in Chicago for more than a year, and you still missed every special day and all but three visits!" Her voice was rising, and she forced herself to lower it so Justin couldn't overhear. "Is it asking too much that you send him a card at Christmas or call him on his birthday?"

"You know I'm busy," he said defensively.

"Yes, I'm sure that at your age, keeping up with Carrie must be a full-time job."

"Her name is Barrie, damn it."

Libby knew that. Even better, Doug knew that she knew. She'd never been one to mix up names. Sighing heavily, she asked, "Will you talk to Justin now?"

"I don't have time. Barrie and I are late for dinner. I just wanted to tell you that you'll have your money in a few days, so you can get off my back. And next time, Libby, call me instead of that pompous ass of an attorney."

"Next time, Doug," she said sweetly, "why don't you send the damn check on time?" With that she slammed the phone down, only to have it ring again almost immediately. Speed dialing, she thought with a scowl, and an ex-husband who couldn't stand not getting the last word in. She jerked the receiver off the hook and snapped out a cross, "What?"

There was a moment's silence, then a puzzled question. "How did you do that? How did you know it was me?"

Joe. For an instant, before the memory of yesterday afternoon came rushing back, she smiled, happy to hear his voice. Then she remembered the things he'd said, the things *she'd* said, the lies she'd told, his big date last night, and her smile slowly slipped. "I'm sorry. I thought you were my ex-husband calling again."

"*I'm* sorry," he replied. "Problems?"

"He never even asked about Justin." She sank onto a padded hassock, then stood and removed the toy soldiers there before sitting down again. "The last time he showed any interest in Justin was when we went to court for the divorce. First he said he wanted custody. Of course he didn't. He was just trying to make things difficult for me. Then he insisted on generous visitation rights. He's supposed to have Justin every other weekend, all summer and on holidays. He showed up for his first three visits, and Justin hasn't seen him since." She broke off for a moment, and when she spoke again, her voice was unsteady. "He called, and he wouldn't even speak to his son because he was late for dinner with his girlfriend."

"I'm sorry," Joe repeated, more somberly this time. "Does Justin know?"

"No. He's in his room playing. He's gotten so used to Doug's treatment that I'm not even sure he would care anymore, but I'm not going to find out." She rubbed her temples with her free hand, trying to ease the ache that Doug had started there. "What did you want?"

"To apologize."

"For what?" she asked guardedly.

"I don't know. Because the sun didn't shine today. Because your ex-husband's a bastard and a lousy father. For the problems of the world." After a pause, he continued more seriously. "For whatever happened yesterday. For being too pushy. For trying to force you to talk about something that you obviously didn't want to talk about. For whatever."

Libby closed her eyes and sat in silence. She appreciated the apology. Doug had never apologized when he was wrong, and he'd certainly never taken the blame for something that wasn't entirely his fault. Now she had one more bit of evidence that he wasn't half the man Joe Mathison was.

"Libby?"

She sighed. "Thank you. I'm sorry it happened, too."

"Then how about if we take Justin to a movie tomorrow evening? I know his bedtime is eight o'clock, but we can have him home by eight-thirty. What do you think?"

After last night's tossing and turning, she knew immediately what her answer had to be, but when she opened her mouth to give it, it came out all wrong. "I think it would be fun. Justin loves going to the movies. So do I."

"Okay," he agreed slowly. Regretting his invitation already? she wondered. Or surprised that for once she didn't have to be coaxed into accepting? "There are several kids' movies over near the mall that start between five-thirty and six. We can choose from those, then get some dinner afterward."

"I don't know if I can get off work at five, drive home, pick up Justin at the baby-sitter's, change clothes and make it to the mall by six."

"Let me pick him up. I'm taking off at four tomorrow. Then we can meet at your office."

"All right. I'll tell Mrs. Franklin to expect you." She gave him the addresses for Justin's baby-sitter and the Greene Street building where she worked.

There was a moment's silence while he wrote down the addresses, then he said, "Tell me about your job, Libby."

The request surprised her until she remembered what she'd told him yesterday. *You want to ask me about my job, go ahead.... You want to know about the places I've lived or the people I've known or the way I grew up, I'll tell you about those, too.* "I work for an accounting firm. It's a small office, the kind where everyone knows everything about everyone else. Kind of like family."

"Kind of like the Army."

"Yeah, I guess so." Then, realizing that she'd never shown any interest in his job, either, she asked about it.

"I'm the first sergeant for Charlie Company, 65th Signal Battalion, 15th Signal Brigade."

"What does a first sergeant do? What are a company, a battalion and a brigade? And what does a signal brigade do?"

His laugh at her query was good-natured and kind, lacking all the mockery and sarcasm that Doug had shown anytime she wasn't as well-informed as he would have liked. "Justin could answer all those questions for you. Basically, the first sergeant runs the company. My company has a captain in command, but I take care of the everyday routine. As for the rest, a brigade is made up of battalions, which are made up of companies. And the signal brigade handles everything that has to do with communications."

"Sounds like a big job—being first sergeant, I mean."

"I spent twenty years getting ready for it." Joe settled more comfortably on his sofa, studying the ceiling for a long moment. Then he quietly said, "See, Libby? I'm not so hard to talk to."

"No," she agreed just as quietly. "You aren't."

There was another brief silence. Maybe he should have kept his mouth shut, he thought, because she didn't seem to have anything left to say to him. Finally he asked to speak to Justin, and she sounded relieved. Because, unlike her ex, he wasn't too busy to talk to the kid? Or because it meant *their* conversation was ending?

He talked to Justin—or, rather, listened to him—for a long time, until finally he heard Libby call that dinner was ready.

"I've got to go," the boy said. "Are you coming to school tomorrow?"

"You know I wouldn't miss it."

"Good. I'll see you then. Bye, Joe."

Yes, he would see Justin then, Joe thought as he hung up. And after school and work were finished, he would see Libby. He would get to spend at least part of the evening with her. He would get another chance to convince her that they *could* be friends, and enough chances like that could lead to the big one.

Because he'd meant every word said yesterday and apologized for today. He wanted more than friendship from her. He wanted caring, sharing and commitment. He wanted affection and desire and plain old lust. He wanted romance. He wanted a future. He wanted love.

He wanted a chance at those things.

He wanted it all.

"My father called last night."

Justin's announcement came, as his important announcements usually did, out of the blue, with no warning whatsoever to prepare Joe. For a moment he didn't know how to respond, and in that moment, the plane he was flying on the video game in the theater lobby crashed and burned. Ignoring the "Game Over" message flashing on the screen, he turned his attention to Justin. "Did you talk to him?" he asked, making an effort to keep his voice neutral.

"Nah. He was busy with his girlfriend. He's always busy with her." Justin picked up the last quarter they'd laid on the machine, inserted it into the slot and pressed the Start button.

Joe glanced uneasily over his shoulder to the bench where Libby was sitting. She had turned down his offer to join them in a game of air combat while they waited for the movie to begin and had chosen instead to read the movie magazine she'd picked up from the lobby display. Part of him wished that she was over here so she could take control of this conversation, but he knew from past experience that if she *had* joined them, Justin would have remained quiet. He would never discuss his father's girlfriend in front of his mother.

"I'm sorry," he said at last. The words sounded inadequate, but he didn't know what else to say. How was he supposed to respond to such adult-sounding acceptance in such a little boy?

"It doesn't really matter. I don't have much to say to him anyway. I don't even hardly remember what he looks like, except when I look at the picture Mom gave me."

"It's nice that you have the picture." Nice that Libby tolerated a photograph of the man in her house, he thought bitterly.

Justin was quiet for a moment, absorbed in his game; then he said, "She lives with him, you know, only she's not my stepmother, 'cause they aren't married or nothing. I don't want a stepmother, anyway. Mom's the only mother I want. Besides, Barrie's too young. She'd be more like sort of a sister."

His father's girlfriend was young enough to be *sort of a sister* to Justin? Joe hoped he was exaggerating. Libby had commented Saturday that Justin had trouble comprehending age. But she had also started to say something about some problem her ex had had with her age, then had blushed and shut up. He had even suspected at the time that Harper had left her for a younger woman—but for one young enough for Justin to consider her *sort of a sister?*

"I wish things were better between you and your father," he said honestly, sincerely. "I'm sorry they're not."

"When you were a kid, did you live with your dad?"

"Yeah, I did. I still go home and see him and my mom whenever I can."

Justin finished the first round. While he waited for the second to start, he gave Joe a solemn look. "Do they have any grandsons?"

Joe's smile was hesitant. "Yeah. Last I counted, they had about ten."

"Oh." He resumed play with the launching of his aircraft, but after a moment he turned away from the machine. "Let's go ask Mom if I can have some popcorn before dinner."

Joe followed him across the lobby. Halfway to the bench, Justin broke into a run. Libby barely managed to move her magazine in time for him to leap onto her lap. "I know that look," she said with a smile as she tickled him. "You saved the free world from evil, and now you want a reward... like popcorn and a soda. Am I right?"

"A big one," Justin replied, giggling and wriggling away from her questing fingers. "With butter."

"How about a small one? We're going to dinner when we leave here."

She reached for her purse, but Joe had already drawn some money from his wallet. "Can you get it by yourself, partner?"

"Yes, sir." He slid free and went to the concession stand, leaving them alone for the first time.

Joe spent the first few moments simply looking at her. Her hair was in a sleek style that kept it off her neck and away from her face, and she was still wearing the very businesslike dress and jacket she'd worn to work, along with black heels that put her almost eye-to-eye with him. She should have looked very elegant, cool and untouchable, and she did manage elegant. But cool? She looked about as cool as he felt, and *he* was starting to burn inside. And untouchable? His hands ached to touch her, to test her warmth, to caress her softness, to—

Resolutely he focused his gaze on the movie poster behind her. This wasn't the place to be thinking such thoughts. Not in a well-lit theater lobby. Not when he was already starting to feel the results. Not when Libby would surely notice, too, if she looked at him.

All he had to do was get through the next few minutes. Once the movie started, he wouldn't be able to look at her or have time to think about her. He would concentrate on the film and not on her. Not on touching her and not on wanting her.

Most definitely not on wanting her.

After dinner Joe dropped Libby off at her car, the only one left in the office parking lot downtown, then followed her home to North Augusta. She pulled into the driveway, then walked back to the Mustang to collect Justin and to offer an invitation. "Do you want to come in, Joe?"

He gave her a strange look in the yellow glow of the street lamp. "What's wrong?" she asked.

"That's the first time you've called me by my name," he replied. "Except, of course, when you opened your front door on Thanksgiving and said, *'Joe?'*"

He did a perfect imitation of the shock that had colored her voice that day, and it made her laugh. "Keep in mind that I expected you to be about this tall." She demonstrated with her hand in the air level with his waist. "If I sounded shocked, it's because I was." Shocked, surprised, disbelieving—she'd been all those things. But not disappointed. No, there was nothing there to disappoint a healthy, intelligent woman—and she was very definitely all three.

She got the mail and the evening paper, then unlocked the door and stepped inside, turning on the hall light right away.

"You ought to leave a light burning when you know you'll be home after dark."

"I meant to." She paused in the living-room doorway to remove her shoes. "I also meant to take some jeans and tennis shoes to work so I could change before the movie, but I forgot. Justin, hang up your coat, then go jump in the shower, okay?''

"Oh, Mom, do I have to?''

Before she could respond, Joe did. "Remember the deal we made last night?''

"Yeah, I remember,'' Justin said with an impatient sigh as he removed his jacket and hung it on a low hook attached to the inside closet door. He stopped in front of Joe and looked up. "Thanks for taking us to the movie and to dinner and everything.''

Joe crouched down to his level. "You're welcome.''

Justin started to walk away, but then he turned back and wrapped his arms around Joe's neck in a hug. "Come say good-night before you leave,'' he commanded when he released him and started toward the bathroom.

It was a touching sight, Libby thought: the little blue-eyed, blond-haired boy clinging to the big blue-eyed, sandy-haired man. A stranger witnessing it would think he was seeing an outstanding example of father-son devotion. If only Justin's father had been capable of such devotion. Their lives would have been so different. Maybe she and Doug still would have gotten divorced, but she would have remained in Chicago so Justin could be close to him. And with a father who loved him, Justin wouldn't have needed a surrogate. They never would have moved back to North Augusta, and they never would have met Joe.

She found that thought disquieting.

Realizing suddenly that they were still standing awkwardly in the hallway, she turned on the overhead light in the living room and invited him inside. "What deal did you and Justin make?'' she asked as she settled down on the sofa, folding her feet beneath her and smoothing her skirt down.

"What? Oh, we agreed last night that if you let him stay up late, then he wouldn't fuss about going to bed when we got home.''

"Good idea. I'd try it myself, but there's a certain sense of respect in his dealings with you that's missing with me.''

"Kids respect their parents a lot more than they let on."
Joe removed his jacket, then sat down in the armchair closest to her. "I think you should know, Libby, that Justin knows his father called last night. He must have overheard you talking to either him or me."

She felt a discomfort low in her stomach. It was the feeling she always got when she answered the phone and Justin's principal or teacher was on the line. Dread. Apprehension. "What did he say?"

"That his father was too busy with his girlfriend to talk to him. That he wouldn't have anything to say to him anyway." He paused. "He's eavesdropped on your conversations before. He asked me once what child support was. He said you had argued with his father about it being late."

Libby felt her face turn as red as the dress she wore. "There's something so tacky about arguing over money," she confessed.

Joe shrugged. "Raising a kid's an expensive proposition. Most single parents need that money to make it."

"I can cover the essentials on my salary, and we can live without the luxuries, if necessary. Most of Doug's checks go into Justin's college fund. But it's not the money, it's the principle. He has an obligation to that child, whether he wants to acknowledge it or not, and I intend to see that he meets it. So... every other month we fight." She sighed deeply. "Maybe that's why Doug refused to talk to Justin last night. I had complained to my attorney in Chicago, and he'd gone to see Doug—he collected both this month's and next month's support payments in person. Doug can't stand my lawyer—Jeffrey doesn't think much of deadbeat fathers—and he was angry that I'd called him."

"He didn't talk to Justin last night because he's a bastard," Joe said quietly. "You said yourself that Justin hasn't seen him since right after the divorce. That's been, what? A year and a half?" He waited for her nod. "The guy can't have been angry about child support all that time."

She sighed wearily. "I'm glad I know he overheard. If he says anything—"

"He won't."

"How can you be so sure?"

"He didn't tell you when he heard you arguing with his dad before, did he?" He waited, but she didn't answer. "He told *me*. He told me this time, too. I think he feels safer discussing it with me than with you."

"Why?" she asked. Then, aware that the blunt question sounded like a challenge when she was simply curious, she tried to soften it. "You've never even met Doug. You don't know anything about our marriage or our divorce."

"Precisely. I wasn't involved in your marriage or your divorce. I didn't know any of you then. As far as Justin's concerned, I'm an objective third party. He can talk to me without being afraid of hurting my feelings or making me feel guilty or reminding me of bad times. He doesn't have to worry about upsetting me or making me cry."

Libby looked away, staring at the array of toy soldiers on the coffee table without really seeing them. Joe was right. In the first few months following the divorce, she'd done all those things—had been hurt and felt guilty, had avoided any reminders of bad times. She had been easily upset and had often cried. She had sent her son the message that he couldn't talk about his own hurts, his own fears and concerns, without arousing hers. She had made him keep his own pain inside.

"I'm not criticizing you," he said quietly. "I'm just telling you how Justin feels. God knows, divorces are never easy, especially when there's a kid involved. Theresa and I didn't have any children, and it was still one of the toughest things I've gone through."

After a moment she glanced at him. "How long ago was that?"

"Fourteen years."

"Did *you* leave *her*?"

He shook his head.

It was hard for her to imagine that any woman would walk away from Joe. But maybe the ex-Mrs. Mathison hadn't been able to accept the military life-style. Maybe the transience, the impermanence, had been more than she could bear. Maybe she'd had a longing for a home to call her own. Maybe she'd needed familiar things—people and places—around her.

Libby could understand that. Hadn't those same longings brought her back to North Augusta? Back home?

But her situation was hardly the same. *She* hadn't left a loving husband behind. *She* hadn't left anything behind but pain and heartache and bad memories. All those years she and Doug had moved from state to state, the pull of home had been strong, but never strong enough to make her consider leaving her husband and her marriage.

"Why did she leave you?" She didn't realize she'd asked the question aloud until she saw the way Joe was looking at her. He wasn't offended by her presumption that she had the right to ask such a question, but amused. After the way she'd acted Sunday afternoon at the river, he was entitled to a far stronger response than amusement. "I'm sorry," she said quickly, blushing again. "That's none of my business."

He propped one foot, then the other, on the edge of the coffee table. "I don't mind discussing my ex-wife with you, Libby, because whether you agree with me or not, I *do* consider you a friend."

She knew she should tell him that, friends or not, the details of his divorce didn't matter. That offering them wouldn't result in a similar offer from her. That she really didn't want to know something that personal about him.

But she *did* want to know. She wanted to know how a woman could marry this man and live with him and love him and not see the answer to every single woman's prayers when she looked at him. She wanted to know what had made Theresa Mathison walk away from him. She wanted to know what Theresa had wanted that was more important than *him*.

Joe was silent for a moment. Why had Theresa left him? There were several simple, pat answers that he usually used whenever the subject came up, answers that absolved them both of any responsibility of guilt, answers that magically erased any hurt. *We grew apart. We wanted different things*

*from life. We decided marriage wasn't for us. Things just
didn't work out.*

But those answers weren't entirely true. He'd had no idea
that they were growing apart until the gulf between them
was too wide to bridge. They *had* wanted different things,
all right. He'd wanted her, love and marriage, children,
forever, and she had wanted out. *She* had made the deter-
mination that the marriage wasn't working out. *She* had
wanted the divorce.

"Three years before we were divorced, we had promised
to love and honor each other forever," he said with a quiet
sigh. "But somewhere along the way she stopped loving me.
She pretended as long as she could, but one day she just gave
up. She didn't want to stay married. She didn't want to have
children. She didn't want to move from post to post. She
didn't want to live on a soldier's salary. She didn't want to
be a soldier's wife. She didn't want to be *my* wife."

The silence that followed his last words was broken only
by the sound of the shower. Then Joe smiled ruefully. "But
that was a long time ago. I learned pretty quickly that you
don't die of a broken heart. Divorce doesn't kill you, either. It only *feels* like it will."

"Don't I know it," Libby agreed.

He waited to see if she would finally trust him with the
reasons behind her own divorce, but she said nothing else.
Would she *ever* trust him? he wondered in frustration.

"Well," he began abruptly, letting his feet fall to the
floor, "it's getting late. I'd better tell Justin good-night, then
head on home."

He went down the hall and tapped at the bathroom door.
Justin opened it a moment later, wrapped in a big towel and
dripping water all over the rug.

"I've got to go now, partner," Joe said.

"I wish you could stay longer."

"I can't tonight. Besides, you've got to get to bed. I'll call
you tomorrow, okay?"

"Okay. G'night, Joe."

"Good night, Justin." When he returned to the front
door, he found Libby waiting there. She'd put her heels on

again, which made it too damn easy to look into those dark brown eyes of hers…and too damn tempting to kiss her lips. He cleared his throat and dropped his gaze, only to find more temptation in the softly rounded curves of her breasts beneath the red dress. He cleared his throat again, but his voice still came out hoarse when he spoke. "I, uh, I'll see you."

"Okay." She hesitated, then said, "I had a good time tonight, Joe."

I had a good time, not *Justin* did. That was the first encouraging sign he'd received, and he took far more pleasure in it than he should have. Meeting her gaze, he smiled and quietly murmured, "So did I."

He fastened the bottom few snaps of his jacket, then opened the door before he finally gave in to the urge—the need—to touch her. It was a simple brush of his fingers against her cheek. Nothing prolonged. Nothing intimate. And certainly nothing very satisfying, because that simple touch made him want more, made him want to draw her close and touch her all over.

But it was enough for tonight, because it had to be. He withdrew his hand, gave her a regretful smile and stepped onto the porch. "Good night, Libby."

Chapter 4

"So... how was Thanksgiving?"

Libby glanced at Denise Tucker across the table. They met for lunch every Friday, but since last Friday had been a holiday from work for both of them, it had been two weeks since their last get-together. What an interesting week the last one had been, Libby thought with a secretive smile. For once *she* had something to tell, instead of being the one to listen. "It was fine," she replied casually. "How was it for you? Did you get along any better with your stepmother?"

"No. But I managed to spend two nights at their house without screaming hysterically, brandishing any sharp weapons or throwing any heavy objects at her." Denise picked up a cheese-stuffed potato skin and slathered it with sour cream. Libby watched and wished she could eat so much and still stay slim, but she'd been born five pounds heavier than Denise and had stayed at least that all their lives. "I wish I had canceled and stayed with you and Justin. The two of you would have been much more pleasant company."

"Actually, three of us. Justin's friend Joe came over for dinner."

"Thanksgiving dinner with two seven-year-olds—and boys, no less. That must have been pleasant. I'm not sure you had it any better than I did."

"Oh, I think I did." Libby cleared her throat. "You see, Justin's friend Joe is about forty years old, around six feet two and a first sergeant stationed out at Fort Gordon."

Denise was surprised into silence. It wasn't often that happened, and Libby enjoyed watching it now. She took advantage of it to explain how Justin and Joe had met and become friends, relating her own surprise at opening the door to a man instead of another little boy. But somehow she left out any mention of Saturday's fishing trip... or Sunday's lunch... or Monday's phone call and Tuesday's movie and Wednesday's call and the outing they had planned for tomorrow.

"What do you think of him?"

"He's... nice." It was a perfectly adequate answer—a perfectly truthful one—but inwardly she groaned. Was that the best she could come up with? What about charming? Sweet? Smart? Patient? Gentle? Handsome? Appealing? Sexy?

"Is that nice as in you hope you never have to see the guy again?" Denise asked. "Or *nice?*" She paused, but not long enough for Libby to respond. "Is he single? Does he really like Justin? Did he show any interest in you other than as Justin's mother? Did he elevate your heart rate, make your blood pump a little faster, make it pump a little hotter? Come on, Libby, tell me the good stuff."

"You act as if this is the first time I've looked at or spoken to a man since the divorce," Libby protested. "And it isn't."

"Fathers, brothers-in-law and bosses don't count," Denise said matter-of-factly. "Why are you trying to avoid talking about Joe? Is he that bad... or that good?"

There was a part of her that wanted to stay quiet, to say nothing else about Joe, to keep him her own little secret.

But, as she'd told him Sunday, Denise knew everything there was to know about her: every triumph and every failure, every schoolgirl crush and budding romance, every hurt and every heartache. And she never betrayed Libby's secrets.

"Well, he's single—divorced, but a long time ago. He seems genuinely fond of Justin. He has a great deal of patience with him, and he treats him with respect. Um . . ."

"The next question was did he notice that you're a woman—an attractive, single woman—and not just Justin's mother?" Denise provided helpfully.

Libby thought of the way he looked at her sometimes, of his gentleness when he'd touched her last night. She thought of the things he'd said about getting to know her and being more than her friend. She thought of how much more than friendship she would like to have from him, and a blush warmed her cheeks. "Uh . . ."

"Oh, he *did,*" Denise said delightedly. "So you really like this guy, huh? And he's attracted to you, and you're hot for him. Libby, you are one lucky—"

"Denise, I didn't say any of that!" Libby protested again.

"Not in so many words, but I can tell—"

"Not in *any* words."

"Minor detail," Denise said, waving it away. "After thirty-two years of best friendship, I can read you like a book. I haven't seen you blush and stammer and stutter like this since the first time good ol' Doug asked you out in tenth grade. At least this time it *seems* to be for somebody worth stammering and stuttering over."

"You never did like Doug," Libby accused.

"Nope," her friend admitted freely. "I've known him all my life, and I never understood what you saw in him in high school or why you married him or why it took you so darn long to divorce him."

"Just to keep the record straight, *he* divorced *me.*"

"Yes, you poor fool, you'd still be married to him if he hadn't met Barrie—and probably hating every minute of it."

"I *loved* Doug," Libby objected.

"Did you? Really? *When?* He was always working late or gone on business trips or entertaining business clients. Or he was out with the boys or partying with his pals or sleeping with his secretaries. When was he around for you to love?"

Libby gave in to the temptation of the potato skins, dipping one into the sour cream and biting into it. "You know, that's a very annoying habit you have," she said sternly when she could speak again.

"What? Remembering everything you tell me?" Denise grinned. "Twenty years from now I'll probably find an occasion to trot out the details of *this* conversation—maybe on the nineteenth anniversary of your marriage to Justin's friend Joe."

Although she laughed, Libby didn't find the comment particularly amusing. She would like to fall in love and marry again, but the man in her fantasies was always nameless, always faceless. It was too scary a proposition to put a specific man—to put Joe—into the role of husband and lover, even jokingly. The fantasy might never come true, and that could hurt. Then again, it just might, as it had with Doug, and that had hurt, too.

In spite of Denise's skepticism, she really had loved Doug. Even though everything Denise had said was true. Even though, after Justin's birth, he'd spent increasingly less time playing husband and virtually none playing father. Even though he had found excuses to cut not only their son, but also Libby, out of his life. She had loved him dearly and had believed she would love him forever.

Until that night two weeks after their twelfth anniversary. The night he'd come home and told her that he was moving out of their house and into his new condo with his secretary. His *secretary,* for heaven's sake! And as long as he was admitting to this affair, he'd gone on, he might as well confess to the others. She had held herself together by sheer will until he'd packed a bag and left, and then she'd locked herself in the bathroom and had cried—for herself and Justin, for her marriage, for Barrie and all the others.

The fact that he'd taken some perverse pleasure in telling her about his affairs had damaged her love beyond repair. She had never asked much of him. She hadn't complained about their frequent moves or his long hours or his heavy social calendar that always excluded Justin and too often left her out, too. She hadn't fussed about his out-of-town trips or his lack of interest in their son or his vocal resistance to her occasional efforts to find a job.

All she had expected was love. Companionship. Fidelity. Those weren't too much to ask of her husband.

But they'd been more than he was willing to give.

And if his infidelity had damaged her love, the way he'd treated Justin since the divorce had destroyed it. She had no affection, no fondness, no sympathy, no respect and no admiration for the man she'd spent nearly half her life with. After eighteen months of his neglect of Justin, she could barely tolerate him.

"So...forget about Doug and tell me more about Joe," Denise invited. "What does he look like?"

Libby waited until their salads were served and they were alone again to answer. "He has the bluest eyes I've ever seen."

"Like Doug. And Billy Taggert. I should have known. You're a sucker for a pair of baby blues." Denise finished picking out the chunks of blue cheese from her salad, then pushed the plate away without touching the lettuce. "I take it you've seen him more than once."

She nodded.

"How many times more?"

"We took Justin fishing at Clarks Hill—I mean, Thurmond Lake—last weekend. And to Riverwalk on Sunday. And to a movie on Tuesday."

"Oh."

Only Denise could put so much meaning into such a tiny word, Libby thought as she speared a cucumber with her fork. It wasn't just "oh," but "oh, you misled me from the beginning," and "oh, why didn't you admit this sooner?"

and "oh, this must be really special if you're withholding details."

"When are you going out alone with him?"

"He hasn't asked me."

"Knowing you, you probably haven't given him any reason to think you'd accept. Would you?"

Lunch forgotten, Libby stared out the window for a moment. Would she go out on a date with Joe Mathison? She wasn't sure she would know how to behave without the safety barrier of Justin. She wasn't sure she could feel comfortable having Joe's attention all to herself. She wasn't sure she was emotionally ready to deal with the reality of a new relationship, with all the possibilities and risks that involved.

And none of those responses had anything to do with the question. *Would* she go out with Joe? Yes. It might not be the wisest answer in the world, and it certainly wasn't the answer her brain would give. But it was her heart's answer.

Her heart's desire.

Ever since the divorce, Saturdays had been cleaning days, errand days, do-everything-she-couldn't-find-time-for-during-the-week days. But just as she had ditched responsibility for fun last Saturday, Libby did so again this Saturday, without even a hint of guilt.

Joe picked them up late Saturday morning for lunch at an old-fashioned drive-in just a few blocks away. Then they made the drive through Augusta to the fort located southwest of the city.

Justin had never been on a military base before, and he was literally bouncing in the back seat. For that matter, neither had Libby, and although she didn't quite share her son's excitement, she *was* impressed. It was cleaner and neater than she'd expected. More attractive. Some of the buildings that Joe pointed out as barracks were rather depressing in appearance, she thought, although he insisted they were nicer inside than out. But the rest of the buildings—mostly brick and stone, except for the original wooden ones, painted a blinding white—and the grounds were well kept.

"It's like a self-contained little town," she remarked. "You even have your own radio station and newspaper and churches."

"All the comforts of home," Joe agreed with a grin.

Justin leaned forward. "Can we see where you work?"

"That's where we're going now, partner. It'll be on the left up here. Watch and let me know when you see it."

Libby listened to Justin read from the signs in front of each building. When they reached the offices for the 65th Signal Battalion, he didn't hesitate to let them know. The parking lot was empty, so Joe took the space nearest the door. The building was brick, one story and contained four separate offices: headquarters for Companies A, B and C and, at the end, Supply.

"What are those buildings?" she asked, gesturing to the ones in back when she got out of the car.

"Barracks for the permanent party personnel."

"Which are?"

"Units that are permanently assigned here. Fort Gordon is primarily a training command for the Signal Corps. Most of the young kids you see around the post are trainees. They're here for however long their particular school lasts, then they transfer out," he explained. "Only a few of the signal units are permanent party. We handle communications here, and some of our people are instructors at the school."

"The barracks look empty," she said.

He glanced over his shoulder at them for a moment, then quietly replied, "They are. The 65th is the only signal permanent party that hasn't been deployed to Africa yet."

Yet. Wishing she hadn't asked, Libby dropped her gaze to the ground. That was a subject she would rather avoid. Every time she watched the news or read the papers, she got an anxious feeling deep in her stomach. If she ignored it, she always thought it would go away, and of course it did. But it always came back. Soon she was afraid the time would come when ignoring it wouldn't work, when it would always be with her.

Justin led the way around front to the third door. The signs for the first two were more formal: Company A and Company B. The third one said simply Charlie Company. The offices were small and cramped, and the decor strictly Army issue. If it wasn't gray and battered, Libby thought, it was olive drab and peeling—or, in the case of the plants, yellow and dying.

Joe's office was about half the size of hers at work, but it was neat and uncluttered. There were few personal items present: a framed photograph on the file cabinet of what appeared to be a Mathison family reunion, a yellow ceramic coffee mug on his desk and a crayon drawing of a man, a boy and a fish bigger than both of them tacked to the bulletin board. She recognized the artist's style and wondered when her son had given it to him.

Justin took a seat in the chair behind the desk and swiveled from side to side while asking questions about everything he saw. Libby quit listening to the questions or the answers and wandered over to study the photograph instead. Joe had mentioned brothers at the lake last weekend, but she hadn't asked how many. It was easy to identify them, though, because they all looked like him. Including him, there were five boys and one girl in the Mathison family, all sandy-haired and blue-eyed, all tall and lean and muscular—yes, even his sister, she thought with a smile.

"That's the annual Mathison Fourth of July barbecue."

She glanced over her shoulder and wondered how long he'd been standing behind her. She hadn't heard his conversation with her son fade away to be replaced by Justin's hunting and pecking at the typewriter in the corner, hadn't heard him move, hadn't felt him come so close.

Then she looked back at the photograph and congratulated herself for not tensing—not visibly, at least—when he came even closer to look at it with her. "You have a nice family."

"I have a *big* family," he corrected. Then he smiled. She could hear it in his voice. "And nice. Every one of them."

"Nice nieces and nephews, too." Finally she turned to face him and casually took a step back. She didn't succeed at putting any distance between them, though, because he immediately took a step forward. "Don't your parents nag you about when you're going to add to the bunch?"

"Are you kidding? In the past ten years they've introduced me to every single woman in the county."

"But no luck, huh?" Her palms were getting damp, and she unobtrusively rubbed them on her jeans.

"No chemistry."

Now her palms were dry, and so was her throat, too dry to swallow. And she could swear the temperature in the building had gone up at least ten degrees in the past few minutes. While the room had been chilly enough when they'd come in for her to leave her jacket on, now she was uncomfortably warm. "They'll find the right woman eventually."

"Maybe I'll find her first."

"Maybe." She sounded hoarse, but clearing her throat wouldn't help. Nothing would, she suspected, short of a cold shower or a timely interruption by Justin, but he was concentrating intently on the typewriter and paying no attention at all to them. "How about your date the other night?"

That broke the spell—or, more precisely, his laughter at it did. "Candace?" he asked, both amused and dismayed.

She'd had a neighbor named Candace, she remembered. All through grade school and junior high and even into high school, she'd wanted to *be* Candace when she grew up. The other girl had been everything desirable—beautiful, intelligent, charming, sweet, popular, funny and kind. The boys had worshiped her, and the girls had adored her. To a six-years-younger Libby, she had embodied perfection. But from the time she'd realized that she was never going to achieve perfection herself, she'd hated the name Candace.

"After Sunday night, I doubt Candace will ever speak to me again. She felt I didn't give her the attention she deserved." Joe paused, then added, "My mind was on someone else all evening. Someone I had unintentionally offended, who I thought might never agree to see me again."

"Would that be such a great loss?"

He reached out to touch her hair, and she let him, standing absolutely motionless. He made a long, gentle stroke all the way to the ends where they curled on her shoulder, a caress so light that she barely felt it, yet so powerful that she quivered inside from it. He started to repeat the action, then instead slid his hand beneath her hair and around to her neck in back, slowly pulling her toward him. "Fishing for compliments, Libby?" he asked softly as he bent toward her.

"How do you do that?"

Justin's question registered somewhere on the hazy edges of Libby's mind, but she couldn't even understand it, much less consider answering it, when Joe was this close to kissing her. But suddenly he wasn't so close anymore. A small, warm, wriggly body had maneuvered between them, clamoring for attention and leaving her feeling dazed. Disappointed. Cheated.

"*Joe*. How do you fish for compliments?" Justin repeated.

Joe watched Libby turn away, her cheeks a sweet shade of pink. Then, smiling ruefully, he turned his attention to her son. By the time he'd finished answering Justin's question, along with the half dozen more his explanation prompted, she was less flustered, more in control. That meant less approachable. Less willing to simply pick up where they'd left off. He would have to wait until next time, and he would make certain that no one could interrupt them then.

They left the office and walked back to the car. On the way, Joe noticed, Libby's attention was focused once more on the empty barracks. Knowing that the troops who lived there were in East Africa bothered her. It bothered him, too, although not because he dreaded getting sent there himself.

He fully expected orders for the 65th. It was just a matter of time.

He had no problems with shipping out, and he didn't object to fighting a war, if it came to that. He'd spent a year in Vietnam, and he'd done his time in Panama. Of course he didn't *like* combat, but he'd survived it before, and if he had to, he could survive it again. It was his job. His duty.

But the empty barracks bothered him, too. Too many of his friends were over in the desert now. If the buildup escalated into war, some of them would probably die over there.

And what would orders do to his chances of a relationship with Libby? he wondered. Being in the Army had already put one strike against him in her opinion, because of the life-style military service required. He might be able to change her mind about moving every few years, but how could he ever convince her to accept destinations that included possible war zones?

"Do you live in the barracks?" she asked when he stopped beside her to unlock the car door.

"No, I have an apartment in town." He grinned as he opened the door for her. "If you don't object to takeout, I'll invite you over for dinner sometime."

"Why takeout? Don't you cook?"

"I don't cook. I don't buy groceries. I don't even own dishes. The only appliances I use in my kitchen are the refrigerator and the microwave, and only for snacks." He waited until she and Justin were both settled inside, then closed the door and walked around to the driver's side.

"How can you be as old as you are and not know how to cook?" Libby asked when he slid in beside her.

"I *do* know how. I just don't do it. Cooking was one of the things my mother insisted on teaching all of us before we were out of school, along with sorting laundry, sewing on buttons and basic housekeeping."

"If you don't cook at home, where do you eat?"

"In the chow hall, Mom," Justin said from the back seat with an exaggerated patience that earned him a dry look from his mother. In the rearview mirror Joe watched him smile sweetly at her before he asked, "Can we see your apartment now, Joe?"

"That's up to your mother." He listened to Justin try to persuade her, but he said nothing himself. He would like to take them to his apartment, of course—anything to prolong their afternoon together—but he wasn't going to pressure her. But when she finally gave in to her son's cajoling, he was privately as pleased—and relieved—as Justin.

The apartment complex was located just off the expressway. Joe parked in front of the building just inside the entrance and led them to the end unit. Justin raced through the rooms ahead of them, examining everything at once, while Libby followed more slowly. Joe had no doubts what Justin thought of the place—the boy wasn't at all shy about expressing his opinions of the great stone fireplace or the small, cramped kitchen or the tiny bathroom—but Libby was far more restrained in her comments. He would like to know what she saw, if she recognized the rental furniture for what it was, if she felt the transitory air about the apartment, if she could tell that it wasn't a home but merely a place to stay.

After the brief tour, they wound up back in the living room while Justin explored the small patio out back. "This is nice," Libby said, taking a seat on one of the stools at the counter that separated the living room and kitchen.

"It's okay for a one-bedroom apartment," he agreed, straddling the other stool. "I usually live on post, but senior NCOs can't do that here, so I rented this place and the furniture. It serves its purpose."

"You like to travel light, don't you?" she asked as she glanced around. Again he wondered what she saw, what she was thinking, what she was feeling.

"When Theresa and I were married, we had our full limit of household goods. When she left, she took everything with her. I moved back into the barracks, so I didn't need any of it. Right now I own a few boxes of personal things, my clothes, a television, a stereo and a VCR. When I move, I can load everything into the Mustang and go.''

"I sold most of our furniture before we left Chicago, but I still had to hire movers to take everything that was left over.''

Her unspoken message came through clearly: this was one more difference between them. She was settled, with a houseful of possessions, while he was rootless, owning nothing more than what would fit in his car. Moving was a chore for her, while he could simply take off. Her belongings gave her a feeling of permanence, while his lack of them made him seem just the opposite.

"That doesn't mean we're so different, Libby," he said quietly. "I live the way I do because, under the circumstances, it's easier—and I don't mean because I move every few years. If I had a family, I'd have a truckload of furniture, dishes, books and keepsakes, too. But I don't. I live alone. That doesn't mean I prefer it that way. It doesn't mean that I *want* to be able to load everything I own into one small car.''

"Do you ever want to settle down?''

"Of course. I've always planned to go back to Kentucky when I retire. I want to buy a piece of land near my parents' farm and get to know my brothers' wives and my sister's husband. I'd like to learn more about my nieces and nephews than I've found out through Mom's letters and once- or twice-a-year visits. I'd like to spend time with my father now that he's not so busy on the farm.''

"But you could retire right now, couldn't you?''

"I have enough time in, yes.''

"Then if you want those things, why don't you retire and do them?''

"Because I still want to be a soldier, too. I want to see a few more places. I want to see if I make sergeant major when I become eligible. I want to be sure when I retire that I'm ready for it.''

His response sounded logical, Libby thought. Common sense dictated that you didn't give up a career you'd invested twenty-two years in unless you were certain that was what you wanted. Until you had achieved all your goals.

But the words also sounded like a smoke screen, an excuse to camouflage the fact that he was no more ready to put down roots than *she* was to take up a gypsy life-style again.

She slid to the floor and wandered over to the fireplace, studying the family photographs on the mantle there. "I can't imagine continuing to move the way you do when you could go home and spend time with your family again."

"You came home to spend time with your family, and look what happened," he reminded her.

She smiled wryly over her shoulder, then gestured to the photographs. "But what are the chances of something like that happening with this bunch? One or two might move away, but all of them?"

As he'd done in the office earlier, he went to look at the pictures with her. "This is one subject we'll have to agree to disagree on, Libby," he said, forcing a grin to lighten the mood. "You see moving as a negative experience—leaving a familiar home and saying goodbye to old friends. I see it as just the opposite—finding a new home and making new friends. If I had retired when I reached twenty years and gone home to Kentucky, the way you think I should have, I never would have come to Fort Gordon. I would have missed out on meeting Justin, and I would have missed meeting you."

She repeated her earlier question from the office. "Would that be such a great loss?"

He studied her for a long time before solemnly answering, "Yes, Libby. I think it would."

Libby was quietly thoughtful all the way home to North Augusta. Probably brooding over what he'd said and looking for ways to push him away for saying it, Joe thought. When they reached her little white house, he expected her to politely thank him for a pleasant afternoon, then send him on his way.

But she didn't. Her invitation to stay for dinner with them took him by surprise, and for a moment he simply sat there, saying nothing. A funny, wary look appeared in her eyes, and just as he opened his mouth to accept, she stiffly said, "Of course, if you have other plans—"

There was a faint current of jealousy underlying her words. Joe recognized it instantly. It was so unexpected and so damn pleasant that it made him grin. "Other plans? You mean like a date?"

She just looked at him, her mouth set in a grimly disapproving line.

"If I were seeing someone else, Libby, I wouldn't be spending so much time with you," he said gently. Then, almost immediately, he amended that. "No, that's not true. If I'd been seeing someone else, I would have stopped when I met you." After giving those words a moment to sink in, he continued, "I would like to stay for dinner."

She got out of the car and unlocked the door, then collected the mail from the box. He watched her thumb through it, then smile unexpectedly. It was a postcard that had cheered her, one from her parents, he supposed, as they made their way around the country. She glanced at the picture, a scenic view of the Grand Canyon, he saw over her shoulder before she flipped it to read the note on the back.

Inside, she handed the card to Justin after he'd removed his coat. "Here's a postcard from your grandparents."

With a whoop of excitement, Justin dropped his jacket on the floor, grabbed the card and went rushing into the living room, where he plopped onto the sofa nearest the lamp and studied both the picture and the hand-printed message.

While Libby scanned the rest of the envelopes, Joe bent to pick up Justin's jacket. He hung it on the hook inside the closet door, then removed his own jacket and slipped it onto a hanger.

The last letter also seemed to please Libby, he noticed as he reached for her blazer. "Good news?"

She glanced blankly at him, then shifted the mail to her other hand so she could pull her coat off that arm.

"Thanks," she murmured, carefully opening the envelope. Inside was a typewritten note and a check. The missing child support from Harper, Joe thought.

"Since Doug was feeling generous enough to send two months at once, maybe I should remind him that Christmas is coming up," she said, tapping the check against one hand. "He 'forgot' last year... although he remembered in time to arrange a Caribbean cruise for himself and Barrie."

"Would it really mean anything?" he asked, closing the closet door and leaning against it to face her. "If you called and argued with him about it and he sent his secretary—or his girlfriend—out to buy a present for Justin and had the store wrap it and the mailroom ship it, would it really have any meaning?"

"No," she admitted, laying the mail, including the check, on the desk just inside the living room. "But sometimes I just get the urge to *make* him acknowledge that he's got a son."

"You can't make him care, Libby. Some people just aren't capable of caring about anything but themselves." He knew what he was saying was true, but it was hard to imagine that Libby had married a man like that. She was so warm, so generous. How had she endured years of marriage to a man as selfish as Harper? She must have given and given until she had little left to give, and she'd apparently gotten nothing from him in return... except Justin. A gift like that could have made up for a lot.

"I'm going to see about dinner," Libby said with a sigh. "Go on in and amuse my child for a while."

He started across the hall, but he stopped right in front of her, lifting her chin with his fingers. "Don't worry about it, Libby," he said quietly. "Justin's not suffering from a lack of love. He's got you, your parents, your family...and he's got me."

She reached for his hand—not to push it away, as he expected, but to clasp it in hers. "Thanks, Joe." Then she released him, forced a parting smile and turned toward the kitchen.

When she was out of sight, he joined Justin on the sofa. The boy scooted over to sit half on his lap. "What's that word?" he asked, pointing to the caption on the card.

"Spectacular."

"What does it mean?"

Joe considered it for a moment, then said, "When you look at something and say, 'Wow,' that means it's spectacular."

Justin turned the card over and looked at the picture again. "Yeah," he agreed. "Have you ever been there?"

"Just once, a long time ago."

"I have postcards from all over. Want to see them?"

"Sure."

He left to retrieve his collection from his bedroom, and Joe took advantage of the moment to study the living room. It was as homey as his apartment wasn't. The furniture was expensive and solid—quality pieces, unlike the stuff in his apartment, whose primary virtue was its indestructability. The walls were hung with pictures, and the shelves and tables were filled with knickknacks, souvenirs, little treasures. He could pack up everything he owned and be out of his apartment in less time than it would take to box even half the things in this room. He knew Justin's room was the same, as were the kitchen and the dining room, with its cherry hutch and all the fragile dishes displayed there.

Libby had made herself and her son a home, one that she didn't intend to budge from.

Justin returned, carrying a binder in both arms. "This is my scrapbook," he said, automatically climbing onto Joe's lap once again. "I used to have a real one that you tape stuff in, but then you couldn't see the back, and it tore if you tried to take it out, so Mom made this one for me."

It was a large notebook filled with clear vinyl sleeves, and inside the sleeves he had arranged postcards, letters, photographs, ticket stubs from baseball games and other souvenirs. Joe held it so Justin could turn the pages and explain what everything was. After the last page, which included a certificate for improved behavior from school, Justin sighed. "And that's all."

But through the empty vinyl pages that followed, Joe could see that the final page in the back held something. When he asked about it, Justin sighed again and flipped the pages back. It was an eight-by-ten photograph of a smiling, blond-haired, blue-eyed man. "That's my father," he said flatly.

Doug Harper was what the young women who worked for Joe would describe as a hunk. He was almost pretty... but his face lacked character. Almost charming... but his smile bordered on predatory. Almost friendly... but his eyes were cold and distant. If he'd never heard a thing about him, upon meeting him Joe would have called him insincere. Sly. Untrustworthy. Knowing something about him, he silently labeled him a bastard.

"Mom says I look like him," Justin continued, "but it's only 'cause our hair and eyes are the same color. I look just as much like you."

The resemblance went deeper than hair and eyes, Joe thought. The shape of Justin's face and his nose and the almost delicate bone structure were reflected in his father's photograph. Only the warm, loving nature his mother had given him saved him from his father's coldness, his insincerity. But Joe said nothing. If Justin wanted to believe their likenesses were superficial, who was he to argue with him?

Joe closed the binder and leaned forward to set it on the table, then settled back on the sofa with Justin. "You know what's coming up in a few weeks?"

The boy giggled. "Christmas. We're going to put our tree up soon. I have my own decorations that Mom started buying for me when I was a baby, only now I get to help pick them out. She says when I'm all grown up and I move away, I can have them to put on my own Christmas tree."

"That's nice. What are you going to get for Christmas?"

Justin launched into a list of all the military toys he didn't yet have, only to interrupt himself with a sigh. "I wish we could go to my Aunt Renee's for Christmas. All my cousins are going to be there. It'll be kind of lonesome here with just Mom and me." Then he brightened. "Could you come over for Christmas, Joe? Like you did at Thanksgiving? It'd be a lot more fun. You could open presents with us and have dinner and play with my new toys with me."

"Maybe he wants to go home and spend Christmas with his family," Libby said from the doorway. "Come on in, guys. Dinner's ready. And, Justin, wash your hands."

Joe carried Justin as far as the bathroom door, then followed Libby into the dining room. She was restocking the wooden napkin holder—a gift from Justin, he thought, judging from the paint job—on the table. She glanced up at him as she returned the package of napkins to the china hutch cabinet. "I assume you *are* going home for Christmas?"

"I had planned to, but a week after my leave was approved, the commanding general canceled all holiday leave." He said it without sounding sorry for himself, although he'd certainly felt it when he'd been notified by the captain. His mother had cried when he'd called to tell her, and she'd fretted over him spending Christmas alone, even though he'd done it before and would do it again. "A lot of our trainees are shipping out to Africa as soon as they complete their schools, so the Christmas break was canceled for everyone."

"I'm sorry. Of course you're welcome to have dinner with us. Justin *does* get lonesome without a crowd."

"Do you get lonesome, Libby?"

She paused in the act of sliding her chair out and just looked at him for a moment. When he'd asked leading questions like that before, she'd found some way around answering them truthfully. This time she didn't even try to think of some lighthearted evasion. "Yes, I do," she admitted. "I used to think it was because of the divorce, but it wasn't. I was lonely before then, too. In fact, the only real change the divorce brought was that Doug went from being an occasional part of our lives to a rare one."

"He didn't have much time for you?" he asked.

She shook her head. "He had time for everyone in the world except us—especially every female. He supported us and paid our bills, and in his eyes, that was the end of his obligation to us." She smiled when Justin came in and climbed onto the seat at the head of the table. He had washed not only his hands but also his face, and she used a napkin to dry the water that still dripped from his hair.

They talked while they ate, a lively conversation that allowed Justin to participate, too. Libby was surprised all over again by how well Joe related to her son, especially now that she knew his only regular exposure to kids, besides at school, was on his rare visits with his nieces and nephews. He never talked down to him, never ignored him or brushed off his comments as unimportant simply because they came from a child.

If some women were meant to be mothers, then Joe was a natural father. Someday he would find the woman he and his parents were looking for, and together they would raise the happiest, best loved and most well adjusted kids anywhere.

Libby felt a twinge of regret that she couldn't possibly be that woman. All she could be was his friend, because no matter how sweet and patient and gentle he was, he was still a soldier. A man with no home, no roots and no ties to this community or any other he'd lived in. A man who could be here today and gone tomorrow if that was the Army's command.

Hadn't seeing his apartment this afternoon confirmed that for her? In less time than it would take her to pack Justin's toys, Joe could be gone, all trace of the months he'd spent in that apartment wiped away. She didn't want to know how many months he'd lived there, or how many other places he'd lived, or how many other places he would see in the future. She didn't even want to know how many more months he would have *here*. She'd rather remain ignorant.

"Mom?"

At Justin's tug on her arm, Libby snapped out of her thoughts and focused her gaze on him. "What, sweetheart?"

"You're not paying attention," he accused. "We asked if we do the dishes for you, then can we walk over to the ice-cream shop and get dessert?"

"Do you think you need dessert?"

He nodded vigorously. "Washing dishes is hard work, isn't it, Joe?"

She tousled Justin's hair. "Don't ask a man who doesn't even own any dishes. Ask your mother who washes them seven days a week."

"Can we, Mom, please?"

She gave in with a great sigh. "All right. But when we get back, it'll be time for you to—"

"I know. Take a bath, wash my hair, brush my teeth and go to bed." His sigh matched her own; then he grinned. "Hey, Joe, you can read me my bedtime story. I've got some neat war stories that Mom doesn't like to read. Okay?"

Joe glanced at her, and she consented with a nod. "Okay, partner," he said. "But first we've got to clean up here. Why don't you start by taking your plate in the kitchen?"

Libby scooted her chair back and began stacking the remaining dishes. But Joe took them from her, and when she reached for the silverware, he took that, too. "Go in the living room and sit down. I may not own any dishes, but I'm perfectly capable of washing yours."

"I don't mind helping," she protested.

"That's not the point. I wouldn't have minded helping you cook, but you did it alone. So go and sit down, and we'll do this."

She laughed softly. "Why am I arguing? The last time anyone offered to do my dishes for me, I had given birth to Justin just three days before. I'll be relaxing on the couch if you need anything."

And that was precisely where she was when they came into the living room fifteen minutes later—stretched out on the sofa, a soft tape on the stereo. Justin ran across the room and leaped, and she caught him just before he landed. "Let's go, Mom. The dishes are all done, and the ice cream is calling."

"Okay, sweetie. Get your jacket." She sat up and slid her feet into her shoes, then joined them at the closet to get her own jacket. No sooner did she take it off the hanger than Joe tugged it away, then held it while she slipped into it. Finally she'd found something he and Doug had in common, she thought with a smile. Because it had been expected by the people he socialized with, her ex-husband had been quite chivalrous. But because it had always been done for effect, she had considered it a less than pleasing habit. It made a world of difference when it was simply a thoughtful gesture, like now.

She followed them outside, turned on the porch light and locked the door, then slid her keys into her jeans pocket. It was chillier than she'd expected, and she quickly snapped her jacket while Joe performed the same service for Justin. "I can't believe we're walking two blocks in this cold to get an ice-cream cone," she fussed good-naturedly.

"It's only a little more than a block, Mom," Justin reminded her.

"Besides, the walk will get you warm," Joe added.

She could think of a few definitely more pleasant ways to raise her body temperature, she thought dryly as she turned the collar of her jacket up. Moving closer to Joe was one. Heavens, simply *thinking* about him was already turning up the temperature. And when he took her hand as they crossed the street and tucked it into his coat pocket with his, she could have been on fire for all the heat she was generating.

This was ridiculous, she told herself sternly. She was a grown woman—a *mother,* for heaven's sake. She wasn't supposed to be having these thoughts about their friend. She wasn't supposed to be feeling these feelings for *any* man right now, especially not this one. She wasn't ready for that yet.

But it was so nice. She hadn't felt these giddy, tingly sensations in so long—not since her wedding night with Doug.

They made her feel alive and young and special and feminine, and as long as she didn't do anything about them,
there was nothing wrong with them....

Chapter 5

She was thankful when they reached the ice-cream shop before she had to find an answer to that. While Joe and Justin went to the counter, she chose a small table in the corner and removed her jacket. Joe ordered bubblegum for Justin and chocolate chip for himself, then turned to her. "What do you want?"

She shook her head. "I don't want any."

"Are you sure?"

This time she nodded.

"I never met anyone who didn't like ice cream," he said when he joined her a moment later. Justin had chosen to sit on a stool at the counter instead, swiveling in never-ending circles while he licked his ice cream cone.

Just as he had called her on the cooking remark earlier, she corrected him on this one. "I didn't say I didn't like it, just that I didn't want any. Justin races around enough to burn up the calories from ice cream and pie and everything else, and I assume that, being in the Army, you work out or something."

"I run one lap a day around the track on post," he said with a grin as he sat down in the seat closest to her, his knee bumping hers beneath the table.

"One lap? And it keeps you in shape?" she asked in a woeful tone.

"On that particular track, one lap is five miles, sweetheart."

"Oh." Forcing herself to ignore the endearment, she went on. "I lead a rather sedentary life-style myself. I don't run when I can walk, and I don't walk when I can sit on the sofa. And that means I don't eat ice cream . . . or ices . . . or buttered popcorn. Just an occasional chocolate chip cookie."

"So I can't tempt you."

She had started to settle more comfortably in the small chair, but at Joe's teasing remark, she became still. She had to bite her tongue to keep from responding, to stop herself from telling him that he tempted her in ways no man ever had, not even Doug. He tempted her to forget good sense and reason, to pretend her promise to Justin that there would be no more moves had never been made, to overlook her son's need for stability as well her own. He tempted her to forget every lesson Doug had ever taught her, to trust again, to think about caring again. He tempted her to think about loving again.

When she did finally speak, she didn't say the things that were on her mind, or the things that were in her heart. Instead, in a voice that was hoarser than she would have liked, she said, "Not with ice cream, you can't."

He leaned forward, so close that all she could see was his eyes. His gorgeous blue eyes. "What *can* I tempt you with, Libby?" he asked softly. "Don't I have anything at all that you'd like to have?"

She was trembling inside—and outside, too, she realized when she looked down at her hands. She clasped them together in her lap, and she forced a smile that didn't fool either of them. "You've got to stop doing this, Joe," she said, making an effort to keep her tone light and casual. "We're friends, right? Wasn't that what you said you wanted?"

He leaned back. "It's a start."

"No, it's *all*. Friends . . . for Justin's sake."

He took a long, leisurely taste of his ice cream. She couldn't stop herself from watching. Then he said, "For a moment, forget about Justin. Forget about what he needs and think of yourself. What do *you* need, Libby?"

She watched her son across the room for a moment, then looked back at Joe. "I can't do that. I can't separate my needs from his. I need whatever he needs, whatever makes him happy and safe and satisfied."

"So Libby the woman ceased to exist when Libby the mother came into being seven years ago?" He gave a disgusted shake of his head. "No wonder your ex wanted a divorce."

The harshness of his words stung more sharply than they should have. She stared at him for a moment, unable to hide the hurt in her eyes; then she abruptly stood up, grabbed her jacket and started to walk away.

Joe scrambled to his feet and blocked her way. "Wait, Libby, please . . ." When she stopped, he dragged his hand through his hair, muttered a curse, then said, "That was out of line. I shouldn't have said it. I'm sorry."

She scowled at his chest. He was right: he *had* been out of line. It was none of his business why Doug had left her. He had no right to speculate about it, no right to taunt her with it.

Then, slowly, unexpectedly, her anger drained away. Just before dinner she had smugly congratulated herself on giving him an honest answer when he'd asked if she ever got lonely. But when his question had become more personal, what had she done? She'd fallen back into the habit of avoidance, giving him an answer that was not quite the truth and not quite a lie.

Well, all right, she admitted, this time it *was* a lie. She *could* separate her needs from her son's. It would take more than simply happiness for Justin to make her life complete.

She needed to remember that she was a woman and not just Justin's mother. She needed to put herself first once in a while. She needed adult companionship. Male companionship.

Denise wouldn't dance around the issue this way, she thought with a touch of envy. Her friend would state it bluntly: after eighteen months of abstinence, Libby needed a man. She needed a wild, passionate romance. She needed sex. It was nothing to be embarrassed about, nothing to be afraid of.

But Libby *was* embarrassed, and she was definitely afraid. And so she played the role of devoted mother, sacrificing her own needs for her child's—or, more accurately, using her son's needs as an excuse not to acknowledge her own. But she had them, and they were growing steadily stronger.

Yes, she needed a man in her life. She needed romance. She needed to see a future for herself with companionship and trust and love and, yes, sex.

But not with *this* man. Not with her friend. Certainly not with Justin's friend. And not with a soldier. Not with a man who was here only temporarily, for a few more months or, maybe if they were lucky, a few more years. Not with a man who was only temporarily in their lives.

"Libby?" Joe looked worried, and sounded it, too. "I *am* sorry."

She managed a rueful smile. "It's okay." She sat down again, clenching her hands together underneath her jacket. "In fact, you're partly right. I gave up my identity as a woman quite a while ago. It's safer being just a mother. Mothers don't get involved with men. They don't have affairs. They don't get hurt." She paused. "I *have* made Justin the center of my life. From the time he was born, he's always been with me. Doug hardly ever was. Justin was all I had, and I'm all he has. But that didn't have anything to do with my divorce."

Slowly he sat down also. "That was just the frustration talking, Libby. I didn't mean—"

She gently interrupted him. "You told me about your marriage—or, at least, your divorce. Let me tell you about mine." It took her a moment to gather her thoughts, to decide where to start. She wanted the words to be right, because once she started, she wasn't going to stop until it was all said.

After a moment, she began. "We were married for twelve years. For the most part, I was ... satisfied. I loved my husband, and he loved me—or so I thought. Ours was a very traditional marriage. Doug was the breadwinner, and I was the devoted wife and mother. I tried very hard to be everything he wanted—wife, lover, friend, assistant, chauffeur, cook, housekeeper. But one day he decided that he wanted something I couldn't be."

"What was that?"

Libby smiled. She had thought this would be harder, had thought that telling anyone besides Denise the details of her divorce would be shameful and difficult. She had thought telling Joe would be impossible. But it wasn't. She wasn't ashamed—chagrined, perhaps, but not ashamed. "Nineteen and blond. He left me for his nineteen-year-old secretary. And she wasn't his first affair. He'd been with countless women since before Justin was born."

Joe was staring at her as if he'd misunderstood. "Nineteen?" he echoed.

She nodded. "That did wonders for my self-esteem. I mean, how does a thirty-one-year-old housewife and mother compete with a nineteen-year-old? Have you seen what nineteen-year-old women look like these days?" Like centerfold models. Impossibly slim and curvy and sleek and lean. Gorgeous bodies and unlined faces. No stretch marks, no five extra pounds and no need for modesty.

"Yeah," he replied dryly. "They look like the daughter I could have had if I'd settled down sooner."

Libby sank back in her chair and felt the tension seeping away. He couldn't have found better words to soothe her still-tender ego.

"Don't confuse me with Doug, Libby," he continued, his voice quiet and steady, his gaze intense. "I'm not interested in little girls. I don't want you to be anything except what you are. And I would never hurt you. Can you trust me on that?"

She searched his eyes for a moment, then nodded. Yes, she trusted him. Not woman to special man, but friend to friend. Justin's mother to Justin's buddy. That was all.

Those three little words saddened her with their finality. No matter what else he wanted, no matter what else *she* wanted, friendship was all they could have.

Denise plopped down on the sofa, kicked her shoes off, then balanced a huge bowl of popcorn on her lap. "Do you want to talk before the movie or after?" she asked as she reached into the bowl for a handful.

With each breath she took, Libby could smell the salt and the tangy aroma of the cheese that coated every kernel. Plain popcorn she could turn down without a problem, but the fancy stuff gave her cravings. Just to be safe, she moved from the couch to the armchair, drawing her feet into the seat. "What makes you think I want to talk at all?"

"I don't get spur-of-the-moment invitations to your house unless there's something on your mind and you need to spill it all out to dear Auntie Denise."

"You don't get spur-of-the-moment invitations because you don't *wait* for invitations," Libby replied with a scowl. "You just drop in whenever it suits you. Like the time you came by at two o'clock in the morning to tell me that you were in love."

Denise winced at the memory. "That was the champagne talking. Besides, how was I to know that my prince would turn into a frog at dawn's early light?"

"That's putting it kindly," Libby agreed, remembering the man who had accompanied Denise on that early-morning visit. The world's second worst bastard, she had called him once she'd sobered up. First place honors, of course, went to Doug.

"But I'm here to talk about *your* prince," Denise said. "Why aren't you with him and Justin instead of here with me? Didn't he invite you?"

He had, but he hadn't pressured her when she'd begged off. She had too much housework to do, she'd claimed, but in reality she hadn't been prepared for a quiet afternoon at his apartment while he and Justin watched one of Justin's favorite movies on cable TV.

Ignoring her friend's questions, she asked one of her own. "Have you ever been in love, Denise?"

"At least a dozen times."

"Come on, I'm serious."

"So am I. Maybe they weren't what you'd call the real thing, but they were as real as it ever gets for me. I love falling in love, and I love being in love, but after a while it ends. And that's okay, because there's always someone new to fall in love with all over again." She smiled sympathetically. "But it's not that way for you, is it? You fall in love, and you expect to stay there forever and ever. You don't know how to be just a little in love. You have to go all the way."

"How do you do that—be just a little in love? How can you care for someone and have a relationship with him without falling head over heels for him and being heartbroken when it ends?"

Denise gave her a long, steady look. "Who says it has to end?"

"It would," Libby said stubbornly without explaining. "It just would."

"No doubts, huh?" Denise ate her way through a big helping of fluffy kernels before continuing. "Well...I guess you just risk it. Broken hearts aren't fatal—you and I are proof of that. They mend just as strong as ever."

Libby shook her head. "Maybe yours does, but I have doubts about mine. I won't go through that again, Denise. It's not worth the pain."

"So what are you going to do? Spend the rest of your life alone? Never have a lover? Never have a *love?* Because those things don't come with guarantees, Libby. The man of your dreams today might be the man of your nightmares tomorrow. The man who promises to love and honor you for always might become the man who buys a new condo and installs his teenage secretary in it before he remembers to tell you that he doesn't love you anymore.''

When her friend paused for breath, Libby stiffly said, "If I got desperate, I could always have an affair. You don't have to be in love with someone to go to bed with him.''

"Oh, tell me about it,'' Denise said sarcastically. "Give me the benefit of your vast experience in this area.'' She broke off to swear disgustedly. "Come on, Lib, counting the years you dated, you spent half your life with Doug the twit. You've never been to bed with anyone but him. You don't know how to have an affair.''

"Maybe I can learn. Not every relationship has to be *the* relationship. Not every romance has to last forever.''

"Is Justin's pal behind this? Did he come on to you? Did he suggest that you ditch the kid with a sitter and run away for a weekend of hot, steamy, toe-curling passion? Did he offer to ease the loneliness of eighteen months of divorce?'' Denise shook her head. "I thought you said he was a nice guy.''

"He didn't do any of those things. He *is* nice.''

"So what made you start thinking like this?''

Libby wrapped her arms around her knees and rested her chin on them. She wasn't going to tell Denise that Joe had almost—only almost—kissed her. That he'd held her hand and asked how he could tempt her and promised never to hurt her. That when he'd left last night, he had pulled her into his arms for a moment and had simply held her—no kisses, no caresses, just the warm comfort of his embrace.

To her friend, who'd been in love at least a dozen times, who'd had more romances before she was twenty-five than Libby would ever have, it would all sound so tame. So innocent. So meaningless.

But it wasn't.

"He didn't do anything,'' she muttered.

"So I can assume that your hormones have finally come back to life. It sure took them long enough." Denise's scowl faded and was replaced by her usual cheery smile. "And I also assume that they zeroed in on Justin's pal Joe, since he *is* the only man in your life right now. So you like the guy, and he likes you, but you can't just go to bed with him, because you're not made that way. You can't make love with a man you don't deeply care for, and you're afraid to let yourself care for Joe, because you're afraid you'll get hurt all over again." She smiled triumphantly. "Auntie Denise's analysis in one hundred words or less. Guaranteed one hundred percent accurate."

Libby groaned, hiding her face in her hands for a moment. "Why are you so smug? And why do I continue confiding in you when I know you're going to be smug?"

"Because I know you better than you know yourself," Denise answered. Growing serious, she rolled into a sitting position and faced her friend. "You know, Libby, *the* relationship—the romance that lasts forever—doesn't just spring into life full-blown. It has to develop. You have to get to know the guy, learn to trust him, find out what you have in common and what you're willing to overlook or adjust to. You can't expect to know within a week and a half of meeting him if he's the one you're going to grow old with. You have to give it some time. And you have to take some risks. Maybe you'll get hurt, or maybe you won't. It's a gamble."

"I'm not much of a gambler, Denise. I gave it a shot with Doug, and I lost more than I could afford."

Her friend sounded impatient when she responded. "This guy isn't Doug."

No, he wasn't. But he also wasn't the man she wanted to fall for. He wasn't the man she wanted to get involved with. He wasn't the man she wanted to have to say goodbye to a couple of months or years down the line. "So..." She sighed glumly. "I guess a casual affair is out of the question."

"Casual affairs are *my* province, Libby," Denise said quietly, with a touch of sadness. "Believe me, they're not for you. Look, kiddo, if Joe is as nice as you say, he deserves every chance you can give him. I mean, seriously, what more could you ask for? He adores your kid. He's interested in you and you're obviously interested in him. You'd be a fool to toss this one away—and I'm much too wise to have a fool for a best friend.''

She could ask for a man with roots. A man who wouldn't leave them. A man who would always be there, not only for Justin, but for her, too.

But she didn't tell Denise those things. She simply pressed the Play button for the VCR, then laid the remote on the table.

The conversation had disappointed her. She'd wanted solutions, but all she'd gotten was confirmation of things she'd already known. Just as she couldn't be just a little in love, she couldn't be just a little involved. She couldn't have guarantees. She couldn't have a meaningless, destined-to-end-soon affair.

Denise was right. Love was a gamble, full of risks, with big wins and bigger losses.

And *she* couldn't afford to play.

Long after Justin had gone to bed that evening, Joe and Libby sat in the living room at opposite ends of the sofa. The television was tuned to a network movie, but he doubted that she was following it any more closely than he was. Frankly he was finding it difficult to concentrate when she was almost close enough to touch.

When she had walked out onto the porch last night to tell him goodbye, he had given in to impulse and drawn her close, and she had come without resistance. He'd known it had been a long time since she had let any man get that close, and even though he'd wanted more—just a kiss would have satisfied him—he hadn't tried to take it.

But he doubted that if he reached for her now she would be so cooperative. But if he didn't do something to distract himself, he was damn sure going to find out.

Turning slightly so he could see her as well as the television, he asked, "Why wouldn't you go with us today?"

She'd told him that she had to do housework, but he had believed it was just an excuse when she'd offered it, and he believed that now. The house couldn't possibly have needed an entire afternoon of cleaning.

But then, she hadn't been alone the entire afternoon. Her friend Denise had been here when he and Justin had gotten back, and she'd been here long enough to finish off an entire big bowl of popcorn by herself. He had enjoyed meeting the black-haired woman, even if her frankly appreciative looks had made him a bit uncomfortable. He had somehow expected Libby's best friend to be more like Libby herself, but they couldn't have been more different.

At the other end of the sofa, Libby sighed and answered his question. "I just needed some time off."

Time away from him, she meant. The idea that she felt she needed a break from him disturbed him, although he hid it behind a grin when he asked, "Getting tired of me?"

"No, not at all."

"Are you still angry about last night?"

"Last night?" she echoed, sounding puzzled. Then she remembered his crack about her divorce, and she smiled. It was sweet and lovely and hit him like an actual physical blow. "No, I'm not angry," she assured him. "I appreciate you taking Justin off my hands for the afternoon and watching that movie with him. He has awful taste in films. Sometimes it's all I can do to sit through the shows when I take him to the theater."

"That's where grandparents come in handy. My folks will sit through anything for their grandkids."

"My dad will, but Mom's a little squeamish. She doesn't care for Justin's taste in movies, either."

He saw her eyes soften when she mentioned her parents, and he asked, "Do you miss them?"

"Yes," she admitted, turning to face him. "They'd been planning this trip for months. I knew all the details long before we left Chicago, but it never really registered that they were going to take off so soon after Justin and I came back. I miss them a lot."

He could sympathize with her; after all, he missed his own parents. He wished he could see them more often, without having to rely on letters and phone calls to keep in touch, especially now that they were getting older. Still, he was selfishly glad that her folks had left when they did. He was even glad that her sisters and their families had moved away. If they had all remained here, Justin would have had all the love and companionship and father figures any kid could need. He certainly wouldn't have needed Joe.

And without Justin, he never would have met Libby.

It was amazing how important she'd become to him in the short time since they'd met. He remembered all too well what his life had been like before he'd met her: work, an occasional date and a lot of time alone. He hadn't been unhappy—he had too many friends at the fort for that—but he'd often been lonely in a way that friends couldn't help. He had often found himself wishing that he had someone to come home to after work, someone to share his bed, someone to share his life.

But now it wasn't some anonymous woman he wished for. It was Libby. He wanted to spend more evenings like this one, quiet and peaceful. He wanted to help her raise her son, wanted to become a permanent part of their family. He wanted to tell her about his day at work and listen to the details of hers. He wanted to know that every evening she would be here waiting, welcoming.

And, heaven help him, he wanted her in his bed. He wanted to hold her, to feel her against him when she slept. He wanted to see her lying beside him when he awakened. He wanted to make love to her gently and tenderly, the way she needed, and hard and fast and deep, the way *he* needed. He wanted to love her.

It was torture to think of making love to her when she was sitting only a few feet away but out of his reach. But it was the sweetest torture he'd ever known, because he fully believed that one day soon it would become reality. Someday Libby would trust him not only with her friendship and her son, but with herself. With her body. With her love.

Until then, he would enjoy the pleasure and the pain of the fantasy.

Libby turned abruptly to the television when the ten o'clock newsbreak came on during a set of commercials. "Another reserve unit prepares to leave Fort Gordon for Africa," the pretty anchorwoman announced. "We'll have the story for you at eleven."

She seemed more tense when she turned back to him. "When this buildup in Africa first started, I watched all the broadcasts and read all the newspaper stories. Now I'm at the point that I don't want to hear anything else about it except that it's over. I was just a kid when we were in Vietnam. I don't remember what it's like for the United States to be at war. I had hoped I would never find out."

He wondered if she *really* didn't want to hear anything more about the prospect of war. Did that mean he couldn't discuss with her the very real possibility that the 65th would get called up within the next month or two? That he couldn't tell her how much he would miss her and Justin when that happened? That he couldn't assure her that he would come back to them? "Nobody *wants* a war, Libby," he said quietly. "But if it comes to that, we'll be ready."

"Please . . ." Her laughter sounded fake, and her smile appeared forced. "Let's discuss something more pleasant."

He guessed she really did mean it. With a sigh, he leaned forward and grasped her hand, pulling her to her feet as he stood up also. "I've got to get home, so come to the door and tell me good-night."

She followed him willingly, her small hand tucked securely in his. He released her only to put on his leather jacket. Then, before he could consider the consequences, before she could even suspect what he was planning, he pulled her close for a kiss. He didn't allow himself time to savor it, didn't leisurely slide his tongue into her mouth, didn't even let himself think about what he was doing, because his body's response would come too swiftly, too boldly, to be ignored, and *that* might be more than Libby was ready to deal with.

It ended too quickly, and it made a liar of him. Just last night he'd thought a kiss, one kiss, would satisfy him. It didn't. A hundred kisses couldn't satisfy the need growing inside him. Only the intimacy of burying himself deep inside her could do that, and even then he would need a lifetime of it.

"Oh, Libby," he whispered, brushing his mouth over her ear and making her shiver. He forced himself to take a step back, then another, and yet one more for good measure. Her dark eyes were soft and hazy, and her lips were slightly parted. She looked surprised, but not angry or annoyed or taken advantage of. That was good. The more she would take from him, the more he was going to give her, until she'd taken everything.

Including his love.

As kisses went, on a scale of one to ten, it had ranked a ten in innocence. Total strangers exchanged more ardent kisses than that. Libby kept reminding herself of that all day Monday and well into Tuesday afternoon. Now she sat in the break room at work, a cup of coffee forgotten on the table in front of her, a notepad and pen equally forgotten, and let her thoughts wander to it once again.

It hadn't meant a thing. It certainly wasn't cause for concern. So he had kissed her good-night. So she had liked it. So she had spent the past two nights fantasizing about it. It was no big deal.

But there had been such promise behind it. That there was a lot more where that had come from, and none of it innocent. That this simple kiss had merely been a prelude to one that would probably curl her toes, as Denise had put it. That even if she sometimes had trouble remembering that Justin's mother had a feminine, sexual side, Joe certainly didn't.

And that *was* cause for concern. He kept forgetting that they were only friends, and she kept letting him. She didn't want to endanger his friendship with Justin—her son counted on him too much—but she had to put a stop to this.

She didn't want to lead him on. She didn't want to let him think that she was willing to let anything develop between them.

Biting back a tiny groan, she let her head sink forward until it was resting on the tabletop. And just how did she think she was going to put a stop to it? She couldn't even convince *herself* that she didn't want a relationship with Joe, so how was she ever going to convince him? She knew all the reasons why he was wrong for her, but that didn't stop her from thinking about him all the time. It didn't stop her from wanting him. It didn't stop that ache deep inside that she recognized—from ancient memory, Denise would insist—as arousal. Desire.

Need.

With a sigh, she sat up and forced her thoughts from him back to the gift list she'd started making a few minutes ago. Christmas was only three weeks away, and her gifts for Faith's and Renee's families had to be shipped to Pennsylvania in plenty of time. She had to quit worrying over her personal life, do her shopping and wrapping, and get the presents in the mail.

Because there were so many kids, she and her sisters bought for families instead. Being the only child, that meant Justin got his own gift from each aunt, while Libby had to find something suitable for all five of Faith's kids and all four of Renee's. Faith's kids loved board games, and it wasn't difficult to find one that would suit the littlest to the biggest. And Renee's brood loved to read and be read to, so a couple of nice books would fit the bill with them.

She skimmed over her list. It was headed by Justin, of course. To keep from overspending, maybe she should make a detailed list and swear not to buy one single item that wasn't on it...although she doubted that would work. It was too much fun buying for him. She wanted to give him everything.

Her parents, next on the list, could be checked off, since she'd bought their gifts last fall. In fact, she had already shipped them to the distant cousin in West Texas where they would spend the holidays.

Nieces and nephews, Renee and Faith and their husbands, Denise and Mrs. Franklin, Justin's baby-sitter, rounded out the list. After a moment, she picked up the pen and wrote Joe's name at the bottom. She couldn't very well invite him to spend Christmas with them without having a gift for him, could she?

That one, tiny three-letter addition made her list seem suddenly impossible. What kind of gift was appropriate for their kind of friendship? Clothing was too personal and a gift certificate too *im*personal. She didn't know if he read for pleasure, or what kind of movies or music he enjoyed, or whether he liked sports.

"So what *do* you know about him?" she muttered, then made a list on her notepad. He liked to fish. He liked sweets. He liked Justin. And he seemed to like *her*.

Her shy smile faded as quickly as it had come. Maybe she should take the easy way out and simply let Justin choose fishing gear or something like that for him.

The ticking of the clock on the wall drew her gaze to it. Her fifteen-minute break would be over in another minute, and she had accomplished basically nothing. Closing her pad, she got up from the table and headed back to her office, which was just about the only perk her title of office manager afforded. As she passed one of the secretaries, the woman gestured to the phone she held to her ear. "Hold on a minute. She just came back." She placed the call on hold, then grinned at Libby. "You have a call on line three."

That grin could mean only one thing, Libby thought grimly as she went into her office. The caller was a man, and it wasn't business. Otherwise, Sandi wouldn't be so pleased. And the only men who would be calling her here were Justin's principal, if her son had gotten into trouble again, or Joe. As she picked up the phone, she found herself half hoping it was the principal.

It wasn't. "How about having dinner with me tomorrow night?"

She delayed answering by asking her own question. "How did you know where I worked?"

"Because Justin and I picked you up in front of the building last week," he reminded her. "I looked in the phone book to see what accounting firms were located in that building. Yours is the only one."

"Oh. Okay."

"Okay, that makes sense, or okay, you'll have dinner with me?"

Stretching the phone cord, she closed her office door, then sat down behind the desk. "Both. We'd like to have dinner with you. Justin will love going out on a school night again."

"Uh, Libby... This time I'd like to take just you." He was silent for a moment; then he asked, "Does that change your answer?"

Just her. That made it a date. Her first date since the divorce. Heavens, her first date in thirteen years. Did it change her answer? In a flash. She wanted to tell him, gee, sorry, but she had other plans. She wanted to tell him that if he was asking her as a friend—if she could drive her own car, meet him at the restaurant, pay her own tab and go home without so much as a serious glance passing between them—she would go.

No, she wouldn't, she decided, feeling panicky and hot. Despite what she'd decided when Denise had asked her, she wouldn't go without Justin. Not without the protection of her talkative, outgoing, possessive-of-Joe's-attention son.

"Libby?"

"I, uh, I don't know if I can get a baby-sitter. After spending the entire day surrounded by kids, Mrs. Franklin doesn't like to keep them in the evenings, too."

"What about Denise? She and Justin seemed to get along well Sunday evening."

"She might be busy. She usually is." But if she was, Libby silently acknowledged, she would probably generously offer to cancel her plans in order to get a date for poor, naive, abstinent-too-long Libby.

There was a long, heavy silence on the phone, and she couldn't think of anything to fill it. When Joe finally spoke, he sounded disappointed in her. "If you don't want to go out with me, Libby, have the decency to say so. Don't make excuses."

"I'll call Denise this evening, then let you know."

Libby swiveled her chair around to face the gilt-framed mirror behind her desk. Had those words really come out of her mouth? *How?* When she was intent on not accepting a date, how had she managed to do just the opposite? Because he had seen through her excuses and been disappointed in her lack of honesty? Because his disappointment had hurt her?

Or because she really wanted to go out with him?

"All right. Justin has my home number." He still sounded guarded. "Speaking of Justin, I just got back from the school."

She was relieved to have an easier subject on hand. "That's right. I forgot today was Tuesday. Was he behaving?"

"Of course. We played a trivia game in class today. He's a smart kid, Libby."

"Yes, he got that from me," she said. "The mean streak came from his father." Then she scowled fiercely. "I'm sorry. I shouldn't say things like that."

"You're entitled. And I don't think there's much chance of Justin eavesdropping this time."

She sighed softly. "For a long time I tried to tell him only good things about his father, but there wasn't much good to tell. He was a terrible father, and he wasn't much better as a husband." She remembered the angry words she and Joe had exchanged at Riverwalk that day when he'd asked her if Doug had been as bad a husband as he was a father. He'd been a little impatient in asking. Ten days later, here she was volunteering the information. "He was a good provider financially. I guess that's something."

"Yeah," Joe agreed. "He could have been a lousy father and a lousy husband *and* left you starving in the streets."

"I have to remind myself from time to time that, for all his shortcomings, Doug *did* give me Justin. He's responsible for at least a portion of who and what Justin is. Although Justin doesn't want to see it, there's a lot of Doug Harper in him."

"Doesn't Justin have any relatives on his father's side—aunts, uncles, grandparents? Someone who could undo the damage his father did?"

Libby sighed again. "Doug is an only child, and he had a serious falling-out with his parents before Justin was born. They know they have a grandson; they just don't care to have anything to do with him. I don't even know where they live anymore. They moved away from here right after we did."

"I don't blame you for being overly cautious in your relationships now."

The remark caught her off guard. "What do you mean?"

"You made a hell of a bad choice last time, sweetheart."

"Yes, I did," she agreed. "But I learn from my lessons. It won't happen again."

It was Joe's turn to wonder what she meant. What wouldn't happen again? A bad choice? Or any choice at all?

Sunday night, when she'd let him kiss her, he had thought things were finally progressing. Now he didn't know. She sounded distant. Wary. Maybe the kiss had made her realize that they were headed in a direction she didn't want to go. Maybe it had scared her. Maybe...

He sighed. Because of the visits to Justin's school, Tuesday afternoons always found him behind on his work. He didn't have time to speculate about the reason for Libby's reaction. That would have to wait until his own time. "I've got to get back to work. Call me this evening, will you?"

"Sure. Goodbye, Joe."

He hung up, but he didn't get right to work. Instead he took the photograph of his family from the file cabinet, propped his feet on his desk and studied it.

Things weren't supposed to be this difficult. According to his father, the moment he'd laid eyes on Joe's mother, he'd known he was going to marry her—although his mother always insisted that it had taken her a few weeks to reach the same decision. All four of his brothers had grown up with the girls they'd married. They had all dated through high school and, with the exception of Pete, who'd been drafted upon graduation, they had all married before they were twenty. His sister Karen had met her husband in college and had been married and a mother within two years. It had all been so simple—and so permanent—for them.

It hadn't been that easy for him. First Theresa and the divorce, now Libby. Why couldn't he like the nice, easy-going, uncomplicated type? Why did the only woman who attracted him have to come complete with a set of fears and insecurities that he might not be able to overcome? And why did she have to matter so damn much?

He could almost hear his father's gruff voice answering that. *Anything worth having is worth working for,* he'd always said whenever something had seemed unattainable.

But Libby wasn't a goal he'd set for himself, like making the high-school football team or earning enough money to buy his first car. She wasn't a prize he could win if he tried hard enough. She was a woman who'd been badly hurt by the man she had loved and trusted. A woman whose pride and self-esteem and self-confidence had been nearly destroyed. A woman who offered friendship grudgingly, hesitantly, because she didn't want to be hurt again.

And whether he liked it or not, she was the only woman who attracted him.

The only woman who mattered so damn much.

Chapter 6

Joe had thought Libby might not call. He'd thought that if she did call, it would only be to say that Denise was busy, so she couldn't go out with him. And he had thought it would probably be a lie.

But she *had* called, and she had said that her friend could take Justin anytime after six-thirty. And so here he stood on the front porch of Libby's little white house, waiting for her or Justin to answer the door and wondering just how well this evening would go. Through the door, he heard the click of heels on the wooden floor, then, as the lock turned, a sharp command from Libby to *please* stop doing that.

Then she was standing in front of him, only the screen door between them. She looked a little frazzled, wearing a bathrobe, only one earring and no lipstick, and with her hair tangled and mussed.

She looked beautiful.

"I'm sorry I'm running late. Come on in." She unlatched the screen door, then turned toward the living room. "Sit down and be quiet *now*," she commanded.

He'd never heard her speak that firmly to Justin, and he suspected he knew why it was necessary now. This was the first time in two weeks that Justin had been left out of their plans, and apparently the kid wasn't taking it too well.

"I'll be ready in about five minutes."

"Take your time." He pulled his jacket off and hung it on the doorknob, then went into the living room. Justin was wedged into a corner of the sofa, his arms folded over his chest and his face set in a mutinously dark expression. "Hey, Justin."

The boy looked at him. "Mom won't let me go tonight," he said, his tone accusing, his lower lip trembling. "I *want* to. I don't want to go over to Miss Denise's. I want to go with you. Talk to her, Joe. Tell her I can come."

Joe sat down near him. "I can't do that, partner. You and I spend a lot of time together, don't we?"

"Yeah, but—"

He held his hand up, stopping Justin in midsentence. "We do, and I like that, but tonight I want to spend a little time with your mom. That's why I invited her to dinner, and that's why I asked her if you could stay with Miss Denise."

Justin stared at him as if he'd been betrayed. "You mean *you* won't let me go?" he asked in dismay. "Why?"

"I told you. I want to spend some time with your mother. It doesn't have anything to do with you and me. You know you're not usually allowed to go out on school nights anyway, don't you?"

Justin nodded glumly.

"And we'll still do something on Saturday and go to the Christmas parade on Sunday, right?"

That brought him another nod.

"We're still friends, partner, but there are going to be times—" with any luck, he added silently "—when I want to see your mom, just like sometimes it'll be just you and me, and sometimes it'll be all three of us. Do you understand?"

"Yes, sir," the boy said grudgingly. "But I still don't want to go to Miss Denise's."

Joe settled back on the sofa. "I guess she must be pretty mean. She probably yells at you a lot, doesn't she?"

Justin's giggle came unwillingly. "Of course not. She plays games with me and lets me watch movies, and she helps me with my homework, and she lets me have ice cream sundaes for dinner and brownies for dessert—but don't tell Mom that. Mom says that the way Miss Denise eats is disgraceful, and Miss Denise says Mom's just jealous because *she* can't eat that way without getting fat."

There was a noise from across the room, and they looked up to see Libby standing there, her arms folded exactly like Justin's. "I leave the room for five minutes, and when I come back, you're talking about me getting fat?" she asked, feigning dismay. "You're such a sweet son."

She had nothing to worry about, Joe thought. She had traded the bathrobe for a navy-blue dress that fit snugly from her shoulders to two inches above her knees. It couldn't camouflage so much as one extra ounce, if there were one, and it showed off her gorgeous long legs. Her hair was pulled back in a style that reminded him of the old forties' movies his mother loved to watch, fastened at her nape with a wide gold clasp, all sleek and smooth and pretty. She'd added a second gold earring to match the one she'd already put in, a gold chain bracelet and a fragrance that was elusive and teasing and sexy as hell.

"You look pretty, Mom," Justin said, leaving the couch and crossing the room to her. "You're not fat at all."

"Thank you, sweetheart." Chuckling softly, she brushed a kiss across his forehead. "Get your jacket and your backpack, okay?"

Joe also stood up and approached her. "You *do* look pretty," he said softly.

Her smile slipped and quivered a little, but remained in place on her rose-colored lips. "Thank you." Leaving the living room lights burning, she went to the closet to get her coat. It was dove gray, long and oversized and loosely belted at the waist. It gave no hint of the lovely dress—and the lovelier body—it was covering, he thought regretfully as he held it for her.

It was three blocks to Denise's apartment, a Wedge-wood-blue duplex with a wide porch and a light shining. Joe remained in the car while Libby hustled Justin inside. In less than two minutes she was back in the seat beside him. "You certainly cheered him up," she remarked as he backed out of the driveway. "We'd been arguing ever since I told him that I was having dinner with you and he was eating with Denise."

"I wish I could handle his mother as well," he murmured. From the quick look she gave him, he knew she'd heard, but she apparently decided to pretend otherwise.

"Where are we going?" she asked.

"Do you have any preferences?"

"I like everything—Mexican, Italian, French, Chinese, barbecue."

"How about Mexican, then?"

"That's fine." Libby wrapped her hands around her purse and stared out the window, trying desperately to think of something to say. She wanted to thank him for taking care of Justin's temper tantrum. She wanted to tell him that he looked nice, too, in khakis and an emerald-green sweater. She wanted to point out that this was the first time she'd been out on a date since before she and Doug were married; to say she was nervous was a major understatement.

And she wanted to tell him that he *could* handle Justin's mother. Better than anyone ever had. Better than she wanted to be handled.

"How many times today did you consider breaking this date?"

Her fingers clutched the leather handbag tighter, and color spread slowly up her throat and into her face. "Only ten or twelve," she admitted guiltily.

"Why didn't you?"

She looked at him. He never took his gaze off the road, never directed that steady, measuring look her way. "I didn't know how to get hold of you," she replied honestly. "I didn't want you to think badly of me. And . . . I didn't really want to break it."

"Does it matter what I think of you?"

"Yes. Friends' opinions are always important."

"Back to that, are we?"

She sighed and looked out the side window again. He hadn't sounded sarcastic. Just skeptical. Slightly mocking. He was entitled to that. After all, he'd made his opinion of limiting their relationship strictly to friendship quiet clear.

What if she gave it to him in ultimatum form? No kisses, no embraces, no leading remarks, no intimate looks—or no friendship. Would he agree to that? Maybe. And he might say so long, too, to Justin as well as to her. She couldn't risk that.

But she couldn't risk falling for a man who was all wrong for her, either. Joe Mathison was a fine friend, but in the long run, he wasn't the man she wanted in her and Justin's lives. He couldn't give them the things they needed—the security, the stability—and she couldn't settle for anything less. She had promised Justin a home, roots. She had promised herself that.

It was one promise she would never break.

It was still barely eight o'clock when they finished their dinner and left the restaurant. Libby was silently wondering if he would take her home now and maybe spend a little time with Justin when he suddenly said, "There's a toy store just a couple of blocks from here. Do you mind if I make a quick stop? I need to pick up some things for the family."

She smiled. "You strike me as the organized type who would have already bought, wrapped and shipped all his Christmas presents."

"I haven't even started. What about you?"

"I made a list yesterday of the people I need to buy gifts for. That's about the extent of it." She was glad he wasn't taking her straight home, she realized as she got into the car. Glad that he wasn't eager to trade her company for her son's. But she shouldn't be. That was a dangerous way to think.

But even knowing that, she was still glad.

They turned the "quick stop" into a full-fledged shopping trip, filling the cart with gifts for Joe's nieces and nephews along with her own purchases for Justin. He was fun to shop with, unlike Doug, who had never, as far as she knew, set foot in a toy store. He seemed to know more about her son's likes and dislikes than she did, and after being corrected several times on her selection of toys, she scowled at him. "How do you know that Justin wants that game and not this one?"

"He ran his wish list by me the other day."

"Oh." She replaced the one she'd chosen on the shelf and accepted the one he held.

He watched her drop it into the cart, then surveyed the collection there. "And you accused *me* of indulging him," he said softly.

"Am I buying too much?"

"You have to decide that."

"That's the cowardly way out."

"It's called diplomacy, sweetheart. If you want to spend a fortune on him for Christmas, that's your business."

She separated her purchases from his and gave each a second consideration. She'd made a lot of selections, some only a few dollars, but too many of the others in double digits. *Far* too many.

"Libby?" He touched her hand until she looked at him, then drew his back. "Buying him a lot of presents isn't going to make him forget that his father doesn't care."

Was that what she was doing? Trying to make sure he had so many gifts to open that he wouldn't realize there wasn't anything there from Doug? So he wouldn't notice that his father had forgotten him *again?* With a sigh, she looked down at the brightly packaged toys. "I did this last Christmas," she admitted. "And for his birthday. And it did make him forget . . . for a few days."

"I understand that you want to protect Justin. But Doug's his father. That's a fact that can't be changed. And he's a lousy father. Sooner or later you've got to come to terms with that."

"And what about Justin? He's just a little boy. How is he supposed to come to terms with something that *I* have trouble with?" She replaced one of the toys on the shelf where she'd gotten it, then began pushing the cart down the aisle.

"I think Justin's dealt with it pretty well for a seven-year-old."

"He doesn't have a father anymore. How can he deal well with that?" she challenged.

"Because from everything you've told me and everything Justin's said, he *never* had a father, not really." He paused as if considering the wisdom of what he was about to say, then decided to say it anyway. "You know what he misses, Libby?"

She set another of the toys back on the shelf before looking at him for an answer.

"A dad."

She looked blankly at him.

"The words mean different things to Justin. A father is a stranger who doesn't live with his kids, never sees them, never talks to them and has nothing in common with them. That's what Justin has. A dad, on the other hand, lives with his kids, plays games with them, takes them fishing, tells them stories, loves them and never leaves them. That's what you and I have. *That's* what he wants. Not Harper."

She sorted through the remaining toys and games in the cart, picking the ones Justin would enjoy most and returning the others while she considered what Joe had said. She had never given it much thought before, but Justin *did* seem to have different concepts for the words. Although he often talked about his friends' dads or her own, she'd never heard him use the word in reference to his. Doug was always *my father*. And Doug was the only father who'd earned that label from him.

"So what you're saying is that the way Doug treats Justin doesn't bother *him* as much as it does *me*," she said slowly as she turned the cart toward the checkouts at the front.

"I don't think it does." He shrugged. "I'm not sure Justin even knows to expect anything different from him."

"So even if Doug sent him cards and gifts and letters and talked to him on the phone, Justin would still need . . ." She paused, thought about it, then used Joe's phrasing. "A dad."

He nodded.

It was a nice theory, one she would like to believe. It would ease some of her guilt for giving him such a rotten father to begin with. It would mean that if she ever remarried, Justin would probably adjust beautifully to his stepfather. He wouldn't miss the father who had abandoned him. He wouldn't be permanently scarred by Doug's rejection.

They paid for their purchases and carried the big bags out to the Mustang. "Could you keep these at your apartment until I can find a place to hide them at home?" she asked, shivering while he unlocked the door.

"No problem." He set both bags in the back seat, then waited for her to get inside. When he joined her, he started the engine and turned the heater to high. "Do you mind if we drop them off now? There's something I'd like to show you. Something I'd like your opinion on."

She could hear Denise now. *So he took you to his apartment. My, my, he does move fast. Give me all the details.* She shook her head to clear away the thought and murmured her agreement.

It was a short drive on winding streets to the complex. The apartment, she noticed, was dark and chilly. Coming home to an empty place was no fun, but at least her house offered a little more welcome than this.

She stood near the cold fireplace, her hands tucked inside her coat pockets, and longingly gazed at the woodbox full of hickory logs while Joe took the toys into the bedroom.

"Libby? Could you come in here?"

To his apartment and straight into his bedroom—without even giving you a chance to remove your coat. Very fast, indeed. Resolutely ignoring her best friend's ghostly tauntings, she went down the short hall and into the bedroom. Joe was standing in front of the tall chest of drawers. When he heard her enter, he moved aside.

There across the top stood a half-dozen mounted tin soldiers, the tallest only three inches high. Three were dressed in the soft gray uniform of the Confederate Army, the other three in Yankee blue. They were exquisitely detailed, down to the braid on the uniforms and the mustaches and tiny fingers on the soldiers.

"These are beautiful," she said, examining one, then replacing it. The rearing horse balanced perfectly on two legs.

"They belonged to my granddad. He had several hundred of them. He was a Civil War buff, and he was always building battlefields and reenacting skirmishes. Before he died, he divided them among all his children. My dad split his six ways." He picked one up and studied it for a moment, then wrapped his fingers around it as he said, "I'd like to give these to Justin for Christmas."

Libby stared at him. "Joe, you can't do that," she blurted out.

"Why not?"

"You should save these for *your* children."

"I don't have any children. I may never have any. Besides, this is only part of my share. I'd like Justin to have them."

"That's too much."

He didn't say anything.

"This is really nice, but..." She trailed off and moistened her lips. "What if you find the woman you're looking for? You'd have that much less to give to your own children."

"And what if I never find her, Libby? What if she doesn't want to be found?" He shrugged. "This way I know that at least some of them would be with someone who would value them the way Justin would."

"He would value them because they're beautiful. Because they came from you, he would treasure them." She ran her finger over one horse's mane, then touched its rider's sword.

"So... you don't object?"

She sighed softly. "If it's what you want. Just be sure you won't regret it later."

"I won't."

For a long moment they simply stood there, gazes locked, the tin soldiers forgotten. *Beautiful.* She'd used the word easily, but Joe didn't think she had any idea how easily, how perfectly, it applied to her. She was a beautiful woman, lovely and soft and fragile and strong. She was the most beautiful woman he'd ever known.

He slowly reached for her, smoothing his palm over her hair without disturbing the sleek style. He wished she'd worn it down, wished he could fill his hands with its fragrant softness, wished he could bury his face in its silk. Then, as he traced the outline of her ear and made her shiver, he was glad she'd worn it back like this, giving him access to her ear and to the long, delicate line of her neck.

In a whisper with no sound, no substance, he spoke her name as he drew just the tips of his fingers along her throat. He stopped when he reached the soft gray wool of her coat and, without breaking contact with her, he loosened the belt at her waist.

It took only the light touch of his hands to push the fabric aside. He felt her heat as he moved a step closer and settled his hands on her waist.

He was too close, Libby thought, and looking at her too intently, touching her too intimately. She should push him away, should turn and run away, but she couldn't. Her brain seemed unable to command, her legs unable to obey... or were they merely unwilling? Nothing had felt so good in longer than she could remember. Her heart hadn't beat like this, her breasts hadn't ached like this, her body hadn't throbbed like this, in months. Years. Forever. She couldn't deny herself such pleasure yet. She couldn't stop him.

When he raised his hand, she sensed it without breaking his gaze. She knew he was going to touch her breast, and she almost whimpered when he did. For a moment he simply laid his hand, big and narrow-fingered, over her breast; then he began a slow, easy, bone-melting caress. She couldn't hold her eyes open any longer. She couldn't hold her moan back, couldn't stop from arching, pressing herself harder against his palm.

Her breast was soft, and her nipple hard and aching. Even through her clothing, the contrast further aroused Joe, stirring his own ache. He longed to undress her, to remove each piece of clothing one at a time until she was naked and weak from wanting. He hungered to remove his clothes and fill the warm, tight, moist place inside her, to join with her so deeply that they could never truly be apart again.

Moving closer still, he continued to tease and tantalize her, to tease and torment himself. He slid his arm around her waist, gently encouraging her with his hand at her breast to lean back, to let him support her, and when she did, he took advantage of her position to leave a trail of heated, wet kisses along her throat to her ear.

Libby shuddered when he bit gently at her earlobe, and she groaned aloud when his tongue dipped inside. Restlessly she shifted against him, bracing her hands on his chest, seeking more warmth, more contact, more—

Abruptly she became still when her hips met his. His arousal was swollen and heavy and potent, pressing like a brand against her belly. This wasn't the kind of innocent necking she and Doug had indulged in when they were kids, she thought in sudden panic. This was a man, fully aroused and fully willing and ready to carry what they'd started to its natural conclusion.

And that couldn't happen. She was aroused, too—heaven help her, so aroused that even her toes ached with it—but she wasn't willing. She wasn't ready. She couldn't do this.

"Oh, Libby," he whispered, his voice thick and warm with need. Need that she couldn't satisfy. Need that she shouldn't even have stirred.

Before she could give in once more to the pleasure, before she could betray herself with weakness and hunger and her own need, she wrenched herself out of his embrace and fled the room, not stopping until she was safely at the front door.

Joe stood motionless for a long time, then ground out a frustrated curse as he brought his fist down on the chest. Five of the six tin horses teetered, then fell with a metallic clatter to their sides. He'd known there was no way Libby was going to make love with him tonight, but damn it, why had she run away like that? Why hadn't she let them enjoy just that small intimacy?

Squeezing his eyes shut, he forced himself to breathe deeply in an effort to ease the knot of tension inside him. The momentary anger faded, but the frustration was stronger, and the arousal... It would take a hell of a lot more than deep breathing to ease that. It would be with him a long time.

Opening his eyes again, he woodenly replaced the six soldiers in the top drawer, then turned off the light and went into the living room. Libby was waiting at the door, her coat belted tightly, her arms folded across her chest. He didn't need to know anything about body language to understand her unspoken message. Keep back. Don't touch.

They left without speaking, and they remained silent on the trip to North Augusta. After pulling into Denise's driveway, Joe turned off the engine. "I'll go in. Justin's probably asleep," he said flatly. "It'll be easier for me to carry him." Without waiting for her approval, he got out, slamming the door hard enough to rock the car from side to side.

Denise opened the door as he crossed the porch and ushered him inside. "Justin's conked out on the couch," she said, directing him into the living room. "Did you and Libby have a good time?"

He considered lying or offering a casual, breezy brush-off, but instead he told her the truth. "*I* enjoyed it, but it's hard to tell with Libby, since she's not speaking to me right now."

"What happened?" Denise asked sympathetically.

"It was my fault, I guess. After all this time, I thought it was all right to touch her." He bitterly shook his head. "I guess I was wrong."

"You're not going to give up, are you?"

He stopped beside the sofa and picked up Justin's backpack, dangling it by one strap over his shoulder. Then for a moment he simply looked at the little boy snuggled under a yellow-and-red quilt. He was already wearing his pajamas, and his hair was standing on end, and he looked younger, more fragile and more innocent, than usual. Giving up on Libby meant giving up Justin, too. He couldn't do that. He didn't want to lose Libby, but he *couldn't* lose Justin. "No," he said on a sigh. "I'm not giving up."

"Go ahead and take the quilt with you. It'll be easier than getting his jacket on him." She waited until he picked up Justin; then she tucked the blanket around him. "Joe, Libby's just scared. She needs a lot of gentleness and patience."

Justin settled against him without waking, and for a moment Joe simply looked at him. He found a strong, deep pleasure in holding the boy, the kind of pleasure that everyone expected a woman to feel for a child but few ever expected from a man. Just as people expected all women to experience strong yearnings to become a mother, he thought, but seemed surprised when a man had the same kind of yearnings.

He did. He wanted to be a father, wanted to have a child of his own to love. He wanted to love *this* child. He wanted to be a part of Justin's life, to teach him and take care of him and protect him. He wanted to be Justin's dad.

Fat chance. After this evening, his chances of that happening had probably gone from slim to nonexistent.

"I know Libby's scared," he said, stroking Justin's hair. "I know her ex-husband was a son of a bitch. I know he did a number on her self-esteem when he left her. But damn it, I didn't even know the guy. Why am *I* paying for *his* mistakes?"

Denise didn't offer an answer. He was grateful, since the only things she could have said would have been nauseatingly pat.

"Thanks for keeping Justin," he said, stopping so she could open the door for him.

"Anytime." She stood in the door, shivering in the cold, and watched him walk across the porch. "Joe?" she called when he reached the top step. "Libby doesn't give of herself easily... but when she does, it's for keeps. It may not happen as quickly as you'd like, but it'll last forever."

He simply nodded and continued down the steps. Forever. That was exactly what he wanted.

He circled to the passenger side, where Libby had opened her door, and carefully settled Justin in her lap. Then, returning Denise's wave, he slid behind the wheel and started the engine again.

He wanted to say something to Libby, wanted to ask her why she had run from him, why she couldn't accept that little bit of intimacy from him. He wanted to pretend it had never happened, that he hadn't grown hard and felt her become soft. He wanted to do anything that would make things normal between them again. But he couldn't find any words, and in less than three minutes they were at her house, anyway.

Once again he carried Justin, taking him straight to his bedroom. The boy woke up while Joe was tucking him into bed and smiled sleepily. "Hey, Joe," he whispered.

"Hey, partner."

"Read me a story?"

"Sure." But he knew Justin would be asleep again in a matter of minutes. He waited until the soft snoring began again, then bent and kissed his forehead. "Next time," he whispered. "I'll read to you next time."

Libby was waiting in the hallway, still wearing her coat, even though the house was warm. When Joe stopped in front of her, she didn't look at him. She hadn't looked at him since she'd left him in the bedroom at his apartment, he realized bitterly. "I won't apologize for touching you, Libby, or kissing you," he said flatly. "I won't apologize for wanting you."

She lifted her gaze then, but it didn't reach his face. Instead she focused somewhere around his right shoulder. "Thank you for dinner," she said formally, stiltedly. "I...I enjoyed..."

She couldn't get the rest of the lie out. He wanted to shake her, to force her to look at him and acknowledge that he wasn't Doug Harper, to see that he wasn't going to hurt her. But he couldn't force her to do anything. And so he smiled sadly and murmured, "Good night, Libby." He didn't look back at her. He didn't give in to the urge to touch her just once more. He simply walked out the door.

Libby rinsed the last dinner dish and laid it in the drainer with the rest, then reached for a towel to dry her hands. In the living room, Justin was chatting on the phone with Joe, a call that she'd known would come but had hoped to avoid. So far, so good. They'd been talking for fifteen minutes, and Joe hadn't yet asked to speak to her. Maybe he wouldn't.

She just didn't know what to say after last night. "I'm sorry" would make a good start, followed immediately by "It can't happen again." She *was* sorry. Sorry that she hadn't stopped him sooner. Sorry that she'd had to stop him at all. Sorry that she hadn't been able to relax and enjoy and let her emotions take her where they would.

And it *couldn't* happen again. The next time she might not be lucky enough to end it in time. The next time she might be foolish enough to give her emotions free rein. The next time they might wind up in bed, and, Lord, she wasn't ready for that yet.

She might never be ready for that. Not with Joe. He wasn't the man for her. He wasn't the man she needed.

So why did he have to be the only man she wanted?

Refusing to answer that question, she went into her bedroom, closing the door behind her. It was another hour until Justin's bedtime, but she couldn't wait. She needed a little time alone. To think. To brood. To regret.

She hadn't even settled on the bed when there was a knock at the door; then Justin burst inside. "Mom, Joe's on the phone. He wants to talk to you."

She closed her eyes to hide her dismay and wondered how Joe would act if she took his call. As if nothing had happened? As if last night were unimportant? Or as if she had disappointed him one more time?

And how would *she* act? She felt like the world's biggest fool and worst coward. She felt that she had done the right thing in walking—running—away. She wondered if she should run even farther.

"Mom?" Justin leaned over her on the bed, giving her a shake. When she opened her eyes, she found him peering intently into her face. "Joe's on the phone. Don't you want to talk to him?"

She reached up to tousle his hair. "Tell him that I can't come to the phone right now, honey, okay?"

"Why not?"

"Just tell him, sweetie. He'll understand."

But would he? she wondered as Justin went back to the living room. Maybe she should have talked to him ... but what could she possibly say that he didn't already know?

A few minutes later Justin returned to her room. Ignoring her closed eyes and slow, steady breathing, he climbed onto the bed with her and landed the fighter plane he carried on the rumpled spread. "I told Joe you couldn't come to the phone," he announced.

She tried not to ask, but it came out anyway. "What did he say?"

"He asked what you were doing, and I told him lying down, and he didn't say anything else." He paused to let his plane take off again, flew it in a slow circle overhead, then landed it once more. "He's going to call you tomorrow to ask if it's okay if we go out for hamburgers tomorrow night. Since it's Friday, I told him it was probably all right, but he said he'd ask you anyway. Is it okay, Mom?"

Instead of answering his question, she asked one of her own. "You like Joe a lot, don't you?"

"Better than anybody." Then he grinned a near-perfect imitation of Joe's little-boy grin. "Except you."

That grin touched her, the same way it touched her when it was on Joe's face. It also sent a shiver of warning through her. When had Justin picked it up? And what other habits of Joe's was he imitating? Not that there could be anything bad. Joe's behavior around Justin was never less than perfect. But it was just one more sign of the influence he had on her son. One more measure of the depth of Justin's feelings for him. "You've been spending a lot of time with him."

"That's okay, Mom. He *likes* having me around."

She had difficulty swallowing over the lump in her throat. "I know he does, honey. He thinks you're a special kid. But...you understand he won't always be here, don't you?"

Justin nodded solemnly. "He gets orders next May. But we'll always be friends, Mom. Wherever he goes, we can write and call and visit."

Next May. Libby had managed not to learn that little bit of information until now, and the sinking sensation in her stomach made her wish she had avoided learning it at all. Six months, then Joe would be gone. To Justin, of course, that must seem like forever, but she knew how quickly those months would pass. How would it feel not to see Joe again? To know that he was no longer working in that tiny office on post or living in that cramped apartment? To not be able to talk to him or spend time with him?

She found the idea depressing, and she was a grown woman. How much worse would it be for her seven-year-old son?

Six months. She wished she had known sooner. She would have ... What? she sarcastically asked herself. Refused to invite him to Thanksgiving dinner? Of course not. But maybe she could have refused to let him get so involved in Justin's life. Maybe she would have refused to let him get involved in *her* life. Maybe she would have kept him at a distance, would have kept their friendship simple and casual so that neither she nor Justin would miss him too much when he left.

But she hadn't known—hadn't *wanted* to know—and there was nothing simple or casual about her friendship with him, or Justin's. There was nothing she could have done, she suspected, to make it simple and casual. They were all three entirely too involved with each other.

So now it was up to her to minimize the impact he was having on their lives. She could start by cutting back on the amount of time they spent with him. She and Justin hadn't had a weekend alone since Thanksgiving, and the weeknights when they didn't see Joe usually included phone calls with him, like tonight. She could limit those calls, could give him a Saturday or a Sunday, an afternoon or an evening, but not both.

And she could put a complete end to her time alone with him.

That way, when he left, it would be no more traumatic than losing any other friend. Justin would be sorry to see him go, but he would adapt. He would fill his life with the kind of friends little boys should have—other little boys—and he would gradually, eventually grow away from Joe.

She would be sorry to see him go, too. Sorry for what could have been. Sorry that he was both everything she wanted and the one thing she wouldn't let herself have. Sorry that he had no roots and no desire to develop any.

And she would adapt, too. She would even meet someone else someday, someone who was exactly what she wanted. Someone who could give her and Justin everything they needed.

Someone who wasn't Joe.

It all sounded fine—friendship, separation without heartache, someone new.

So why, she wondered bleakly, did it feel so grim?

Chapter 7

Fridays were supposed to be good days. The end of the work week. Thank God it's Friday.

But this one, Libby thought with a scowl, had been miserable. The morning had gone fine, but then she'd had to face lunch with Denise. Denise, who couldn't understand why her friend seemed to be deliberately trying to sabotage the first good thing that had happened to her since the divorce. For the first time in more years than she could remember, Libby had resented Denise's interference. They had come away from lunch barely speaking to each other.

Then she'd returned to her office only to find a message for her from Joe. When she failed to return his call, hoping to avoid putting into practice the plan she'd devised last night, he had, of course, called back. After she'd turned down his invitation to dinner without explanation, his temper was barely under control. When the call ended only a few minutes later, he was hardly speaking to her, either.

And now Justin. *Did Joe tell you where we're going for dinner?* had been his first question when she'd picked him up at Mrs. Franklin's. She had tried not to make a big deal out of it, had simply told him that he would see Joe tomorrow but tonight they were having dinner at home, just the two of them. He had argued, pleaded, cajoled and bargained. But when she hadn't caved in, he'd gone to his room to play. *Loudly.* So loudly that when she'd tried to talk to him a few moments ago, he had pretended not to hear her.

Why couldn't life be simpler? Why couldn't Doug have been a decent husband and a loving father? Why couldn't Joe be the average guy next door, happy to spend the rest of his life in one place? Why did he have to enjoy Army life and the frequent moves it required so damn much? Why couldn't he be settled and stable? Why couldn't he be what she needed?

Why did he have to be what she wanted?

Muttering darkly, she transferred two hamburger patties from the skillet to paper towels to drain, then took the buttered, toasted buns from another skillet. She had considered fixing french fries, too—anything to coax Justin out of his grumpy mood—but she'd drawn the line at bribery. Her son simply had to accept that there would be times when he wouldn't like the decisions she made. He would have to learn to live with that.

"Justin, dinner's ready," she called. Thoughts of bribery aside, she fixed his hamburger the way he liked it, then added a handful of his favorite chips and a big serving of his favorite dip. Instead of the milk he usually got with his dinner, she popped the top on a can of his favorite soda, then carried it all into the dining room. On her way to the kitchen for her own food, she banged on his bedroom door, calling to him again.

She was seated at the table when he finally dragged himself in. He sat down across from her and gave his food a disinterested look. "Why couldn't we have dinner with Joe?"

"Hey, I'll have you know that my hamburgers are as good as any restaurant in the entire CSRA."

He broke a potato chip in two and nibbled on the smaller piece. "What's that stand for?"

"The Central Savannah—"

He finished with her. "River Area. We learned about that in school. That's what they call this whole part of South Carolina and Georgia."

She smiled faintly. Her son was learning things in school that she'd grown up knowing, things that, if he'd ever lived long enough in one place, he also would have grown up knowing. But that was okay. In another ten or twelve years, North Augusta and the entire CSRA would be as familiar to him as if he'd lived there all his life.

"So why couldn't we have dinner with Joe?"

If she'd thought she could distract him, she'd been badly mistaken. Her smile fading, she replied, "Because I wanted to have dinner at home tonight."

"Then why couldn't he have dinner with us? You could have invited him over here. He gets tired of eating in the chow hall and restaurants all the time."

"Because I wanted to have dinner alone with you, and that's the end of this discussion, sweetheart." She took a bite of her hamburger, then asked, "How was school today?"

"Fine."

"Did you learn anything?"

"No."

"Do you have any homework?" She waited patiently for his reply. It was a question she asked every Friday night, and it always earned her the same response: an exaggerated sigh, an upward roll of his eyes and, *It's Friday, Mom. We never have homework on Friday.*

"No," he said listlessly. "Can I go play now?"

She glanced at his plate. He'd eaten less than half of his dinner and hadn't even touched the soda. "After you take your dishes into the kitchen. But if you decide you're hungry later, there won't be any snacks," she warned.

"Yes, ma'am." He left with his plate, then came back for the soda and napkin.

She should have told him last night that they couldn't have dinner with Joe, Libby thought regretfully. Instead she'd kept quiet, and he had looked forward to it all day, only to be disappointed at the last minute. She should have told him.

Or maybe she should have let him go. Joe wouldn't have minded taking just Justin. In fact, he would have enjoyed it. Next week would have been soon enough to start cutting back on the amount of time they spent together. Letting them go out tonight wouldn't have hurt.

Sighing, she pushed her plate away. She didn't have much appetite, either. Except for the battle sounds coming from Justin's room, the house was depressingly quiet. There was no laughter, no lively conversation, no deep masculine voice. . . .

Realizing where her thoughts were heading, she put a stop to them. She carried her dishes into the kitchen, leaving them in the sink instead of immediately washing them, then went to the living room. There she turned on the television and stretched out on the couch, tucking a brightly patterned pillow beneath her head. This was a good night to be lazy, she decided. To lose herself in game shows and gossip. To spend as little time thinking as possible.

Without being told, Justin went in at seven-thirty to take a shower. When he was done, he came into the living room, a bath towel anchored beneath his arms, and his hair—the same sandy color as Joe's when it got wet, Libby noticed—dripping water. He sat down on the coffee table in front of her, blocking her view of the television, and solemnly asked, "Can I ask you something important?"

"Sure, honey." She sat up, used the remote control to mute the TV, then gestured for him to join her, wet towel and all, on the sofa.

He snuggled against her, then sat quietly for a moment. Libby waited patiently for him to begin. Finally, twisting his fingers together and staring at them intently, he asked, "How does a kid get a new dad?" Quickly, before she could respond to the shock, he rushed on. "Some of the kids at school have two dads. They live with one, but they get to spend a lot of time with the other one. Lisa Marie doesn't like one of hers, but Robert Calhoun says it's fun—he's got two dads and two moms. And since my father lives in Chicago and I don't ever see him, I was just wondering if maybe I could get a dad for here. Maybe...maybe someone like Joe.''

Closing her eyes, Libby hugged him tighter. It was a long time before she trusted her voice enough to speak. "Honey, you can't just pick someone out and make him your dad. That's not the way it works. If I get married again, my new husband will be your stepfather, and he'll live with us, and he'll do all the things that—that Joe does with you. *He'll* be your dad."

He reached up to rub his nose, then asked plaintively, "Then couldn't you marry Joe? He likes you, and he likes me, and he'd be a real good dad. And I bet he wouldn't ever leave us the way my father did." He looked up at her, his expression so full of hope. "So couldn't you, Mom? Couldn't you marry Joe so he could be my dad and we could always be together?"

"No, baby," she whispered. "I couldn't."

"Why not?" he pleaded. "Don't you like him?"

She pulled a corner of the towel free and dried the water dripping from his hair. "He's a nice man, sweetheart, but I can't marry someone just because he's nice. There has to be so much more. You have to want the same things and have the same interests and the same goals, and you have to be willing to compromise and sacrifice. And you have to be in love, too."

He ignored the first parts of her reasoning. She doubted he even understood what she meant by interests and goals, compromises and sacrifices. Instead he locked in one the last part. "Couldn't you love Joe someday, Mom? Maybe?"

She sat there for a long time without answering. How could she explain to a seven-year-old that loving Joe would be the biggest mistake she could make? The biggest gamble and the biggest loss she could face? Because as surely as the sun rose each morning, next May was going to come. Joe was going to get orders, and he was going to leave Fort Gordon. He was going to leave *them*.

And as sure he was going to leave, *they* had to stay. This was *home*. This was where they belonged. This was where her heart was. This was where she had promised both Justin and herself that they would always stay.

"I'm sorry, Justin," she said quietly. Sorry she couldn't give him what he wanted. Sorry for all the hurt he'd suffered in the past and for all the hurt he would have to suffer in the future.

Most of all, she was sorry that he would have to say goodbye to Joe—not in May, not in six months when the bond between them had grown even stronger, when the affection her son felt for Joe had become something even deeper. He would have to say goodbye *now*, before the damage was irreparable. Before he cared too much. Before it cost him too much.

She stroked his hair from his forehead and pressed a kiss there. "I really am sorry."

The mild winter weather they'd been having gave way to downright cold on Saturday, but Joe didn't mind. He had always liked winter and felt the holidays weren't quite as special when Christmas shopping could be done in shorts and a T-shirt, when attending the Christmas parade posed a bigger threat of sunburn than frostbite, or when Christmas Day itself was shirtsleeve warm. He wouldn't mind seeing this cold spell last right through New Year's.

He'd left his apartment only a minute ago wearing his usual leather jacket, but before he reached his car, he decided to trade the unlined leather for a down jacket. He and Justin hadn't made any specific plans for today, but whatever they did was sure to include some time outside... which would probably give Libby an excuse to avoid accompanying them, he thought with a scowl. Just as she'd avoided dinner with him last night. And his phone call the night before.

Maybe she was still unnerved by what had happened—
had *almost* happened—Wednesday night. That was the only
excuse he could think of for her behavior. He could deal
with that. If all she wanted, all she could let herself accept
from him at this time, was friendship, then that was all he
would offer. Even if his restraint *was* stretched thin. Even if
not touching her was torture. Even if his need for her had
become almost obsessive.

He would be her friend, and by God, she would *learn* to
trust him. She would rediscover a little of the faith that her
ex-husband had nearly destroyed. She would uncover a little of the desire, too, and affection and eventually even love.
Then they could go beyond friendship. Then they could become lovers and so much more.

When he reached the Harper house, Justin was the one
who answered the door. He was still wearing pajamas,
which were stained in front with what looked and smelled
like chocolate milk when Joe bent to accept his welcoming
hug. "Hey, partner, what are you up to?"

"I'm being quiet. Mom's still asleep. I decided to let her
sleep 'cause she was up late last night. I got my breakfast all
by myself, and I've been watching cartoons, but real quiet,
so I don't wake her."

Joe straightened to remove his jacket, then glanced at his
watch. It was a few minutes until ten. It was unusual for
Libby to sleep that late. She had told him the day they'd
gone fishing that Justin usually woke her around seven on
weekends. He wondered if she was coming down with
something or if she was simply tired. Then the jealous streak
that he'd forgotten he even had began wondering *why* she'd
been up late the night before and why she'd refused to give
him a reason for turning down his dinner invitation. Had
she gone out with someone else? With another man?

He hung his coat in the closet, then turned to Justin.
"Why don't you get dressed and wash your face and
brush—"

"My teeth and comb my hair," Justin finished for him. "Mom tells me every morning. And then I guess I'd better clean up the kitchen. I made kind of a mess."

"I'll help you with that," Joe offered. But first he wanted to check on Libby just to make sure that she was all right.

He knew the front bedroom was a combination guest room and storage area, and the center room belonged to Justin. That meant Libby's bedroom was at the back of the house. The room where the door was always closed when he visited. The only room he hadn't had so much as a peek inside.

The door was closed now, too. He grasped the cut glass knob and turned it, silently swinging the door in. He didn't need to enter the room to assure himself that Libby was all right. Her bed was less than ten feet in front of him, and she was lying on her side facing him, her hair a tangle, her face soft and unlined, her breathing slow and deep and even. She was snuggled beneath a mountain of covers with one bare arm exposed, her hand tucked beneath her pillow, a narrow strap of soft white fabric showing at her shoulder.

She wasn't the sort of woman to sleep naked, he thought regretfully as he watched her. Or the type, he added when his gaze swept her room and landed on a plain white slip discarded on the dresser, to indulge in sexy, skimpy lingerie. He would bet the nightgown she had on beneath the covers was cotton, lace-edged and ruffled, sweet and simple and demure enough to wear on the street.

Had she been with another man last night? He honestly didn't think so. She couldn't deal with the possibility of *one* relationship. There was no way she could handle two at the same time.

She rolled onto her back and tugged the covers higher until all he could see was her forehead. But he'd seen enough already. Enough to stir his arousal and his frustration. His hurt that she wasn't willing to accept what was happening between them and his fear that she might never accept it.

He silently closed the door and went down the hall to the kitchen. He couldn't do anything for her in the bedroom, not without a miracle, but at least he could keep her from facing Justin's mess first thing in the morning.

And it *was* a mess, the kind that only a little boy could make. There was milk on the counter, chocolate powder on the floor, smashed bits of cereal on the rug in front of the sink and sugar everywhere.

"I kind of spilled a few things," Justin said, coming to join him in the doorway.

"Nothing that can't be cleaned up. What did you have for breakfast?"

"Cereal and sugar and chocolate milk and a peanut butter and jelly and syrup sandwich. Mom usually fixes me pancakes and toast and bacon, but I'm not allowed to cook by myself, so I fixed what I wanted."

"After a breakfast like that, you must have pure sugar pumping through your system," Joe said dryly. "Why don't you have a seat over here—" he lifted him up and set him on the only clean counter in the room "—and I'll start by sweeping the floor. Then you can help me with the dishes."

They were just finishing up when Libby wandered into the room. Joe dried Justin's hands, then his own, but his mind wasn't on the task. Instead he watched her—the slow, sleepy way she moved, the warm, loving smile she gave Justin, the smile that appeared, then suddenly faded and was replaced with wariness, when she saw *him*.

Her nightgown *was* cotton, just as he'd suspected, and trimmed at the neck and bodice with narrow rows of white eyelet lace and tiny embroidered flowers. It fell to midcalf and was as modest as any dress could possibly be . . . except when the morning sunlight came through the window behind her, turning the thin cotton nearly transparent, revealing the soft curves of her breasts and the narrow shape of her waist.

He lifted Justin to the floor, then deliberately turned away. He reminded himself that friendship was all she wanted from him right now. Not arousal. Not lust. Not fantasies that made him hard and hot and hungry this early in the day.

"Morning, Mom," Justin said, giving her a hug.

"You forgot to wake me, sweetie," she replied, her voice soft and a bit husky.

"I didn't forget," he chided her. "I fixed breakfast all by myself, and Joe helped me clean up."

"That was nice. Did you thank him?"

Joe gave her a sharp look over his shoulder. That sounded just a bit too formal. She had long since stopped prodding Justin to thank him for everything. He had assumed it was because she had finally accepted him as a friend. Friends didn't have to always say thanks; it was taken for granted. But acquaintances had to say it. Strangers had to.

Apparently Justin shared his viewpoint. "Aw, Mom," he said with a sigh. "He *knows* I 'preciate it. Want some coffee? I can put the water in the microwave."

"Yes, honey, that would be nice." She moved away from the window, coming only marginally closer to Joe. "Good morning."

He risked a glance at her. Without the light, the gown was perfectly modest once more, revealing far less than that gorgeous blue dress she'd worn Wednesday night.

"Have you been here long?"

"A half hour."

She combed her fingers through her hair. "I should have set my alarm, but Justin's never let me sleep in before."

"He said you were up late last night. Something on your mind?"

His question disturbed her—he saw it in her eyes and in the suddenly stiff lines of her body—and he wondered once again if she'd been with another man.

But she gave him no clue. She simply ignored the question and started back toward her room. "I'd better get dressed. Justin, be careful taking that cup out of the microwave."

Joe remained where he was long after her bedroom door closed. That encounter certainly hadn't been encouraging. He wondered how long it would take them to get some level of easiness back into their relationship. Only last week he hadn't given much thought to touching her—nothing serious, merely holding her hand—but if he tried even that now, he suspected she would jerk away as if burned.

She was back in a few minutes, wearing jeans and a sweatshirt. Her hair was pulled back in a ponytail, and all the sleepy softness had disappeared from her face. She fixed a cup of instant coffee with the water Justin had heated for her, then took a seat at the small corner table to drink it. "What do you have planned for today?"

"Nothing. Any suggestions?"

"We could go to a movie," Justin piped up. "Or to the mall."

"Not on a weekend this close to Christmas, kiddo," Libby said.

"Oh, come on, Mom. We could see the Christmas decorations and have some cinnamon rolls and maybe see Santa Claus." Joe watched him turn on his sweetest, most heart-tugging grin. "If you got tired of the crowds, you could wait for us at Joe's apartment. He's got cable TV."

Libby hesitantly glanced his way. "What do you think?"

About the mall? He didn't care. He didn't mind the holiday crowds. About her ditching them for a quiet afternoon alone in his apartment watching TV? Not likely. He wanted this day with her as much as he wanted the time with Justin. "Sounds fine to me."

"Then give me fifteen minutes, and I'll be ready."

Ready to collapse, Libby thought five hours later. They had wound up visiting both of Augusta's malls, parking miles from the buildings, battling their way through what seemed like at least half of the city's population. But Justin had been happy, and that was what counted. He'd gotten in two visits to Santa Claus, as well as a little flirting with the teenage girls who were Santa's elves, added another few hundred dollars' worth of toys to his wish list and had virtually eaten his way through the day.

And now that home and the comfort of her sofa were in sight, he wanted to go to the park. Why not? she thought with a shrug when Joe laid the burden of deciding on her shoulders. That was as good a place as any to say what she'd decided had to be said. It was a public place, though empty in this afternoon's chill, so there could be no scene, no argument, no emotional outburst. And in spite of its openness, it also offered a measure of privacy that couldn't be found in the house, since Justin could be sent off to play on the equipment.

When they reached the park, as she had expected—had hoped—Justin raced off to play. He climbed onto a swing, gripping the chains tightly with gloved hands, and began pumping his short legs, slowly climbing higher. "Hey, Joe, come and push me," he called.

Joe started to obey, but Libby stopped him with her hand on his arm. He seemed surprised when he looked down at her—because for once *she* had been the one to touch *him?* she wondered—and she self-consciously withdrew her hand. "Could I talk to you for a moment?"

He gave her a long wary look, then shrugged. "I'll be there in a minute," he told Justin, then turned back to her. "I'm listening."

She moved away to sit on the nearest picnic table. Joe followed, but chose to remain standing. He looked so serious, almost as if he expected what she was about to say. She wouldn't be surprised. He knew both her and Justin too well. That was the whole point of this talk.

"Well?"

She didn't know how to start or what to say or how to make him understand, so she simply opened her mouth and blurted out her decision. "I don't want you to see Justin anymore."

Joe stared at her, and she shifted uncomfortably on the table. She'd been wrong. He hadn't expected this. If he'd expected it, he wouldn't look so stunned. He wouldn't look like someone had just punched him. "Why?" he demanded after a moment.

"He's getting too involved with you. He cares too much."

"He likes me so much that we can't be friends?" His voice vibrating with disbelief, he repeated his earlier question. "*Why*, Libby?"

"You—you're not what he needs."

"He *needs* a friend," he pointed out. "He needs someone who will spend time with him and listen to him. He needs someone who will care about him and respect him and look out for him. He needs someone who will make up to him for the lousy father you saddled him with."

"He needs someone he can count on," she challenged. "Someone reliable. Someone who will always be here for him."

He moved closer, resting his hands on the table on each side of her. "And you think I'm not reliable, Libby? You think I won't be here when he needs me?"

She had to moisten her lips before she could reply. "Not after next May." She watched him suddenly stiffen, then turn away. "Joe," she began hesitantly, pleadingly, "don't think I made this decision lightly. This is why I was up late last night. I gave it a lot of thought, and I kept reaching the same conclusion. Justin's getting too attached to you. He's already lost so many people from his life. I can't let him lose another. I can't let him go through that again."

He spun around and returned to stand directly in front of her. "*Let* him go through it? You're *putting* him through it, Libby. You think it's going to be any easier on him now than it'll be next May?"

"Yes. If I let him continue seeing you, by the time you leave here, he's going to love you like a father, and that—"

Angrily Joe interrupted her. "He already loves me like a *dad*." He saw the startled look flash through her eyes and muttered a curse. "You thought I was—what? Too stupid? Too selfish?—to see that, didn't you? I'm not either of those things, Libby. I know exactly what Justin feels for me. And I know that you're a damned fool if you think separating us is going to be any easier on him now than it will be next spring."

He started to walk away, then just as suddenly turned back to her. "Is this because of what happened the other night? Because I touched you? Because I let you know that I wanted to make love to you?"

Her face turned as red as the sweatshirt she wore. "Of course not," she mumbled. "This has nothing to do with you and me."

"Doesn't it?" he challenged. "As long as I kept my distance from you, you didn't mind letting me see Justin. But the first time things got a little intimate, you went running away. You wouldn't talk to me on the phone. You wouldn't let me take you two to dinner. Now you've suddenly decided that Justin doesn't need me, that he can't count on me. And I'm supposed to believe that it has nothing to do with you and me?"

She stood up and moved to the opposite side of the table. "I'm trying to do what's best for my son," she said stiffly.

"For your son." He sounded bitterly skeptical. "What's wrong, Libby? Are you afraid that the next time we're alone I won't be satisfied with just touching your breast?" He paused before adding in an ominously low voice, "Or that *you* won't be?"

She refused to dignify his question with an answer, refused to even consider the possibility that her fears about their relationship had played a part in her decision.

He swore darkly. "Maybe it won't be so easy to stop next time. Maybe you won't find it so easy to run away. Maybe, God forbid, you'll enjoy it and want more. So you're stopping it now. You're running away now."

She folded her arms over her chest and gave him a hard, stony look. "It has nothing to do with you and me," she insisted.

"Fine. I won't touch you or kiss you or even think about making love to you. I won't even see you again. But don't—" He broke off, struggling for control. "Don't keep me away from Justin, Libby. He depends on me. He *needs* me."

"He needs more than you can give him," she said stubbornly. "He needs stability. Security."

"And because I'm in the Army, I can't offer him that? Is that what you believe?" He dragged his fingers through his hair in frustration. "What makes me so damn unstable, Libby? I've had the same job since I was eighteen. I make a decent salary, and I've been able to save a lot of it over the years. I've never been in trouble, never been late paying my bills, and I've never even failed to vote. Granted, I am divorced, but, as you know, that was Theresa's doing, not mine. So please tell me, Libby, what the hell makes me so unsuitable?"

"You've had the same job since you were eighteen, but how many times have you been transferred? How many places have you lived? What's the longest period you've stayed in one place?" She paused for breath. "How many times have you risked your life? How many wars have you been in? How many battles have you fought? How many will you be asked to fight?"

He stared at her, just stared. He couldn't think of anything to say. He certainly couldn't give her the answers to her questions. If she knew all the places he'd been assigned, all the posts he'd been at for a year or two but never more than three, if she knew about all the combat he'd seen in Vietnam and Panama, about the times he'd come too close to dying or about the very real probability that he would come that close again if war broke out in East Africa... If she knew those things, he wouldn't stand a chance.

She took advantage of his silence to try to explain. "You know Doug left us. You know that right after Justin got to know my family, they all left, too. He has a right to know that the people he loves won't leave him. That they won't get transferred away. That they will always be right here when he needs them, not hundreds or thousands of miles away."

"And he has a right to be loved," Joe countered. "He has a right to trust that his mother won't send away the only other person right now who does love him. Do you think he's going to thank you for this? Do you think he's going to forgive you for it?"

"He'll be hurt," she admitted. "But he'll get over it a lot easier now than six months from now. He knows you'll be transferred then, but to him six months is forever. He doesn't really understand what it'll be like when you're gone. I *know* how hard it was for him when his grandparents left on their trip, and I know how tough it was when his uncles moved away." She wiped away a tear that had gotten caught in her lashes. "And I know that that pain was nothing compared to what he would feel when you leave next spring. That's why it has to end now."

Finally he took a seat on the table she had abandoned. "So who have you picked to take my place?" he asked dully, recognizing the defeat in his voice.

"What do you mean?"

"Your family took his father's place. When they left, I took their place. Who's going to replace me? Haven't you picked out someone?"

She wouldn't look at him. "Of course not."

"So you think he's better off with no one than with me." He shook his head in dismay, then quietly said, "He's your son. Obviously you can do whatever you think is best for him. But you're wrong this time, Libby. You're damn wrong. Unfortunately, Justin is the one who will have to pay the price for your mistake."

They sat in uncomfortable silence for a moment; then he stood up and faced her, their gazes locking. "All right. You win. I'll get out of his life. I'll get out of *your* life. But *you* tell him. *You* tell him why you decided that we can't be friends anymore. *You* tell him why he has to lose one more person who he's counted on."

She swallowed visibly. "I will." Once again she reached toward him, but this time he backed away before she could touch him. She swallowed again. "I'm sorry, Joe."

Cynically, he smiled. "I don't think so. I think you'll be glad to see the last of me. You won't have to deal with your fears or your insecurities or your desires. You won't have to worry about feeling or thinking or acting like a woman. You can go back to playing the only role you know anymore, the devoted, sacrificing mother.''

He walked a few feet away, then turned for one last time. ''I'll bring Justin home when he's through playing. Go back to the house, Libby. We don't need you here.''

He joined Justin at the swings and pushed him, warning him to hold on tight as he soared sky-high and making up a story to explain his longer-than-a-minute delay. He didn't risk a look back at the table until Justin was ready to move on to something else. When he did look, she was gone.

He felt cold inside. Angry. Empty. Hurt. Oh, God, it hurt. He wasn't prepared for this, wasn't prepared to lose the two most important people in his life. He wasn't ready to tell them goodbye.

He would never be ready to tell them that.

He was disappointed in Libby. He had misjudged her. He had thought she was someone special, someone who had been through some difficult times but had survived them and come through stronger and braver. But she hadn't survived at all. She had given in to the fear and the hurt and the distrust. She was letting them run her life. Worse, she was letting them run Justin's life. *Ruin* Justin's life.

And he was disappointed in himself. He had thought he could earn her trust, but he couldn't. He'd thought he had a chance to build a relationship with her, something permanent, something to be cherished, but he hadn't.

Deliberately he drew out this last visit with Justin. They played and talked and exchanged jokes. They scuffed through the fallen leaves and sat on top of the picnic table and talked some more. Finally, when Justin was tired and the cold had become too much to endure, Joe suggested they go home.

''Will you stay and have dinner with us?'' Justin asked as they trudged up the hill. ''Mom won't mind.''

''I can't, partner. I'm sorry.'' Joe reached for his hand as they crossed the street and started toward the house.

''Do you have a girlfriend?''

Joe forced a light note into his voice. ''Nope. Do you?''

"Ashley Raye says she's my girlfriend," Justin replied matter-of-factly as he rubbed his nose with the back of his hand. "But I'm not her boyfriend. Do you like my mom?"

Not at this moment. Hiding his pain inside, Joe grinned down at him. "Ask me something else."

"Do you think she's pretty?"

"She's very pretty."

Only a few feet from the edge of the yard, Justin stopped and crouched beside the road to watch a column of ants as they marched along. "She's never going back to my father. Ashley Raye's mom and dad are divorced, and she hopes they get back together, but my mom won't ever do that. I don't want her to. I'd rather have a new dad."

Joe moved him away from the road, then joined him on the ground. "Justin, listen to me. You're the best kid I've ever known, and the best friend I've ever had, but I can't be your dad. I wish I could... but it's just not possible."

His big blue eyes sad, Justin sighed. "That's what Mom said."

"You told her that was what you wanted?"

He nodded. "Last night."

At least that explained the timing, Joe thought grimly. Justin's talk last night about making him his dad must have frightened Libby into taking action.

And he would bet that not once had she considered positive action—giving the kid what he so badly wanted. *He* would have been willing to give it a try.

"Even if I can't be your dad, Justin—" *even if I can't ever see you again* "—I'll always be your friend. Don't ever forget that, okay? If you ever need me—" He broke off, unable to continue. Justin needed him *now,* but that didn't seem to matter to Libby. Of course, Justin would also need him in the future, but she would make sure that Joe never knew about it. For all her fears that he would let Justin down, now when it was actually happening, it was *her* fault, not his.

Justin stood up, smiling sweetly, and leaned forward to hug him. "You'll always be my *best* friend," he corrected him. "I know that. Come on. We're almost home." He tugged Joe to his feet, then slipped his hand inside Joe's bigger, warmer palm.

At the house, Justin invited him inside, but Joe turned him down. "I'd better go," he said, crouching in front of him, brushing his hand over Justin's hair.

"Thank you for staying with me at the park," the boy said gravely.

He sounded so formal, so *grown*. In spite of his mood, Joe couldn't help but smile. "You're welcome." Then, one last time, he gathered Justin into his arms for a fierce embrace. He didn't try to speak over the lump in his throat, didn't try to find the words to say what he wanted, needed, to say. He simply held him close.

Then the door opened, and Libby stepped onto the porch. Joe automatically loosened his hold. "Honey, your grandfather's on the phone. Run in and say hello."

The grown-up little person disappeared and the boy returned. "Okay. See you, Joe." With a grin and a wave, he pulled away and ran inside. Out of sight. Out of Joe's life.

Joe slowly got to his feet, and for a long moment he simply stood there, watching Libby, who watched him in turn. He wanted to shake her, to curse her, to kiss some sense into her. But he didn't do any of that. He simply walked away. He got into his car and drove down the street, never looking back.

Maybe that was the way to deal with it, he thought without hope. Never look back. Go on with his life as if he'd never met Justin. As if that one scrawny little kid hadn't meant any more to him than all the other scrawny little kids at the school.

And Libby, too. Pretend that he'd never met her, either. That he'd never come to care for her. That he'd never spent these past few weeks with her. That he'd never touched her, kissed her, held her, wanted her.

Pretend that he hadn't left some part of his life, some part of his future, back there in that little white house.

Pretend that he hadn't lost some part of his soul.

Chapter 8

She was a first-class coward.

Libby had told herself that repeatedly since Saturday evening. Every time she had gathered the courage to tell Justin that Joe wouldn't be back. Every time she had listened to one more "Joe says" or "Joe likes" or "Joe thinks." Every time she saw that so-much-like-Joe grin on her son's face.

A major first-class coward.

She had let Saturday evening pass without a word, thinking she would tell him Sunday. Sunday she had made up some excuse for why Joe couldn't attend the Christmas parade with them and had drafted Denise to go instead, and she had guiltily promised herself that Monday would be the day. But Monday she hadn't managed, either.

Tonight, she promised herself. Definitely tonight. As soon as they'd had dinner and homework was out of the way. Before bath and bedtime.

Definitely tonight.

She went inside the house and traded the wool blazer she'd worn to work for a heavier jacket, then took the flashlight from the hall table. In Chicago and half the other places she'd lived, she wouldn't have dreamed of an after-dark walk through the neighborhood. But this was North Augusta. This was *home*. The local criminals seemed to prefer doing their business out of town, while Augusta's criminals didn't want to bother crossing the river to do what could just as easily be done at home.

At Mrs. Franklin's house, Libby waited just inside the door while Justin got his things together. He didn't come running to greet her as he normally did, and his manner when he did appear was definitely subdued. "Hi, Mom," he said dejectedly, raising his cheek for her kiss.

Uh-oh. She bent to zip his jacket, called goodbye to Mrs. Franklin and led Justin out the door. "How was school today?"

"It was okay," he replied in a tone that clearly indicated otherwise.

She paused to switch on the flashlight. The light from the street lamps located at each end of the block didn't reach to the middle here, where it was pitch-black. "Did you get in trouble today?" she asked conversationally, thinking how long it had been since that had been a routine after-school question, usually with a routine affirmative answer.

"No." As they approached their house, he looked up at her, the expression in his eyes pure sadness. "Today was the day the company came to school."

"The company?"

"The soldiers. Charlie Company and the others."

"Oh." How had she forgotten that? And how had Joe handled it? Had he already told Justin what she had asked—no, demanded? He must have been furious with her for not breaking the news to her son herself, for letting the task fall to him, and he wouldn't be impressed with her excuse that she just hadn't found the courage yet.

"Joe didn't come, Mom," he said anxiously. "He's never missed before, not once. And he didn't even give one of the soldiers a message for me. I asked and asked, but no one knew anything. And he didn't call yesterday, and he missed going to the Christmas parade with us Sunday when he *promised* he'd go, and he wouldn't stay for dinner Saturday. Mom, do you think he's tired of me? Do you think he got bored with me and doesn't want to see me anymore?''

Feeling sick, Libby scooped him into her arms and carried him up the steps to the porch. "No, honey," she whispered. "That's not the problem at all. Joe liked you. He could never get tired of you."

"Then what's wrong? Why hasn't he called me? Why didn't he come to school today?"

She set him down to unlock the door, then followed him inside. "Come into the living room, sweetie," she requested as she slipped out of her coat. "There's something I want to tell you."

Still wearing his jacket and backpack, Justin took a seat on the coffee table. He looked so small, all bundled up like that, she thought as she sat down on the sofa. So small and vulnerable.

"I asked—" Her voice quavered. She took a deep breath to steady it, but it didn't help much. "Honey, I asked Joe not to come over here or call you anymore."

He stared at her, his eyes wide in disbelief. "You what?"

She flushed guiltily, even though she told herself she'd done nothing to be ashamed of. She had to look out for her son's best interests. She'd had no choice but to do what she had. "You were getting so involved with him. We hardly ever had time for just ourselves anymore. And I just didn't think it was a good idea for you to spend so much time with someone who's going to be moving away soon."

"But he's *not* moving away soon!" Justin protested. "Not until next May!"

Just as she'd told Joe, Justin had no understanding of how quickly next May would be here. There was no way she could make him see how much harder it would be to go through this then.

"Mom, he's my *friend!* He's my *best* friend! And you made him go away?"

"You're a little boy, Justin. You need friends your own age. You need to spend time with other kids, not a grown man. I realize you like Joe a lot, but—"

"I *have* friends my age," he interrupted. "I have lots of friends at school and at Mrs. Franklin's. But I want Joe!"

"Sweetheart—"

"It's because you don't like him, isn't it?" His lower lip was starting to tremble, and his eyes filled with tears. "You don't like him. You don't like *anyone*."

"Honey, that's not true. Joe is a nice man, but—"

"You made my father go away, and now you made Joe go away. You probably made Grandpa and Uncle Travis and Uncle Rich leave, too." He jumped up from the table and shouted, "I wish *you* would go away! You're mean, and I don't want you to be my mother anymore! I hate you!"

He was gone before Libby recovered from his outburst, flying down the hall and into his bedroom, the door slamming against the frame.

She felt shaken. Justin had lost his temper with her before, but never like this. She had never seen him so angry.

Had she expected it to be easy? she bitterly asked herself and replied immediately, Of course not. But she had expected it to be no more traumatic than the night she'd had to tell him that his father had moved out and wouldn't live with them anymore. Or the day she'd had to explain that his grandfather was leaving for a long time and couldn't take him fishing or tell him funny stories about the old days anymore. Or the day that Travis had gotten his orders from the plant, or Rich his. After all, those people were *special* to Justin—his relatives. *Family.*

And Joe wasn't? her little voice asked snidely. Maybe there were no blood ties between them, but there were some bonds stronger than blood. There was love. Joe had admitted that he loved Justin, and he had warned her that Justin loved him, too. But she hadn't wanted to believe it, hadn't wanted to see that the feelings between them already went much deeper than mere friendship.

Wearily, she pushed herself to her feet and went to her bedroom at the back of the house. When she passed Justin's room, she could hear the muffled sounds of his sobs. Had he ever cried over Doug's leaving? she wondered. Not that she could recall. All the tears then had been hers.

She changed clothes, tossing the dress that she'd worn to work into the laundry basket at the back of the closet and putting on a T-shirt and sweatpants. Next she went into the kitchen, concentrating on dinner and not on her son down the hall. She would go in and talk to him if it would do any good, but right now, she thought, the best thing for him was to get it all out. When he calmed down, when the tears were gone, then they could talk. Then he would understand.

In the meantime, she fixed his favorite foods for dinner: fried chicken, mashed potatoes and gravy, and green beans, canned fresh out of Mrs. Franklin's garden last summer. Breaking her own rule, she ignored the table in the dining room and carried their plates into the living room, setting them side by side on the coffee table. Justin loved eating dinner in front of the TV but was rarely allowed to do so. Maybe this small treat would cheer him up, she hoped.

"Justin?" She stopped at his bedroom door, tapping lightly. "Dinner's ready."

There was no response for a long time; then, slowly, the door swung open. He stood there, staring at the floor, his eyes puffy and red, the trails left by his tears still visible on his grimy cheeks.

"We're going to eat in the living room tonight, sweetheart, okay?" She was trying to sound normal—not too desperate, not too anxious to please. In her own ears, she knew she didn't succeed.

He followed her into the living room and sat down beside her, but he hardly touched the food on his plate, and he never even glanced at the television show, one of his favorites. After a while he stood up and, eyes still downcast, asked, "May I be excused?"

"You didn't eat anything."

"I'm not very hungry."

"All right." She watched him walk away, then put her fork down and pushed her own plate away. She wasn't very hungry, either.

"What's going on with you?"

Joe leaned back in his chair and studied the staff sergeant sitting across from him. Max Stanley was one of his best NCOs and, for the two and a half years they'd worked together, he'd been a good friend. But there were disadvantages to being good friends with the people who worked for him, he thought with a scowl. Too often they felt entitled to ignore the rank that made him their supervisor and nosed around in things that were none of their business. Like now.

"You were behind this school program from the very beginning. You made some of us go when we didn't particularly want to. And now you've suddenly decided that you don't want to be involved anymore. Why?"

"I was busy yesterday. I couldn't spare the time."

"Too busy to care that some little kid was disappointed as hell because he didn't get to see you?"

"This doesn't concern you, Sergeant," Joe said stiffly.

"It concerned me when this kid spent the entire time going from soldier to soldier asking why you didn't come or if you'd sent a message for him. What's going on, Joe?"

Joe had turned to stare out the window. Now he looked back at his friend. "Justin's mother told me to stay away from him."

"Why?"

With a sigh Joe told him everything—well, almost everything. He didn't tell him about his one and only date with Libby. He didn't tell him about the scene in his bedroom that had sent her running. He didn't tell him that the days since he'd last seen her and Justin had been the worst days of his life.

He didn't tell him that he'd somehow fallen in love with Justin—and Justin's mother.

"I don't think this was quite what the captain had in mind when he signed us up for the program," Max said quietly.

He was trying not to sound critical, but Joe recognized the subtle censure in his voice anyway.

"I didn't go into that classroom intending to get involved with anyone," Joe said defensively. "And I certainly didn't intend to get *this* involved with Justin. He just—" He broke off and shook his head. "Hell, you remember what he was like in the beginning. He didn't have a friend in the world, he was always in trouble, he was unhappy..."

"And you couldn't resist trying to help him. But maybe you got a little *too* close."

"Libby certainly thinks so."

"But you don't."

He thought about it for a long moment, then shook his head. "No, I don't." As lonely as he'd been the last four days, he still believed Libby was wrong. He still believed Justin needed him in his life, and he knew he needed Justin in his. "Now I know how a father must feel when he gets a divorce and suddenly he can see his kids only on weekends. Only I can't even have that, because Justin's not my kid in the one way that counts."

"Too bad you didn't hit it off with the mother as easily as with the kid," Max said sympathetically as he got up. "Then you could get married, maybe adopt the kid, and everything would be fine." Then he reconsidered what he'd just said. "On the other hand, considering the state of *my* marriage, maybe the way this has turned out has been a blessing in disguise. What do you need with a ready-made family at your age?"

"There's nothing wrong with your marriage except that your wife deserves a better husband," Joe pointed out. "And nothing wrong with my age, either." He picked up the stack of reports he'd been sorting through earlier, then scowled at Max. "Get out of my office, Sergeant, and get some work done."

He intended to take his own advice and get to work, but Justin lingered in his mind. He wondered how the kid was dealing with their separation. It would serve Libby right if he regressed to the destructive behavior that had occupied his days at the beginning of the school year, he thought, then immediately regretted his pettiness. She was only trying to do what she thought was right for her son. Even though she was wrong, even though she was making things harder all around instead of easier, she was trying. What more could he ask of her?

A hell of a lot, he decided with a scowl. He could ask that she show some common sense. That she quit being so damn overprotective. That she give him credit for understanding what his responsibilities to Justin were. That she quit judging him according to her ex-husband's behavior.

Too bad you didn't hit it off with the mother as easily as with the kid. Damn right. Then he wouldn't have spent the last four days alone. He wouldn't have lain awake at night regretting what he'd lost, wondering what he could have done differently, how he could have convinced her to trust him, how he could have convinced her to let him love her. Justin wouldn't be unhappy, and Libby... Maybe she could quit being so scared. Maybe she could start healing the wounds her ex-husband had inflicted on her as well as on their son. Maybe she could learn to trust again, to believe in someone again, to love again.

And maybe dreams came true and wishes were fulfilled and the tooth fairy really did exist.

A few days. Libby had convinced herself that that was all Justin needed to get back to his bright, normal self. But as one day dragged into another, she admitted that she'd been overly optimistic. Saturday was a little bit better—with all the moping, all the gloom, but none of the temper—and Sunday was a little better still. But Monday was worse than ever, because Tuesday was approaching again, and the soldiers would visit the school again, and Joe wouldn't be there again.

And today... Libby winced at the memory of the anger and tears that had greeted her after work, along with the note from his teacher that Justin was falling into old hab-

its. Was there a problem at home, Miss Wilson had wanted
to know, that the school should be aware of?

She wanted to confess everything to Denise, curled at the
other end of the sofa with a big bowl of popcorn and
watching a movie on the VCR, and ask for her opinion, but
she already knew how her friend would respond. She would
be disappointed in Libby, annoyed and irritated. She would
take Justin's side—and Joe's. She would call Libby overprotective, shortsighted and selfish. She would cast serious
doubts on Libby's intelligence, her value system and her
common sense. She would tell her that any fool could have
predicted Justin's response, would remind her that she
should be thankful that a decent guy like Joe had taken an
interest in her son, would accuse her of behaving like a timid
old maid.

And maybe she would be right. On every count.

Denise sighed dreamily and used the remote control to
freeze the movie on a close-up of the hero. "Isn't he gorgeous?"

"Hmm."

"Can you believe he's just a little older than us and has
six kids and supposedly loves his wife to distraction?" She
sighed again. "Why can't I ever meet a guy like that?"

"With six kids?"

Denise scowled at her. "A guy that gorgeous with the capacity to be that devoted. He must be one of a kind. However—" Her familiar lascivious smile returned. "Who do
those eyes remind you of?"

Libby didn't spare even a glance for the television. If she
wanted to see a pair of beautiful blue eyes, all she had to do
was close her own and conjure them up—or go down the
hall to where her son was lying on his bed, drawing gloomy-
colored pictures.

"Have you seen the good sergeant lately?" Denise asked,
ignoring her friend's apparent lack of interest in the subject.

"You don't call a first sergeant 'sergeant,'" Libby replied. That was one of the finer points she'd picked up from Justin in the past few months.

"Oh, well, excuse me for not being up on proper Army protocol. So... have you?"

Libby looked inside the bowl. All that remained were unpopped kernels and plain white popcorn. Denise had picked out every bit of the caramel-coated corn. "I—I told him not to come over anymore."

The silence in the room was heavy, and at last it forced her to meet her friend's gaze. Denise was restraining herself. Clearly there were plenty of things she wanted to say—most of them insulting, Libby knew after a lifetime of friendship—but she kept her mouth shut for a long time. When she did finally speak, her voice was carefully controlled. "Why did you do that?"

Patiently Libby ran through the reasons she'd given Joe and, later, Justin. Denise looked no more impressed, no more understanding, than either of them had.

"You're saying the guy was so good for Justin that you didn't want him around anymore."

"*No.* I'm saying—" She made an impatient gesture. "I knew you wouldn't understand. You don't know what it was like for Justin when Doug left us. Or when my parents took off on their trip. Or when Faith and Travis moved away. Or Renee and Rich. Don't you see? That was why Justin was behaving so horribly at school. He couldn't find any other way to express his pain and anger and rejection."

"And Joe Mathison is the reason Justin finally began acting like a normal kid again. Come on, Lib, you're not dumb. You had to make the connection between Justin meeting Joe and the drastic improvement in his behavior. The guy worked miracles." When Libby started to speak, Denise raised her hand to forestall her. "And don't tell me I don't understand what it's like to lose someone you love. You think it was easy for me when you married Doug and moved five hundred miles away? Or when my mom died? Or when my dad got married again and moved to Savannah?"

"No, of course not. And that's the point I'm trying to make, Denise. Coping with loss is difficult for you, and you're a grown woman. Don't you see how much harder it is for Justin? He's just a little boy. He shouldn't have to constantly be telling the people he loves goodbye."

"So you made him tell Joe goodbye." Then her gaze narrowed suspiciously. "Or did he even get a chance to do that? You didn't wait until after their last visit, then just casually mention, 'Oh, by the way, sweetheart, Joe won't be back'?"

Libby flushed guiltily.

"Oh, Libby, how could you?" she gasped. "No wonder Justin's stayed in his room all evening. He probably can't stand to be in the same room with you."

"He doesn't understand, that's all. And he misses Joe. But he'll get over it."

"Probably. But he may never forgive you for it." Denise turned back to the television, hit the Play button and watched as the movie began running again. But after a moment she glanced back at Libby. "Tell me something, Lib— and remember who you're talking to here—your best friend. The woman who knows all your secrets. The woman who's stood by you through all of your major mistakes, including Doug. Including this one."

Solemnly Libby nodded.

"Do *you* miss Joe?"

Libby suddenly found the fuzzy socks she wore incredibly interesting. "He was Justin's friend, not mine," she mumbled.

"But do you miss him?"

Did she? she wondered, trying desperately to pretend it was a casual question with a casual answer. But there was nothing casual about the way she'd felt ever since that afternoon in the park. When she should have felt relief that their friendship with Joe was ended, she'd felt only a deep sense of loss. When she should have been glad that now her and Justin's lives could get back to normal, she had faced the frightening possibility that there could be no "normal" without Joe. When she should have been proud that she had recognized a serious problem and immediately resolved it, she had suspected that she'd merely made a serious mistake.

Yes, she admitted, she missed Joe more than she'd thought possible. She tried her best not to think about him, but she couldn't keep him out of her mind. She kept remembering him sweet and charming, gentle and patient, solemn and aroused, angry and hurt. She kept seeing the haunted expression on his face when he'd hugged Justin just before he'd left that Saturday afternoon—the same expression that she knew would be on *her* face if someone forced *her* to tell her son goodbye.

She kept remembering that she'd hurt him.

She didn't answer Denise's question, but her friend didn't need an answer to confirm what she already knew. "I never thought you could be so foolish, Lib," she said grimly. "And I certainly never thought you could be so selfish."

Libby didn't even have the energy to be offended. "What do you mean?"

"You sent Joe away because you were falling for him, didn't you? It wasn't because Justin was too fond of him or because he'll be moving away from here next spring or because you wanted to protect Justin from getting hurt. It was because *you* were too fond of him. You wanted to protect *yourself* from getting hurt, even if it meant hurting Justin. Even if it meant hurting Joe."

Denise shut off the movie and pressed the Rewind button, then began putting on her shoes. When they were laced, she looked at Libby again. "You *are* foolish, Libby, and you're selfish, and you know what? For the first time in thirty-two years, I'm ashamed to call you my friend."

Libby sat at her desk Wednesday afternoon, her fingers motionless on the keyboard of her computer. The cursor on the dark screen was blinking rhythmically, encouraging her to quit letting her mind wander and turn to work instead, but she ignored it.

Denise's comments had haunted her all last night, leaving her no peace for sleep, and hovered in the back of her mind all morning. Of course she had known that Denise would take Joe's side—that it was herself she was concerned for and not Justin—but her friend hadn't known that that was Joe's side. If two people reached the same conclusion independently, wasn't it possible that the conclusion held some validity?

Maybe she *was* afraid for herself. Afraid, after all the pain Doug had caused her, of getting involved with another man. Afraid of committing herself to a relationship, even short-term. Afraid of learning to care for a man who couldn't give Justin the things he needed. No, she corrected that. No more hiding behind Justin. A man who couldn't give *her* the things that she craved in her heart.

You sent Joe away because you were falling for him. You wanted to protect yourself from getting hurt.

She wished she could deny that Denise had been right, but she couldn't. She had lied to everyone else. The least she could do now was be honest with herself. She *had* been falling for Joe, and she *had* been afraid of getting hurt.

But that was the only possible outcome she could foresee. They didn't share the same goals. He wanted to spend more time in the Army, to see a few more places and to get that last promotion, while she wanted to spend the rest of her life right here. He couldn't compromise on his career, and she couldn't sacrifice her dreams of having a home and roots sunk deep in the Carolina soil.

So, under those circumstances, what could they have? A short-term affair that would end when the Army sent him someplace new? Maybe a longer, long-distance affair, if his next assignment kept him in the South. After all, Army posts were plentiful in this part of the country.

Maybe an affair long-term enough, she thought with a humorless smile, for him to see all those places, get that promotion, retire and come back here. She could just imagine herself waiting year after year, afraid to fully commit herself until he could give her everything she wanted.

Denise had been right again, she admitted. She wanted Joe to make all the compromises. She wanted him to make all the sacrifices. She *was* selfish.

Leaving herself out of it, had she been fair to Justin? Was shutting Joe out of his life now, when he still seemed to need him so much, really in his best interest? Was it really easier for him to deal with the end of their friendship now than it would be next spring when Joe transferred away?

Easy wasn't the right word to use. There was nothing *easy* about any of this—just different degrees of difficulty. And right now she was having trouble believing that anything could be more difficult than the past ten days. Although Justin had told her last night at bedtime that he loved her— the first time since last week's outburst—this morning when she'd dropped him off at school with an admonition to behave, he had given her an angry look. "I'm being haved," he had said in his most grown-up little voice. "You're the one who's been bad."

Had she been bad? Had she made a bad decision based not on what Justin needed but on her own fears? So far the vote was three ayes—Joe, Justin and Denise—and one undecided—herself. Heavens, she couldn't even give herself a vote of confidence that she'd done the right thing.

Because she knew deep in her heart that she hadn't.

So the next obvious step was to correct her mistake. To call Joe and apologize. To tell him exactly what she was afraid of—of caring for him, then losing him. To ask him to please come back into Justin's life and into her own.

But what if he'd decided in the past week and a half that she was more trouble than she was worth? What if he told her that he would see Justin but not her? What if he was no longer interested in her?

It was a gamble, and, as she'd told Denise, she'd never been much of a gambler. She had never known how to take risks. She'd never known how to take chances.

So wasn't it time she learned?

She was reaching for the phone when it rang, sharp and shrill in her small office. It was Justin's school. Come pick up your son, the principal told her. He's been suspended for the rest of the week.

Libby made the drive to the school in record time. Justin was waiting for her in the office, his face dirty and streaked with blood around his nose. His eye was swollen, his shirt torn, his knuckles skinned, and he wore the most sullen expression she'd ever seen. Seated across the room from him was another boy, a few inches taller and fifteen pounds heavier, in similar condition.

She didn't trust herself to speak to Justin right away. Instead she went into the principal's office and listened to the few details of the fight that he could provide; neither Justin nor the other boy would admit what they had fought about.

"I realize that Justin got off to a rocky start here," the principal said, flipping through the records in front of him. "But for the past few months everything's been fine. He seemed to have adjusted to the school and the kids, he made friends, and his grades improved significantly. Now..." He shrugged helplessly. "Do you have any idea what's wrong, Mrs. Harper?"

She closed her eyes for a moment. Oh, she knew, all right. If she needed any further proof that she had been wrong in sending Joe away, now she had it.

And if she needed any further proof that calling Joe and apologizing was the best thing she could do, she had that, too.

Aware that the principal was waiting for her answer, she opened her eyes and smiled grimly. "I'll talk to him, Mr. McKie."

He stood up and escorted her out again. "The secretary has some papers for you to sign, Mrs. Harper. Justin, we'll see you after the holidays."

Libby signed the suspension forms, then turned to her son. "Let's go, Justin."

He walked to the car at her side, clutching his backpack in both hands and never looking at her. On the short drive home she expected a few sniffles, maybe an apology or a vow, as he'd given her so many times before, that it would never happen again, but he said nothing. He simply sat beside her and ignored her.

At home she stopped him before he could escape to his bedroom. "What happened?"

"Nothing."

With both hands on his shoulders, she marched him into the bathroom and turned him to face the mirror. "This isn't 'nothing,'" she said sharply, tilting his face so he could see the grime and the blood and the bruising around his eye. "Neither is this—" she tugged at his torn shirt "—or this." She held up his bruised knuckles. "What happened?"

Suddenly the belligerence drained away and he was just a miserable, battered little boy. "Robert said Joe doesn't like me anymore. He said he quit coming to school with the others because of me, so he wouldn't have to see me. He says I messed up everything for the whole class, 'cause they all liked Joe a bunch, and now they can't see him anymore, and it's all my fault for being so stupid."

Kneeling on the fuzzy rug, Libby gathered him into her arms and let him cry, unmindful of the dirt he smeared on her blouse. "That's not true, honey," she whispered, stroking his hair. "You know that's not true. It's not your fault, sweetheart, it's *mine*. I'm so sorry."

When his tears faded away to occasional shudders, she pushed him back and brushed his hair from his forehead, then kissed him. "Listen, baby, I want you to take a quick bath and wash your face really good. Then I've got to go back to work, so I'm going to leave you at Mrs. Franklin's, okay?"

He nodded glumly and began pulling off his ripped shirt. "Mama?"

She paused in the doorway. Just as he had different meanings for father and dad, he had different names for her, too. She was always Mom except when he was especially sad, when he reverted to the more childish Mama. "What?"

"I'm sorry I caused so much trouble and got kicked out of school."

"We'll talk about it later. Go ahead and get in the tub."
She closed the door, then went into her bedroom to change
blouses. Then she headed straight for the phone.

Her hands were trembling when she dialed the number she
got from the post operator, and her throat tightened so that
she could barely swallow when the phone began to ring.

A young man answered on the second ring, rattling off
the company and battalion, followed by his name and rank,
so quickly that she barely understood. The rest of his greeting—"Can I help you, sir?"—left her off balance for a
moment. Then she gave herself a mental shake and, sounding far too hesitant, asked, "Could I speak to First Sergeant Mathison?"

"Can I tell him who's calling, ma'am?"

She wanted to tell him no, afraid that Joe might refuse the
call if he knew it was her. But after a moment's hesitation
she gave him her name. "Libby Harper."

"One moment."

He put her on hold, and she contemplated hanging up like
the coward that she was. But it was too late. Even if she did,
the young man would pass her name along to Joe, and he
would think even less of her than he already must for not
having the courage to talk to him.

"Hello, Libby."

She gripped the receiver tighter. If she had expected him
to be happy to hear from her, he was wasting no time in
disillusioning her. There wasn't one bit of the warmth she
remembered so well in his voice. In fact, he sounded the way
she must on the rare occasions when she answered the phone
and found Doug at the other end. "If you could see me
through the phone, you'd see that I'm waving a tiny white
flag," she said in a hesitant, hopeful voice.

"A white flag?"

"Isn't that the way you people surrender?"

"'You people'?"

She bit back a sigh. If all he did was echo her words, they
would never get anywhere. "You know, soldiers? Army
types?"

"I wouldn't know. I've never surrendered."

"I bet you haven't," she muttered, carrying the phone into the living room and sinking into the nearest chair. "*I* have. I've given in or given up more times than I care to remember."

Gripping the telephone tighter, Joe stifled the urge to tell her that *he* didn't want to make her surrender or give in. He didn't want to triumph over her, to defeat her in any way. He only wanted to be part of her life.

But *she* didn't want that.

"Is everything okay with Justin?" he asked, unable to keep the stiff, wary tone from his voice.

"No, not really." She cleared her throat. "Listen, Joe, could you meet me for lunch? I need to talk to you."

Every bit of common sense he had told him not to agree, not yet, not without knowing what she wanted from him and what she was offering in return. Not when he'd finally learned to live without her and Justin. Not when he'd finally accepted that they were no longer a part of his life. But he ignored his common sense and went instead with his instinct. With his heart. "Why don't you meet me near the shaved-ice stand at Riverwalk in half an hour?" he suggested. It was close to her office and offered more privacy than a restaurant would. Then, if either of them felt like it after their talk, they could decide about lunch.

"Okay." She paused. "Thank you, Joe."

After he hung up, he got up from his desk and slipped into his coat, then picked up his service cap. He told the corporal who'd taken the call that he was going to lunch, then left the building, putting his cap on as he walked outside.

What was it Libby wanted? he wondered on the way to his car. He knew Justin had been in trouble again at school. Several of his soldiers had mentioned it after yesterday's visit. He also knew Justin missed him a lot. Practically all of them had mentioned that. Had Libby found some way to blame that on him?

Maybe she had reconsidered her position. Maybe she had realized that she'd been wrong. Maybe *she* had missed him, too. She *had* mentioned that white flag.

Or maybe she was simply looking for an easy way out of the situation she'd gotten herself into. He had helped Justin deal with his problems before. Maybe she expected him to help again.

He left the post through Gate One, then took Gordon Highway downtown. The lot closest to the main Riverwalk entrance was practically empty, probably because it was too chilly for a casual walk along the river. The fountain was turned on, the light breeze blowing a fine spray around the edges, but the vendors who normally set up shop near the entrance were absent today. So was the shaved-ice man, he noticed as he walked through the levee breach, and just about everyone else.

But Libby was there.

She was leaning against the railing, only a portion of her face visible to him. There on the riverbank the wind was stronger, and it had freed strands of her hair from the wide clip that held it at her nape and now blew them wildly around her face. It tugged at her clothes, too, molding her slim skirt to her thighs, lifting the heavy lace collar at her throat. She should have worn a jacket, he thought, but she didn't seem to notice the cold. What he could see of the expression on her face was distant. Thoughtful. Sad.

She was beautiful, so damn beautiful that it made him ache, and he knew now that he had lied to himself earlier. He hadn't learned to live without her and Justin. He hadn't accepted that they were gone from his life. He had dealt with his loss the way Libby dealt with unpleasant subjects: by ignoring them. By refusing to think about them. By refusing to acknowledge how damn much he missed them.

He moved down the gently sloping hill, taking the steps in a few strides, reaching her before he was ready to, before he knew what he would say, how he would feel.

As he approached, she offered him an uneasy sort of smile, as if she suspected that he might reject it—might reject *her*. He could do that. He could give her a hard time, could make this meeting difficult. He could make the next few minutes damned unpleasant for her.

But he didn't want to. He didn't want to punish her. He didn't want to hurt her. She'd been hurt enough already. They all had been.

"Thank you for coming."

His only response was a nod.

She glanced out across the river, then back at him. "All the way over here, I thought about what I would say and how I would say it. I used to be really good at making apologies. Living with Doug, I had to be." She cleared her throat and swallowed hard. "But most of the apologies I made to Doug were for things I hadn't done, problems I hadn't caused. They were meant to soothe his ego. They weren't real. They weren't important. But this time..."

Again she turned to the river, staring at the muddy flow of the water for a moment before facing him again. "Joe, I—"

He took a step forward, wrapped his arms around her and pulled her close. She was startled into silence, and he took advantage of it to do something he'd wanted to do for a long, long time.

An instant before his lips touched hers, Libby realized what he was going to do, but she made no effort to avoid it. She reached for him instead, bracing her hands against the broad strength of his chest, raising her mouth to his, opening to the warm, hungry invasion of his tongue.

Everything else faded under the passion of his kiss—the cold, the wind, her own anxiety. She barely noticed when he drew her even closer against his hard body. She didn't hear the self-conscious snickers of a couple of kids as they passed. She didn't feel it when his cap bumped against her forehead and he loosened his hold long enough to impatiently yank it off, then crushed it against her back.

All she felt was the heat. The hunger. The unbearable need. All she heard was the rushing of hot blood, the ragged breathing, the tautly controlled groan. All she knew was pleasure. This was what she'd wanted, she thought with a dazed satisfaction. This was what she'd needed. What she'd craved not just with her body but with her heart. With her soul.

She had surprised him, Joe thought numbly. Where he had expected tolerance, he had found a sweet welcome. Where he had expected ice, he'd found fire. Where he had known he would find fear, there was only passion, quick to ignite, slow to burn and impossible, in this place at this time, to temper.

He ended the kiss and raised his head and, for just a moment, looked at her. Her expression was dazed, her eyes dark brown and sleepy, her cheeks flushed a becoming rose. God help him, she was beautiful.

Slowly he kissed her again, a simpler kiss this time, just the brush of his mouth, the tentative touch of his tongue to hers.

Then, quickly, another. There was nothing hesitant about this one. He claimed her mouth again, sliding his tongue inside, probing, stroking, filling her in a poor parody of the way he really longed to fill her. Using his free hand, he loosened the clip that contained her hair and slipped it into his pocket, then tangled his hand in the cold, silky strands. Then he drew her closer, closer still, until not even a breath separated them. Until he could feel all her softness. Until she could feel his hardness.

When the tightness in his chest threatened to explode, when the heat became too much, when his fragile control started to shatter, Joe broke off the kiss once more, but he didn't release her. He couldn't give up this contact with her, not yet. So he pressed her head against his chest, gently stroking her hair, calming the trembling that raced through her.

"I'm sorry," she whispered at last, brushing her cheek against the soft, scratchy fabric of his dress coat. "You were right about Justin. This isn't better for him. He loves you, and he misses you, and he needs you."

He tilted her face up so he could see her, then gently stroked her cheek. Her skin was cold and soft and smooth. He could go on touching it like this forever. "And what about you, Libby? Did you miss me, too?"

"After that kiss, do you have to ask?"

"I want to hear it. I want to hear the words."

She smiled tremulously. "Yes, Joe. I missed you, too."

Chapter 9

Libby felt as if a tremendous burden had been lifted from her with that admission. She had admitted it to herself and had given Denise enough clues to figure it out, but to finally say so to Joe himself made her feel free.

"So does this mean I'm welcome to spend time with you and Justin again?"

"Yes. Whenever you want."

"Does it mean I can kiss you again?" He continued in spite of her shy blush. "That I can touch you? That someday I can make love to you? Because you know that's what I want, Libby. I don't want this relationship to center solely on Justin. I want to be friends with you, too. Lovers."

"You're asking for a lot," she whispered.

"No more than you can give."

This wasn't an easy conversation to have when he was holding her so close that she could still feel his arousal. When her heart still thudded irregularly.

But he was right. He wasn't asking for anything that she couldn't give. That she didn't *want* to give.

"I'm not bargaining with you, Libby. I'll still see Justin even if I can only be friends with you."

When she gently pulled, he released her. Almost immediately she missed his warmth, his closeness. She wanted his arms back around her. But she walked a few feet away before facing him again. "I don't want to be hurt, Joe."

He put his cap on again. In his dress uniform—Class A's, she recalled—he looked so handsome and strong, so serious and determined. He looked like everything she wanted. "I would never hurt you, Libby," he promised.

"What about when you leave?"

"We'll work something out."

By that, she assumed, he meant that if things got serious enough between them, she could be persuaded to give up her home and go with him. Or maybe that he had considered the same options she had only a few hours ago. But she didn't ask. She would rather not know, she decided. For once she would prefer to go with her heart instead of her head and believe that something really could be "worked out."

"Libby?"

She smiled uneasily. "You know, you scare me half to death."

"I don't think so," he disagreed. "I think what you feel scares you. I think getting involved with someone scares you. And I think being a woman again scares you. But not me. You'd feel this way with any man."

"I wouldn't be having this conversation with any other man." She stood motionless for a moment, the wind tangling her hair and sending shivers through her; then she said simply, "Yes."

That was all—just *yes*—but she saw in his gentle smile that he understood. Yes, he could kiss her and touch her. Yes, he could make love to her. Yes, she was going to gamble her heart and her soul on this relationship.

He came to her, bent and brushed his mouth end to end across hers. Then he straightened and claimed her hand, tucking it securely in his bigger palm. "Tell me about Justin."

They walked along the riverbank as she related the details of his suspension. What she found so appalling as Justin's mother, Libby noticed, Joe found mildly amusing. When she finished, he said, "I bet the other kid was twice his size."

"He *was* bigger," she admitted. "How did you know?"

"Justin's an equal opportunity brawler. He takes on the big kids as quickly as those his own size." He looked down at her and grinned. "If you'd ever seen some of the kids he was fighting at the beginning of the school year, you would have been a lot more concerned."

"This isn't supposed to be funny," she reminded him.

"Hey, I had my share of fistfights growing up, and I even got kicked out of school a couple of times for them. And I didn't turn out so badly." He released her hand and slid his arm around her shoulder, pulling her closer. "Libby, boys fight. It's no big deal. Justin was provoked, and he handled it."

"And got kicked out of school less than a week before Christmas." But she wasn't really trying to convince him of the seriousness of Justin's offense. She suspected that her parents and her sisters and their husbands would have the same reactions: the women would be distressed, and the men would agree that fighting was a typical little-boy thing to do. Her father would probably even suggest a few lessons to help Justin avoid another black eye in the future.

They reached the amphitheater, then turned and started back. "He's been really unhappy," she remarked quietly, trailing her hand along the retaining wall that supported the levee. "When I told him that I had asked you to stay away from him, he said that I had made his father go away, too, and that maybe I should just go away myself. He said that he didn't want me to be his mother anymore."

"You know he didn't mean it."

"That night he did," she said with a rueful smile. "He was furious. He's hardly spoken to me since then, and I don't blame him. I really thought not seeing you would be best for him. I can't believe I misjudged the strength of his feelings for you so badly. I misjudged you, too."

"People make mistakes," Joe said with a shrug.

She moved away so she could look at him while they walked. "I'm trying to finish my apology here. Would you quit being so reasonable until I'm done?"

"You already apologized. You said you were sorry."

"And that's enough?" she asked skeptically.

He pivoted suddenly and backed her against the wall, trapping her there with his hands on either side. "I'm *not* your ex-husband, Libby. I'm not going to punish you for being human enough to make a mistake. I'm not going to rub it in. I'm not going to say, 'I told you so.'"

"Even though you did." She smiled the kind of happy, warm smile she hadn't had any use for in a long time. "Well, if you're sure you don't want to gloat, I've got to get back to work."

He moved away, and they returned to the parking lot. At her car, Libby hesitantly touched him. "Will you come over tonight?"

"Sure."

"Anytime after six, all right?" Suddenly somber, she leaned forward and brushed a kiss along his jaw. "Thank you, Joe."

When Joe arrived at their house a few minutes after six that evening, Libby was still wearing the dress she'd worn to work, although she'd traded her heels for fluffy slippers. "We just got here," she said, sorting through the mail she still held. "I had to work late to make up for the time I took off to pick Justin up at school. Give me ten minutes to change and I'll see what we can have for—"

He kissed her, nothing too intimate, just a taste to feed his hunger and to stop her words. Then he smiled. "Hello."

"Hi." She smiled, too. "Justin's in his room. I didn't tell him you were coming over. I thought maybe you could just surprise him."

"Yeah, right," he agreed dryly. "You thought you could avoid having to explain to him why you invited me over when just last week you said I couldn't see him anymore. You're a coward, Libby."

He was just teasing, but she took him seriously. "I know, but I'm working on it. Denise says I need to take more chances, but it's not as easy for me as it is for her."

When she started to turn away, he caught her hand and pulled her back. "You only need to take one chance, Libby. On *me*. I won't let you down if you do."

Her only response was a hesitant smile; then she tugged her hand free and went down the hall to her bedroom. As she passed Justin's door, she tapped on the door. "Justin, there's someone here to see you."

Joe removed his jacket and hung it in the closet, turning just as a bruised and dejected Justin came out of his room. When the boy saw him, his face lit up and he came racing down the hall. "Joe, you came back, you came back!" he shouted, launching himself into Joe's arms. "I thought I would never get to see you again, but you're here!"

Joe hugged him tight, then settled him on one hip while he took a long look at him. "Now *that's* what you call a shiner," he teased, although the extent of the bruising made him better understand why Libby had been so dismayed by Justin's fight. The black eye was an ugly contrast to the angelic smile the little boy wore. "Are you okay?"

"It only hurts a little." His smile faded. "Did Mom tell you I got suspended?"

"Yeah, she did." He carried Justin into the living room and sat down in the armchair, settling him comfortably on his lap. "She told me why you were fighting, too. You know what Robert said isn't true, don't you? The reason I quit coming to the school had nothing to do with you."

Justin leaned back against him. "I know. It was my mom's fault. Did she change her mind?"

Joe again silently called Libby a coward for not dealing with this before he got here. "Sort of. Your mom was concerned about some things, and she just needed to be sure that it was okay for us to spend so much time together.''

''She thinks that when you get orders, you'll forget me like my father did. But I know you won't do that,'' Justin said solemnly with all the faith of a child. ''You're not like my father at all. You're a lot nicer, and you like kids better than he does. All *he* likes is Barrie.''

''No, I won't forget you, not when I transfer, not ever.'' With any luck, when he transferred, they would go with him. And if Libby couldn't be persuaded to give up the security and comfort she'd found in being home, as he'd told her, they could still work something out. If all other options failed, he could forget about making sergeant major and go ahead and retire when his current enlistment was up. He could even forget his plans to return to Kentucky after retiring. He could be happy here if Libby and Justin were here.

''Where's your Christmas tree?'' he asked, glancing around the living room. ''I thought you'd already have it up.''

Justin sighed heavily. ''We didn't feel much like doing it. Maybe we can get it tomorrow. Could you come over and help?''

''Sure, if it's okay with your mom.''

''Do you have a Christmas tree?''

''No. I don't usually get one, since I live alone.''

''That's okay. You can come over and look at ours. And you can come Christmas Eve when we open our presents and Christmas Day for dinner. I made Mom a present at school. Want to see it?''

Justin was on his feet and headed toward his room before Joe could reply. Grinning, he followed, catching a glimpse of Libby in the kitchen on his way.

''Close your eyes,'' Justin commanded before he opened the closet door. ''I made something for you, too, and I don't want you to see it.''

Joe obediently shut his eyes and listened to the boy rustling around in the closet. Finally he came out and placed an object in Joe's hands. It was an ornament in the shape of a Christmas tree, made of cardboard and felt and decorated with glitter and sequins. Across the back it was signed and dated in Justin's best printing. The tree's branches were a little lopsided, and the *9*'s in the year were backward, and there was so much glitter that every movement shook off some of the excess, but of course Libby, like all mothers, would treasure it.

"That's nice," he said, carefully handing it back. "Your mom will like that."

"She keeps stuff like that forever," Justin said matter-of-factly. "She gets it from her mom. You should see some of the stuff Grandma has—old baby shoes and poems and pictures and all sorts of stuff that Mom and Aunt Renee and Aunt Faith made when they were kids." He returned the ornament to its hiding place in the closet, then climbed onto his dresser to study his face in the mirror. "Can I tell you something?"

Joe met his gaze in the mirror. "Of course."

"The stuff Robert said wasn't the only reason I hit him."

Slowly Joe moved away from the door and went to stand behind him. "What was the other reason?"

"I thought maybe if I was bad enough, Mom would let you come back," he admitted sheepishly.

Joe rested his hands on Justin's shoulders. The kid was too smart for his own good, he thought, and easily as manipulative as any adult he'd ever known. "You know that was wrong."

"Yes, sir," he said glumly; then suddenly he grinned. "But it worked."

"Maybe. But it was still wrong. You caused trouble at school, you hurt Robert and got yourself hurt, and you upset your mother."

"It was wrong of her to make you go away."

It was hard to argue with Justin's logic when he agreed with it, Joe thought wryly. No matter what her reasons, Libby *had* been wrong. "But that's not your decision to make, partner. Just because you don't agree with what your mother does, that doesn't mean you have the right to misbehave. You can't cause trouble to try to get your own way. Maybe your mother *was* wrong to say we couldn't see each other, but she didn't mean to hurt anyone. It was a mistake. What you did was worse, because you did it on purpose.''

Justin's glum look returned. "I'm sorry, Joe. I won't do it again.''

''I hope not. I would be disappointed if you did.'' Then, sure that his point had been made, he smiled and picked Justin up, swinging him to the floor. ''Let's see if your mom needs any help.''

All too soon dinner was finished and Justin was in bed. Libby gave him a good-night kiss, then left Joe alone with him while she returned to the living room. Although the house was warm, she was cold, and her hands trembled a little. She was afraid to be alone with Joe, she realized as she sat down on the sofa, tucking her grandmother's quilt over her feet. Would he be content to spend the next hour or two quietly talking, the way they'd spent most of their time together, or would he expect more from her?

What had she agreed to this morning? That eventually they would become lovers. That until that happened, they would do the things that soon-to-be-lovers did. The touching. The kissing. The little intimacies. How much easier it had been that night at his apartment, when it had simply happened, than now, when they had discussed it and determined that it *would* happen. Now she was nervous. She identified the tingly feeling inside her as both anticipation—what living, breathing woman wouldn't anticipate being intimate with Joe?—and dread. What woman who'd been with only one man in her entire life—a man who had later walked out on her—wouldn't be at least a little fearful of her next encounter?

When Joe came into the living room, he didn't join her on the couch, as she expected, but instead chose to sit in the easy chair. He nudged his tennis shoes off without unlacing them, then propped his feet on the edge of the coffee table. "Did Justin tell you he wants to put up the Christmas tree tomorrow?"

"No, he didn't." She gave a relieved sigh. "I tried to get him to do it last weekend, but he wasn't interested. I planned to do it Friday whether he wanted to or not. Want to go with us to pick it out?"

"He already invited me," he said with a smug smile. "He's a lot freer with the invitations than you are."

"Why should I bother asking you when he's usually already done it?" she retorted, but her own smile took the sting out of the words. "You have an open invitation. You can come over tomorrow night, Friday night, Saturday—"

He interrupted her. "Saturday night I want you to go to a party with me."

She hesitated. She couldn't remember the last party, excluding family get-togethers and little boys' birthday parties, that she'd been to. It had been in Chicago, she knew, and it had been connected somehow to Doug's job. The people he'd worked with had been big on celebrations, but at some point she had stopped attending them. Probably about the time he'd begun seeing Barrie, she thought. He'd made no effort to hide his affair from his colleagues. Instead, he'd hidden *her,* finding excuses to exclude her from their gatherings.

"I take it your silence means you don't like parties."

Shutting Doug and Barrie out of her thoughts, she shook her head. "No, I do. I just haven't been to one in so long. What kind of party?"

"You can ask that with Christmas less than a week away?"

"I mean, is it your friends or people you work with?"

"Both. It's mainly the senior NCOs in the 65th. It's for adults only, so we'd have to find a baby-sitter for Justin. Are you interested?"

Was she interested in a party that would add some much-needed cheer to her holiday season? Undoubtedly. Was she interested in attending a party with Joe's friends and coworkers as his date? The answer to that wasn't so easy. There was something intimidating about meeting his friends, about putting in an appearance as a couple. It would make this new relationship of theirs so *official*.

He was waiting for her answer, and she saw from the faint resignation in his eyes that he expected to be turned down. So she gave up analyzing, considered what she wanted to do, then did it. "I'd like to go. I'll ask Denise if she can keep Justin." And if Denise was busy, there were other people she could turn to—Mrs. Franklin and a few casual friends in the neighborhood with sons Justin's age.

The resignation was replaced by relief. "The party's supposed to start at seven. It'll be at the clubhouse at some apartment complex in Augusta."

"Okay," she agreed. As she turned her attention to the television, she smiled secretively. Maybe she'd made the last year and a half harder on herself than she'd had to. She liked leading with her heart instead of her head. She liked it a lot.

It was after ten o'clock when Joe announced that he had to leave, and Libby walked to the door with him. This time she fully expected his kiss, but not the slow, leisurely way he went about it. He laced his fingers with hers, then folded both her hands behind her back, allowing him to bring her body completely into contact with his, her breasts against his chest, her belly soft against his, her thighs rubbing his.

"You're a beautiful woman, Libby," he said softly, shifting from side to side, making her breasts ache, her nipples harden.

She laughed self-consciously. "Tell that to my ex-husband."

"The ex-husband who likes his women so young that they're still little girls?" He gently nipped her ear and made her shiver. "The ex-husband who was so busy looking for something elsewhere that he overlooked what he had at home?" He released her hands, then drew his own up her spine, lifting her hair, revealing the curve of her throat.

That was where he placed his first kiss, and Libby's eyes fluttered shut. The second was a fraction higher, and so was the next, until he reached her jaw. He gave it the same treatment, a long line of little kisses, some wet, some not, but all of them heated, all of them hungry.

By the time his lips brushed hers, she was more than ready. Her muscles were quivering, and her body was growing warmer with each beat of her heart. Her pulse was soaring off the chart, and her lungs were so constricted that breathing was nearly impossible. But she could live without breathing as long as she had the sweet taste of him. She could draw her life from him, could lose herself in him, could sustain herself through him.

How easily she welcomed his tongue and his hands, Joe thought. The first time—the last time, the only time—he had touched her breast, she had run away from him, but now, as he smoothed his palm over the soft cotton fabric of her blouse, as he teased the hard crest of her nipple, she showed no interest in running. Even when he tugged her T-shirt free of her jeans and slid his hand underneath it, even when he caressed across the warm skin of her midriff to her breast, soft and bare, her only response was a helpless moan that vibrated through her and into him. No interest in running at all.

He rocked his hips against hers, seeking to ease the pain of his arousal. But, of course, there could be no relief without release, and there could be no release tonight. Asking her to take him to bed tonight was asking too much, and he had too much at stake here to jeopardize it for sex.

Slowly he withdrew his hand, then ended the kiss. While her eyes were still closed, her lips still moist and slightly parted, he gently stroked his fingertips across her face. "If you could see yourself the way I do," he murmured, "you would know I'm telling the truth. You *are* beautiful, Libby."

Bending, he gave her one last kiss before he walked out the door. It was easier to leave than he'd expected, because even though he didn't want to go, he knew he would be back. One day, one day soon, he would be back to stay.

* * *

Thursday evening found Libby and Joe sitting together on the sofa in the dark living room, but there was nothing, she thought with a faint sigh, the least bit romantic about it. From the end of the room opposite the television came a steady rustling, a few bumps and grunts and an occasional frustrated murmur.

"I *told* him we should leave the lights on until he got everything plugged in," Libby whispered in Joe's ear.

He shifted to lean against the arm of the sofa, then pulled her back against him. "Even though I declined to say 'I told you so' yesterday, you're going to say it now. Where's your sense of fair play?" he whispered back.

Before she could respond, Justin succeeded in inserting the two plugs into the outlet behind the desk, and hundreds of tiny lights of every color lit up the Christmas tree they had just finished decorating. Even though she'd seen the sight dozens of times, she couldn't resist an admiring "Ooh."

Then Justin came across the room and climbed onto her lap. Joe made room for him, lifting his arms to include him in their embrace. "We did a good job," Justin said proudly, looking from the tree to his mother, then to Joe. "Now all it needs is some presents."

"Your presents from Renee and Faith are in my closet," Libby said, mussing his hair. "So are the ones from Grandma and Grandpa."

"And what about my gifts from *you?*" he asked, grinning charmingly.

Libby pretended surprise. "Oh, no, that's what I forgot! I wondered why my Christmas list seemed so short this year. How did that happen?"

Justin giggled. "Oh, Mom... You're not a very good liar."

"Thank you, dear. I have to say, that never was one of my goals. Why don't you get the packages from my closet? And no shaking, rattling or peeking, either," she warned as he wiggled to the floor.

"Now that the tree's up, you won't have to find a hiding place for your presents," Joe said, pulling her a little closer. "Why don't you wrap them at my apartment, then bring them over this weekend?"

"Okay." She rested her head on his shoulder, then sighed. "I love Christmas trees. After we moved away from here and until Justin was born, I always put ours up by myself. Doug never showed much interest in them. He usually watched television in the bedroom or went out or something while I decorated the tree."

"Did he ever show much interest in anything besides himself?"

"What do you mean?"

"When you moved someplace new, did he help you get settled? Did he help you learn your way around? Did he introduce you to the wives of the men he worked with? Did he try to make the adjustment easier for you?"

"Of course not." She laughed softly at the thought. "That wasn't his job."

"No wonder you got tired of moving. It's not like that in the Army. Military wives know what it's like to adjust to a new place, and they stick together. They help each other. And, of course, you have to realize that most husbands don't just drop their wives in a new place, then forget about them. *I* certainly wouldn't."

Libby stiffened for a moment. Maybe he did expect her to change her mind—or expected to change it for her— about moving. She didn't want to spoil this nice, quiet moment by telling him how she abhorred the idea. She had given up her home for Doug, and she'd never been really happy again until she'd come back. She couldn't face the thought of going through that again.

Justin returned then, dragging a box behind him by the flaps. "I got lots of stuff in here, Joe. Come look."

He lifted Libby so he could stand up, then settled her back against the cushions. "Keep my place warm," he murmured.

It wasn't right that she should grow used to the physical contact so rapidly, she thought. It wasn't fair that she missed him already when he'd gone only ten feet away. It wasn't proper that the uneasiness that had accompanied her decision to become lovers with him had so quickly given way to a state of near-constant arousal. After that good-night kiss at the door last night, she had dreamed about him, and she had awakened with her heart pounding, her breasts aching, and heat, potent and damp, pooling between her thighs. All day she had looked forward to this evening, had anticipated more kisses, more caresses, and they would probably lead to steamier dreams...and frustration. And excitement.

And why shouldn't she be frustrated and excited? She had been alone for eighteen months—and, she admitted, her love life prior to those eighteen months hadn't been anything to miss—and she was about to take only her second lover in thirty-two years. If those weren't good reasons for frustration and excitement, she didn't want to know what were.

Justin insisted on leaving off all the lights except the Christmas lights while he and Joe arranged the packages underneath the tree. Even after he went to bed a short while later, the overhead lights remained off. The tiny, colored lights offered more than enough illumination—or, rather, just the right amount, Libby thought with a smile—for what she and Joe were doing. There was something special about necking on the sofa under the glow of a beautifully decorated Christmas tree.

"I've got to go," Joe muttered.

She drew her fingers through his hair. She'd been surprised by how much she liked touching it—not that there was much to touch. When she and Doug had gotten married, it had been a toss-up as to whose hair was longer, and he still had a tendency to keep it shaggy. Who would have thought that she would fall for a man whose hair wasn't much more than a clip away from being gone?

"I *really* have to go."

She smiled lazily. "You've said that four times in the past hour by my count."

"This time I mean it." He tugged her hands away and got to his feet.

"Can I change your mind?" she asked, standing up, too, and placing a slow, sweet kiss on his jaw.

He cupped her face in his hands. "Only by taking me to bed."

She smiled, then realized he was serious. Could she do that? The desire that had long ago spread its warmth through her body said yes, but the butterflies that suddenly appeared in her stomach said no. Not yet. It was too soon for such a momentous step. She needed more of this—the closeness, the kisses, the caresses—a lot more before she could take that step.

His smile was filled with regret. "Not tonight, huh?"

"Justin—"

"Is asleep. He would never know." He rubbed the pad of his thumb across her lips. "Libby, I'm forty years old. That's too old to lie awake at night because I'm too damn aroused to go to sleep. And it's way too old for cold showers."

Chastened, she dropped her gaze to his chest. "I'm sorry."

"Don't be. I like kissing you. I like touching your breasts and lying with you beneath me on the sofa. I just want more. I want to take your clothes off and look at you and touch you and kiss you everywhere. I want to be inside you. I want to show you how sweet and special making love can be." He coaxed her into looking at him again, then kissed both cheeks, then her mouth. "Whenever you're ready, sweetheart. I can be patient."

When Joe left for his apartment Friday night, his patience seemed to remain intact, but *hers*, Libby thought crossly, was shot to hell. Hours after he'd left, she lay in bed, still unable to sleep, unable even to think clearly. Oh, but she could feel. There was nothing wrong with that part of her. And what she felt was . . . edgy. Irritated. Restless. Needy. Empty. Lonely. Heavens, she was lonely!

She wished she had asked him to stay. Her only argument against it—Justin—had been feeble and hadn't even convinced herself. Joe had been right. Justin would never know. If he found Joe there when he woke up the next morning, he would simply assume that he had come over early to spend the day with them. It would never occur to him that he might have spent the night, and even if it did, he wouldn't understand the significance of that.

But no, she hadn't asked him to stay. When he had left her with one last breath-stealing kiss, she had let him go . . . and regretted it ever since.

Why was she avoiding the final step of becoming lovers with Joe? She knew she wanted him. Was she afraid that he would compare her to his other lovers and find her lacking, either physically or in experience?

Maybe, she thought with a reluctant smile. She had never lost those five extra pounds that had plagued her ever since she was a baby, and being pregnant with Justin had certainly left its mark, too. And there was no denying that her self-esteem had suffered a major blow from months of comparing her own body to model-thin, athlete-perfect, teenage Barrie.

But if Joe had wanted thin and perfect, he never would have given her a second glance. He was a bright man. He knew what he was getting with her, and he wanted her anyway.

Was she afraid that he would be disappointed, that he would find the reward hadn't been worth the effort? That once he'd gotten what he wanted, he would lose interest? *No,* on all counts. He wasn't that kind of man.

Maybe she was afraid of making that final commitment. After all, for the kind of woman she was, making love wasn't something to be done lightly. It ranked right up there with falling in love and getting married and forever.

And she wasn't sure she could have forever with Joe.

Considering their differences she wasn't sure she could even dream about marriage.

But there *was* one thing she was sure of. She could love him. Whether for six months, six years or sixty, she could love him.

She already did.

Chapter 10

It was cold when they left the party Saturday night, and a steady rain was falling. When they'd taken Justin over to Denise's, Libby remembered, he had expressed his fondest wish to have snow for Christmas. It would only have to get a little colder, he had insisted, but it wasn't going to happen, and privately she was grateful. She hadn't minded the snow in Chicago and the other places where they'd lived, but she knew from experience that it was such a rarity here that people didn't know how to deal with it. A few inches of snow constituted a major emergency here.

Still, a white Christmas *would* be nice, she thought dreamily as she snuggled closer into Joe's warm embrace. A snug house, snow, Christmas, Justin and Joe—what more could she want?

"You're awfully quiet," Joe remarked as they approached his car.

She glanced up at him and smiled. "I like your friends. They're nice."

He pretended surprise. "What? Libby Harper actually *liked* a bunch of career soldiers? People who have no roots? Who are unreliable, undependable, un—"

She cut him off with her elbow in his ribs. "Don't make fun of me. They're nice people—especially Reba Stanley. I felt like I'd known her forever."

"Yeah, she's nice." They got into the car, and he started the engine. "Her husband Max works for me. They've got twins Justin's age."

"Yes, she told me." She shivered when he turned the heater on and cold air blew on her feet. "I don't think I really understood what a first sergeant does, or I would have been more impressed with you in the beginning."

He claimed her hand and pressed a kiss to the bare skin above the edge of her glove. "Are you impressed now?"

"Absolutely." She fastened her seat belt and looked out the window for a moment. She had reached a decision in the early hours of this morning, and she had acted on it when she'd called Denise this afternoon. Now she needed some way to tell Joe, but she couldn't think of any besides blurting it out, and she couldn't find the courage to do that. Finally she turned toward him and smiled uneasily. "We're not far from your apartment, are we?"

He met her gaze in the dim light, his steady and knowing, hers nervous. "A couple of miles."

Her smile became shakier. "Do you still have some wood for that fireplace?"

"The wood box is full, and there's more covered and dry on the patio."

"Could we go there?"

Joe nodded. That was all—just a nod. He didn't trust himself to say anything. He decided the engine had warmed up enough, and he shifted into gear. The distance to his apartment was closer to five miles, and it seemed to take forever to get there...yet they arrived too soon. Too soon for him to accept what he knew she was going to offer. Too soon to quiet the sudden case of nerves drawing his muscles into tight knots.

He wanted to suggest that they go to her house. He wanted to explain that he wanted to spend the night with her, wanted to sleep beside her and wake up next to her, that he *didn't* want to have to get up and get dressed and take her home all too soon. He wanted all night to love her, to touch and seduce her, not a hurried hour or two.

He pulled into the space closest to his apartment and turned off the engine. For a moment they just sat there, the rain a steady drumming on the car's roof, the warmth of the heater slowly giving way to the night's chill. At last he glanced at her. "What time does Denise expect us?" It was after ten now. If they were lucky, they'd have a couple of hours....

"She doesn't." Libby's voice quavered, and she smiled, embarrassed by that. "Justin's spending the night there. I don't need to pick him up until tomorrow."

His misgivings faded, although the nervousness remained. "Let's go inside, and I'll build that fire."

Just inside the door they removed their coats, and Libby brushed the rain from her hair. She busied herself with hanging up their coats while Joe turned to the fireplace. When he had a bright blaze going, he turned and found her still standing at the door, beside the wooden coat tree. He crossed the room and reached for the light switch next to her, plunging the room into darkness except for the warm golden glow of the fire.

Then he touched her. She shivered and caught her breath, and he laughed softly. He had no need to be nervous, because *she* was nervous enough for both of them. "Don't be afraid, Libby," he whispered as he drew her near. "You know I would never hurt you."

"I know." There was just enough substance to her voice for him to make out the words.

He led her across the room, where they sat on the floor, backs against the sofa, legs stretched out toward the fireplace. For a long time he simply held her close, his cheek against her damp hair, his fingers caressing where they rested.

Slowly Libby relaxed. He could feel the tension draining from her, leaving her soft and warm and easy. It had been difficult for her to decide to do this, he suspected—and even harder still for her to let him know. She couldn't simply say, "I want you to make love to me. I want you inside me," even though *he'd* had no problem making a similar statement to her two nights ago. But then, he had the benefit of more lovers, more experience and the certainty that he was going to spend the rest of his life with *this* lover, while all she had were doubts, fears and lingering hurts, courtesy of Harper.

He nuzzled her hair aside and kissed her forehead. "I'm glad you went to the party with me."

She wiggled her feet out of her shoes and stretched closer to the heat of the fire. "I had a good time."

He had told her the party would be casual, but she'd wanted to wear a dress anyway. Most of the men had worn jeans, like him, and most of the women, too, but a few, including Reba Stanley, had chosen dresses. None of them, though, had come close to matching Libby's beauty or her style or her gorgeous long legs...legs that he would soon feel wrapped around him.

He was in sad shape, he acknowledged, when such a mild thought could cause such an extreme reaction. Already he was aroused, his jeans growing uncomfortably tight, his blood pumping unbearably hot. He wasn't going to be able to take the time he wanted, to seduce her with the gentleness, the patience and tenderness, that she needed, not this time. Not this first time.

Libby shifted against him, bringing her hand up to stroke the nubby knit of his sweater. It was black and soft and fit him superbly. She slid her hand underneath it, then flattened her palm against his chest. His skin was toasty warm and soft, too, a lovely contrast to the hard bone and muscle underneath.

This was the first time she had touched him so intimately, but instead of being nervous, she was simply aroused. After eighteen—no, now it was nineteen—months of celibacy, she was finding she had little patience and a very great need for this man.

About the time her fingers found his nipple, small and hard, he tilted her face up and kissed her, a long, leisurely exploration of her mouth that left her breathless and weak and even needier than before. Wordlessly she protested his leaving, and he returned for another kiss, longer, deeper, hungrier, demanding and taking and giving, making her shiver helplessly, feeding the ache inside her, promising her relief but not delivering it, not yet.

Pushing his sweater out of the way, she stroked his chest and made him shudder. Then, tentatively, she slid her hand lower, from warm, smooth skin to cool leather to soft, faded denim. All her worry over her lack of experience had been for nothing, she discovered. Her fingers knew exactly how to curve around his hardness, just how gently to touch him, just how erotically to stroke him, just how sweetly to make him groan.

Once again she had surprised him, Joe realized. He had expected hesitation, even fear, and she was giving him passion. He had intended the slowest, sweetest, gentlest seduction he was capable of, and she was deliberately hurrying him along.

He gently eased her back, grateful for the thick area rug that covered the wall-to-wall carpet here, then leaned over her, supporting himself on one hand so he could use the other to undo the row of buttons that fastened her dress. It was slower going one-handed than he liked, and when she silently offered her help, he let her finish the task while he turned his attention to more important things.

Gently he nudged the fabric aside, revealing a creamy-shaded bra, all lace and narrow straps and secured between her breasts with a single small hook. He opened it easily and pushed the lace aside, too, revealing her breasts, full and soft and lovely and crested with rosy peaks that invited his kisses. He drew his tongue across one nipple, and she groaned; then he suckled it, and she arched her back, straining against his mouth.

She whimpered his name and reached for him, tugging impatiently, but he resisted. Instead he gave her one last kiss, then sat back on his knees and simply looked at her. She rested her hand on his thigh and questioningly whispered his name. "You're so beautiful," he said hoarsely. "I just want to look at you for a moment."

The love in his steady gaze encouraged her, and the awe emboldened her. She shrugged out of her dress and bra; then, in one long graceful movement, she slipped out of the rest of her clothing. For one brief moment she thought of Barrie and her all-too-perfect body; then she banished the younger woman from her thoughts. Let Doug have his barely-more-than-a-teenager lover. There was no denying that Joe wanted *her*.

Still fully dressed, he moved between her legs, and she opened to him. He caressed her breasts, across her ribs, over her stomach to her thighs, leaving a trail of heat and need behind. When he rubbed across her stomach again, she sucked in her breath and felt her muscles clench and ripple at his touch. And when he stroked between her thighs, through the dark curls and into the heat, she cried out and trembled uncontrollably.

With her last bit of strength, she touched him, molding her hand lovingly to the length of him. "Please, Joe," she whispered. "I need you."

Joe covered her hand with his for a moment, and his eyes closed on the pure pleasure of the sensation. Then he lifted her hand to his mouth, placing a hot, moist kiss in the center of her palm before he laid it on the rug at her side.

He removed his sweater first, then his shoes and socks. He wasn't in any hurry, because Libby was watching him, and he was watching *her*. Slowly he unbuckled his belt, unzipped his jeans, then stood up and drew them down, over his arousal and off. Just as slowly he lowered himself to the floor again and kissed her, biting her lower lip, evading her questing hands and trapping them on the soft rug, moving lower to kiss one breast, then the other, and finally her stomach.

He released her hands to gently stroke her, parting the damp curls, measuring the heat inside her, tenderly testing her. When she cried out his name, her voice was half sob, half laugh and all demand, and he surrendered to it, guiding himself into place, pushing against her, into her, until finally he filled her. Until the heat his fingers had found surrounded him, tight and welcoming. Until he was where he belonged.

Until he was home.

Libby couldn't remember ever feeling the way she did right now. Filled. Warm. Satisfied. Tense and, at the same time, relaxed. *Loved.*

She shifted her legs, twining them with Joe's, then drew her hands over his spine, feeling each bone, each strained muscle, each quivering nerve. When she reached his shoulders, she glided her fingers on up and into his hair, using her gentle grip to tug his head up so she could see his face. His skin was slick from exertion, like hers, and his expression was dazed, like hers, his eyes soft and somewhat surprised.

"Was it supposed to be like that?" she whispered, and he laughed.

"You got me, sweetheart. I was expecting something less..."

Intense? she wondered. Less emotional? Less bonding? Less earth-shattering? So was she. All those years of making love with Doug hadn't prepared her for this. She hadn't known such an experience could even exist.

"But then," Joe continued, bracing himself on both arms so he could look down at her, "I've never made love to a woman I loved the way I love you."

She gave him a long, steady look. She should have been surprised, but she wasn't. She couldn't have experienced the last hour with him and not known that he loved her, just as now he had to know, too, that she was in love with him. But she didn't say anything. She couldn't just yet. Not until she'd considered all the implications, all the possibilities, all the obligations.

"I don't expect a similar declaration," Joe said patiently, "but I would like some kind of response. Considering that you're only the second woman I've ever said that to—and the last I'll ever say it to..."

A tear seeped from the corner of her eye and disappeared into her hair. She blinked, and two new tears welled. She hadn't realized that she wanted to cry, although she had felt the urge during their exquisitely wonderful lovemaking.

"Words given in the heat of passion," she whispered, trailing her fingers down his chest until she was caressing her own skin as well as his.

Joe shook his head. "No. It's not passion, Libby. It's truth. Honesty."

"I know." She wiped away another tear, then drew him down for a kiss. This time she was the aggressor, the one who did the exploring, the tasting. Her kiss, she suspected, lacked polish, but Joe didn't seem to mind. In fact, she felt a distinct stirring deep inside where her body still sheltered his. "Let's go to bed," she whispered between tiny, hungry kisses, "and you can say it again." She caught her breath when he moved inside her. "You can show me again."

Their second loving was slower, lazier, but no less satisfying. Joe sank onto the bed beside her, his face only inches from hers, his arm wrapped around her waist, his leg hooked possessively over hers. The fire's warm glow didn't reach into the bedroom, and he moved only to pull the covers over them before returning to her.

He wasn't as widely experienced as Libby probably believed. He'd never had a meaningless affair, had never been to bed with a woman he didn't care deeply for. But he knew enough to recognize something extraordinary when he saw it—rather, when he *felt* it—and what he and Libby had shared had been extraordinary indeed.

It must be because they were in love, he decided as he lazily stroked her arm and the side of her breast. He did love her, and whether she wanted to acknowledge it or not, he

knew she loved him, too. She couldn't have come here tonight, couldn't have offered herself to him, if she didn't.

So where did they go from here? He knew the next logical step for him: marriage. He wanted to marry Libby, to
have children with her, to grow old with her. He wanted to
be Justin's father, wanted to come home to them every day,
wanted to know that they would always, always be part—the
main part—of his life.

But what did she want? She wouldn't even admit that she
loved him yet. Saying the words would make it so real, so
undeniable. It would mean doing what people in love did:
getting married, having babies, planning the future. In their
case it would almost certainly mean moving, and he knew
how she felt about that.

He moved his slow, soothing caresses from her breast to
her stomach. He knew her ex-husband's preference for his
young secretary had damaged Libby's self-esteem, that too
many times she had compared her body to the younger
woman's, and that she had always judged herself unfavor-
ably. But *he* thought she was beautiful—not boyishly thin
or lean or muscular, but shapely and soft, with full breasts,
a narrow waist, rounded hips and legs to die for.

Stretching his fingers wide, he laid his hand flat across her
stomach. He hadn't used any protection tonight, hadn't
even considered the possibility that he might need it. He
wondered idly if she had been prepared, but he didn't ask
her. If she hadn't, the risk that they'd taken might unnerve
her. Nothing could settle their future as quickly and permanently as a baby on the way. She was too traditional to
become a single parent, and he was too possessive to allow
her to try.

"What are you thinking?" Her voice came from the
darkness, soft and sleepy and close.

"Nothing." Except that they had made love twice tonight. That he had filled her twice. That for a few weeks, at
least, he could hope she was pregnant; he could fantasize
about becoming a father, about forming a family.

"Joe?"

"Hmm."

"Before I fall asleep—" she paused to yawn "—would you tell me again?"

He smiled in the dark, hugged her close and kissed her. "I love you, Libby."

Waking up in a man's bed was a new experience for Libby, but one she could get used to, she decided, even if the man wasn't there, even if he'd been up so long that the sheets where he'd slept were icy cold. She'd slept better than she had in ages, and though it wasn't even eight o'clock, she felt rested and satisfied and only the slightest bit sore.

Sitting up, she looked around the bedroom for something to wear—her clothes or Joe's, it didn't matter—but there was nothing. With a shiver, she peeled the comforter from the rest of the covers, wrapped it around her and went down the hall in search of Joe. She found him in the living room, sitting in front of the fireplace where another fire burned, wearing nothing but a pair of indecently snug jeans and drinking a cup of coffee while he read the Sunday paper.

"Good morning."

He looked up and smiled. There was nothing special about it—just one of his usual charming smiles—but it made her feel warm. Welcome. Beautiful—as if she weren't wearing only a black-and-turquoise comforter, with her hair in a tangle and her face free of makeup.

He set his coffee on the hearth, pushed the newspaper aside and extended his hand to her. "Come and sit with me."

Libby hesitated. "I'll get too warm," she protested. He was leaning right against the stone hearth, the blaze only a few feet behind him.

"That's the idea," he admitted, the smile changing to his mischievous little grin. "Then I can unwrap you and see what's inside."

Gathering the comforter so she could walk more easily, she started toward him, intending to sit beside him. But he stretched his legs out and caught two fistfuls of the down-filled coverlet and pulled her down to straddle his lap. "Is this supposed to get me warm quicker?" she teased, deliberately rubbing against him as she settled into place.

"I don't know about you, sweetheart, but it's already raising *my* temperature." He combed his fingers through her hair, then studied her for a moment. "Any regrets?" he asked gently, solemnly.

She shook her head. "None."

"Except that you wish I wasn't a soldier."

She gave it a moment's serious thought—not easy to do, when she could feel the swelling of his body beneath her. "I'm not sure if you became a soldier because of the man you are, or if you became that man because you're a soldier. Either way, you're very special to me. You know that."

"I won't be in the Army forever."

She smiled at the slightly hopeful tone in his voice, as if he was offering her encouragement that they could, indeed, work something out. "When could you get out if you wanted?"

"My current enlistment is up in about a year and a half, provided that the situation in Africa is back to normal by then."

A chill passed through her that had nothing to do with the cold and the fact that she was naked underneath the blanket. "What does that have to do with it?"

"The Army has put a freeze on all personnel. Service members whose enlistments end or who come up for retirement are extended indefinitely until everything's settled over there. It's no big deal—unless, of course, you're the one being extended."

Steeling herself, she asked the question she should have asked long ago—before falling in love with him, before going to bed with him, before finding out that she wasn't sure she could live without him. "What are the chances that you'll be sent over there?"

She wanted to hear the truth. She wanted to hear a lie. She wanted to hear anything except what he said. "If we go to war...pretty good."

"And what are the chances of that?"

He filled both hands with the blanket and pulled her close. "Your guess is as good as mine, sweetheart." Then he kissed her, long and easy, deliberately trying to distract her, and she let him. "Move over here just a minute," he directed hoarsely when the kiss was done.

Libby blindly obeyed. When he pulled her back, she discovered that he was naked, too, and hot and throbbing, and so was she. She guided him inside her, her body stretching to accommodate him, her earlier soreness forgotten. One way or another, the day would come when they couldn't make love like this anymore—if he got orders and she didn't go with him...or if he got orders and she *couldn't* go with him—and it would probably break her heart. But until then, she would store up memories. She would take what she could have, give what he would take. She would enjoy the pleasures of his company, the pleasures of his body and the very deep pleasures of his love.

And she would love him.

It had been a hectic day, Joe thought Monday evening as he stretched out on Libby's couch with Justin beside him. He had worked until noon, then picked up Justin at Mrs. Franklin's, and they had braved the mall—a first and definite last for him on the day before Christmas. But he'd had to find a gift for Libby, and he'd needed Justin's input. The only idea that had come to *his* mind had been an engagement ring, and he'd known Libby wasn't ready for that. Of course, most of Justin's suggestions had been better suited to a child than his thirty-two-year-old mother. Still, it had been fun having him along.

He felt lazy lying here with Justin, watching an animated Christmas show that he'd seen at least a dozen times before while Libby was in the kitchen fixing dinner, but he didn't get up. He'd offered his help earlier, and she had requested that he simply keep Justin from asking her every five minutes if it was time yet to open the presents. And so he'd done his job—the eager, repetitive questions had come to *him* instead. But after Justin went to bed, he promised himself, he would help her with her preparations for tomorrow's dinner.

And then *they* would go to bed. Libby had invited him to spend the night, and *that,* he thought with a smile, was just about the best gift he could have asked for.

She came into the living room as the show ended, carrying a tray loaded with soft drinks and their dinner: cheeses, crackers, rolls and a selection of meats and, for dessert, a plate of Mrs. Franklin's homemade candies. Joe got up to help her, but the phone rang, and she gestured toward it instead. "Answer that, will you?"

There was a brief pause after he said hello, then a woman's voice. "This is Lorna Howell, Libby's mother. Who am I speaking to?"

"Joe Mathison," he replied.

"And who is Joe Mathison?"

"Libby's friend." After all the time he'd fought against being Libby's *friend,* Joe thought with a grin, here he was describing himself as just that. But it wasn't a lie—they *were* friends—and he knew better than to tell her mother, of all people, exactly how friendly he was with her daughter. "Would you like to speak to her?"

"Yes, I would."

"Just a moment." He laid the phone on the hall table and returned to the living room. "It's your mom, Libby."

She straightened from fixing Justin's plate and went to the phone. For a moment Joe remained motionless, listening to her end of the call, knowing her mother would ask about him and wondering what she would say. It took only a moment to find out.

"Who is Joe?" Libby echoed softly in the hallway. "He's Justin's best friend in the entire world . . . and he's the best thing that ever happened to me."

Grinning, he returned to the sofa and slid in beside Justin. It wasn't "I love you," but she was getting there. It wouldn't be long now until she admitted that she did love him, and then he could ask her to marry him. Then they could start planning their future.

Libby kept the phone call short, chatting for only a few minutes before calling Justin in to talk. "They'll call again tomorrow so they can find out what Justin got and how he likes their gift," she said as she sat down in the easy chair and leaned forward to fix her own plate. "But Mom called tonight because she was worried about us spending Christmas alone, and she wanted to make sure we're all right."

"You look better than all right to me."

She caught his hand and squeezed it tight. "Thank you," she said solemnly.

"For what?"

"Not holding grudges. For being understanding and patient. For giving me a second chance."

He twisted his hand so that *he* was holding hers. "I love you, Libby. I started falling in love with you the day we met." He held her hand a moment longer, then reluctantly released it. "You'd better eat while you have a chance. Justin's got a good head start on you. He'll be ready to start opening his presents as soon as he gets off the phone."

Libby knew he was right. Justin wouldn't cheerfully wait much longer, and, after all, it was after seven o'clock. He'd waited long enough. She sliced a croissant in half with the serrated knife and filled it with cheese and turkey and ham, then turned to look at the Christmas tree while she ate.

There were plenty of packages under it—including a couple of new ones that Joe and Justin had brought back from their afternoon together. Once again there was nothing from Doug, but she didn't think Justin would mind so much, not when Joe's gift was there. Not when Joe himself was here. And this time *she* didn't mind so much. Sooner or later she would have to come to terms with the fact that Doug was a lousy father. Joe had told her so the night they went toy shopping, and, as usual, he'd been right. Fretting and hurting and getting angry over Doug's behaviour didn't change anything; it didn't guarantee that the next birthday or the next Christmas would be any different.

Besides, Justin didn't need Doug or his gifts. He had plenty of people who loved him dearly. He had Joe.

She had just finished her sandwich when Justin came back from the phone. He took one bite of the food on his plate, then announced, "I'm finished eating. *Now* can we open the presents?"

Libby gave in as soon as she retrieved her camera from the bedroom. Impatient as he was, though, Justin didn't tear into his gifts. He examined each one, exclaiming over it and showing it first to Joe, then to her, then laying it aside before turning to the next package. He saved Joe's for last and climbed onto his lap on the sofa before carefully removing the paper and opening the box.

"Wow," he whispered, stroking one horse in its tissue bed. "That's *neat*. They look real old."

"They belonged to my granddad, then my dad, and then me," Joe said. "Now they're yours."

"Can I pick one up?"

"Sure."

He lifted one out and studied it, then returned it to the box and picked up another one. Then he turned and wrapped his arms tightly around Joe's neck. "Thank you, Joe. I'll take *real* good care of them," he promised. "I won't let anything happen to them, and when I'm grown up, I'll give them to my little boy, too."

Libby sat on the floor, her hands trembling after the last few shots she'd taken. One of them, she'd bet, would be the perfect picture of love.

Justin took the metal soldiers into his room, then returned to hand out the remaining packages. Libby had insisted that Joe bring his gifts from his family, and he opened those first, followed by Justin's. It was a frame made of wooden sticks and holding a five-by-seven second-grade portrait of her son. It was the sort of gift that Doug would have dismissed as worthless, but Libby knew she would see it sometime in the future in a place of honor at Joe's apartment or office.

The last box was from her, and she snapped a few more pictures as he unwrapped it. "I didn't know what to get you," she said almost apologetically as he lifted the crew-neck sweater from the box. It was heavy and knitted in an intricate pattern from yarn of the softest blue. "Then I was walking through this store at the mall, and I saw that sweater, and it's the exact same color as your eyes, so..."

He leaned across and kissed her, a heady enough kiss to make Justin giggle self-consciously. "Thank you," he whispered, then took the camera from her hands. "Now it's your turn."

She opened the gifts from her sisters and parents and dutifully oohed over the ornament Justin had made for her, getting up immediately to hang it on the tree. Then she opened the last box, the one with the tag that said, "From Justin and Joe." It was big and flat, and inside was a chocolate chip cookie the size of a large pizza. Decorated with colored frosting, it carried a brief message: *Merry Christmas. Love, J & J.*

"I'm the first *J*," Justin said, leaning over to scoop off a fingerful of frosting. "And Joe's the second. Can I have a bite?"

"Just a little bit. You've already eaten half of Mrs. Franklin's candy." She kissed his forehead, then broke off two chunks of cookie and went to join Joe on the couch, feeding him one piece. When he took it, he nibbled her finger, too. "I *love* chocolate chip cookies," she sighed after tasting her own chunk.

"I know. But the cookie isn't your real gift. You'll get that later."

She gave him a long, leisurely look, from head to toe and back again. "I know," she said huskily. "I'm looking forward to it."

By eleven o'clock the house was quiet, the Christmas pies were baked, and the kitchen was cleaned. Justin had long since gone to bed, and Libby had brought out his final gift, the one from Santa, and placed it in a prominent spot under the tree for tomorrow morning; then she and Joe had stretched out on the sofa. It was a snug fit, but she liked it this way—liked feeling his body pressed against hers, his arms wrapped comfortably around her, his slow, steady breathing stirring her hair.

"Tired?" he murmured, brushing a kiss to her temple.

"Hmm."

"Ready for bed?"

"Hmm."

"Want one last present before we go?"

He released her, leaving her balancing precariously on the edge of the cushions while he retrieved a package from behind the sofa. When he gave it to her, she sat up and carefully peeled the ribbon and paper off the box. Inside was another box, this one made of wood, rich mahogany in the shape of a heart. The workmanship was exquisite, the fit of the lid tight, the seams nearly invisible. The lid was decorated with intricately carved flowers, ribbons and lace, and the interior of the box was lined with crimson velvet. It smelled of fragrant wood, dreams and hopes and intimate secrets.

Nestled into one rounded arch was a small piece of paper, folded in half. She unfolded it and read the message aloud in a quavery voice. "No matter where I go, you'll always have my heart. You'll always share my life. You'll always be my love. Merry Christmas, Libby."

She couldn't remember the last time a gift had been so special that it had made her cry, if ever, but this one did. Clutching the box in both hands, she hid her face against Joe's chest and cried.

"Now I think it's time for bed," he said with a gentle smile, disentangling himself and standing up, then scooping her into his arms.

Laughing through her tears, she wrapped one arm around his neck. "I can walk," she protested.

"Yes, and you do it quite well."

"I'm too heavy for you to carry. Put me down before you hurt yourself."

"In due time." He had to bend his knees so he could open the bedroom door; then he carried her into the cool, dark room and laid her gently on the bed. He followed her down, his body covering hers, resting his weight on his elbows so he could stroke her face. "Thank you for sharing your Christmas with me. It would have been lonely alone."

"Thanks for making it worth sharing. And thank you for the cookie and for the heart—" she still held it tightly "—and for the soldiers you gave Justin and for loving him and especially for loving me when I know I haven't always been very lovable."

He kissed her, then turned on the lamp on the bedside table. She tried to shy away from its light, but his greater strength held her where she was. "I want to make love to you, Libby," he murmured, slowly unfastening each button on her blouse. "I want to look at you. I want to see how beautiful you are."

He undressed her with great care, kissing her skin as it was exposed, caressing and tickling and stroking it. When she was naked, he continued his seduction, slow and loving, making her muscles clench and her nerves quiver and her skin tingle. Her soft moans turned to needy gasps, then breathless pleas, until finally he took pity on her. Lying on his side so he could continue his lazy, hot kisses on her breast, he slid his hand across her stomach, through the dark curls between her thighs and inside her fiery liquid warmth. Long moments and long, talented strokes later, a helpless cry vibrated through her, and she grew rigid and taut.

He tenderly rubbed her face until the tremors eased and the tiny, heated convulsions faded. When she opened her eyes, he smiled smugly. "Not bad, huh?"

"Not bad at all." She summoned the energy to push him onto his back, then rose over him, saying in a throaty voice, "Now it's your turn."

As she removed his shirt and drew her hands over his chest, she understood his pleasure in simply looking. He was lean and muscular, solid and strong, the handsomest man she'd ever known. She liked touching him and watching his muscles ripple. She liked drawing her fingernails lightly across his nipples and seeing them draw up hard and taut. She especially liked sliding her hand lower and feeling him swell to fit it.

Awkwardly she unbuckled his belt, then undid the metal buttons of his jeans. Undressing a man was new to her, as new as the toe-curling passion of making love. She was a little clumsy at sliding his jeans and briefs down his legs, and she forgot to remove his shoes first, and she wound up with a tangle of clothing, but somehow she didn't think Joe minded. In fact, she thought as she knelt beside him and subjected him to the same kind of long, intense inspection he had given her, she was positive he didn't.

She touched him tentatively, tracing an unseen path over the long, hard muscles of one thigh, over the narrow flat expanse of his stomach, finally, hesitantly, coming to rest over his arousal. He responded to her gentle caresses, growing even longer, even thicker, and when she offered him a shy, intimate kiss, he groaned her name aloud.

She moved to lie beside him, wrapping her arms around him, drawing him into place over her. Looking was fun, and touching was a pleasure, but she needed more. She needed him inside her. She needed him loving her. She needed it all.

Joe rolled onto his side and drew Libby closer. From somewhere in the night he heard music—Christmas carols, low and sweet. Raising his head from the pillow, he located her alarm clock across the room on the dresser, its numbers a faint red glow in the dark. It was after midnight. Christmas Day.

He kissed her neck, then offered a sleepy, "Merry Christmas, sweetheart."

She was silent for a moment, and he thought she must be asleep. Then she gave a sigh of contentment. "Joe?"

"Hmm."

"I love you."

He grew still, afraid to breathe, afraid any disturbance would cause the soft echo of her words to disappear.

"You're speechless, aren't you?" She laughed and scooted back so that not even a breath separated them. "Merry Christmas, Joe."

Merry Christmas, Joe. Such simple words didn't even begin to cover it. He'd just been given the one thing he wanted most in life. It was a merry Christmas indeed.

Chapter 11

"I must be a terrible friend," Denise announced over lunch Friday.

Libby gave her a questioning look but didn't speak, because her mouth was full of salad. After Mrs. Franklin's candy, Justin and Joe's giant chocolate chip cookie and Christmas dinner, salad was all she'd allowed herself for lunch the rest of the week. She was sick of it.

"I should be thrilled that you're so disgustingly happy," her friend explained. "But I'm not. I'm nauseated. And jealous. Why is it that *you* found the one decent guy in Augusta when *I've* been looking for so long?"

"Don't look so down," Libby said after a drink of unsweetened tea. "Joe's not your type anyway."

"Let's see...he's gorgeous, smart, nice, reliable, loves kids... Yeah, you're right. Not my type at all." She raised her eyebrows and said in a sexy drawl, "Honey, you should have learned by now that *all* men are my type—with the exception of the strange little guy who lives next door. *Him,* I could do without. So...when's the wedding?"

Libby avoided the question by turning her attention to cutting the cucumber slices in her salad into bite-size pieces, but after a moment Denise put an end to that by taking her knife away.

"You cut those up any smaller and you won't be able to stick a fork into them," she admonished. "Is there a problem? And let me warn you, Libby Harper, if you're thinking about telling me that you have no desire to marry Joe Mathison, I'm just going to shoot you right here, because you won't deserve to live."

Smiling shyly, she looked at her best friend. "I would like to marry Joe," she admitted. It was a decision she'd reached after spending nearly all her free time with him—and the rest of her time thinking about him, missing him. And she knew it was on his mind, too. He'd made too many references to the future—no, to *their* future—in the past week for her to miss the direction of his thoughts.

"So what's the problem?" Denise asked.

"Other than the fact that he hasn't asked me?"

"Minor detail. The man's no fool. He's not going to let you slip away."

Libby's smile slowly faded. "It would mean moving away from here again."

Denise's smile disappeared, too. "Leave it to you to fall in love with another wandering man—and just when I was getting used to having you around again."

"When we came here, I promised Justin we would never move again."

Her friend waved her hand as if erasing that small fact. "He's forgotten by now. Besides, he adores Joe. He won't mind moving if it means moving with him."

"I promised *myself* we would never leave home again," Libby said quietly. "I hated it, Denise. I hated having to make new friends and find new places to shop and bank. I hated looking for new doctors and dentists and mechanics and dry cleaners. And do you have any idea how hard it is to find a good hairstylist in a strange town?"

"You can cut your hair off and keep it short," Denise said gently. "Joe won't mind."

Realizing that tears were forming in her eyes, Libby blinked. "I *want* to get married—no, I want to marry *Joe*. I want to raise a family with him. I want to spend the rest of my life with him. But that would mean spending the next two or four or eight or God knows how many years moving. It would mean *maybe* coming back to North Augusta when he retires, or maybe settling in Kentucky with his family and never living close to mine again."

.Denise was silent for an unusually long time. When she finally spoke, she was totally serious. "Look, Lib, I've never lived anywhere else, so I don't understand why you feel the way you do. In fact, I've always envied you being able to live in other places and experience different ways of life. Honey, the simple fact is you fell in love with a man who *has* to move. You can either make the best of that and go with him and be happy and have that family you want ... or you can stick to your roots and send him off alone and know that you've made the worst mistake of your life."

"He said it would be different," Libby admitted. "He said that military wives stick together and help each other out. He said *he* would help. Doug's idea of helping out was telling me where our new house was in time to meet the movers before he disappeared to work."

"Lib, you *know* Joe's not like Doug. Of course moving with Doug was no picnic. He left you to do everything on your own. For all practical purposes, you weren't half of a couple, you were by yourself. But think of the fun you could have making a new home and exploring new places with Joe."

Her appetite gone, Libby laid her fork down and leaned back in the chair. "I guess," she admitted reluctantly.

"Okay," Denise said, undaunted by her friend's lack of enthusiasm. "Let me put this another way. Think of the loneliness you'll have staying here without him."

* * *

Maybe moving wouldn't be so bad, Libby thought a week later as she carried a box full of Christmas decorations into the spare bedroom. This was the last box, but she wasn't sure where to find room for it. The closet was full, the bed was covered, and the floor space between the bed and the wall was packed. At least when she had moved every year or two she'd learned to keep only what was necessary and to discard the rest.

With careful maneuvering she found a space in the corner for the box, then straightened and glanced at her watch. Joe was taking her out to dinner, and he was due in less than an hour. Denise had already picked up Justin—she was keeping him for the night, she'd announced with a sly smile—so she had time for a relaxing bubble bath before Joe arrived. She suspected that she was going to need the relaxation.

The butterflies in her stomach told her that this would be no ordinary date. She knew Joe had made reservations at one of Augusta's nicest—and, according to Denise, most romantic—restaurants. And although she had made the baby-sitting arrangements with Denise herself, she'd said nothing about Justin spending the night. It wasn't really necessary. In the nearly two weeks since Christmas, Joe had spent practically every night at their house, and Justin was none the wiser. But for some reason Denise had decided that tonight was different.

Libby turned on the water in the bathtub and added a generous amount of bubble bath. One more difference between a single woman and a mother, she thought as she breathed in the sweet fragrance. Denise's bubble bath was expensive and rich and matched the designer perfume she wore. Libby's was a couple of dollars a half gallon and smelled of bubblegum.

After undressing, she pinned her hair up, then stepped into the steamy, soapy water, adjusting the inflatable vinyl pillow beneath her head and closing her eyes.

Tonight, she suspected, Joe was going to ask her to marry him.

And she was going to say yes.

After all her agonizing, all her mental arguments, it was that simple. Yes, she wanted to stay in North Augusta, wanted to hold on to all that was familiar here, wanted to be close to her parents when they returned next spring. But more than that, she wanted to be with Joe. Maybe moving wasn't her favorite thing in the world. Maybe not having a real home, a permanent one, wasn't the best thing for Justin.

But without Joe, they would have no home at all. Just this empty lonely house in this nothing-special little town. Home is where the heart is, the old saying went, and *her* heart was with Joe.

Her *home* was with Joe.

The numbers on the clock radio on the bookshelf flipped over with an audible plop, drawing Joe's attention. He was due at Libby's in half an hour, and he hadn't changed yet. He hadn't even gone home yet. He hadn't done anything in the last two hours but sit at his desk and stare at the two items it held.

One was a small velvet box, opened to reveal the ring inside. Not diamonds, Denise had told him, because Doug had always given her diamonds, and she had gotten rid of every one of them. Choose something flashier, less icy, more fiery, she had recommended.

The emerald had drawn him from the moment he'd seen it. It was large, deep green, a beautiful stone in a simple gold setting. Green fire. It had met with Denise's approval, too. Libby would love it, she had assured him.

Beside the box was a single sheet of paper. He'd received similar documents countless times over his twenty-two-year career, but never before had they concerned him the way this one did.

Never before had they held the potential to destroy his future the way this one did.

With a sigh, he slid the paper into a manila folder, closed the jewelry box with a click and picked them both up. Because of the one he might not have any need of the other, but he took them both with him when he left his office.

Even though he was running late, he stopped at home and changed from his BDUs into the suit he'd laid out this morning. He wasn't comfortable in it—for functions requiring formal wear, he preferred his dress uniform—but he'd thought it appropriate for such an occasion. Although his hopes for the night were shattered, he wore the suit anyway. Who knew? Libby might surprise him and still feel like going to dinner after he told her his news.

Sure. And she might still feel like marrying him, too.

He spent the thirteen miles to her house preparing what to say. He still hadn't found the right words when he got there.

She answered the door, wearing a pretty green dress—emerald green, he noticed, and felt a pain deep inside. Her hair was up, all sleek and smooth, and she smelled erotic and exotic, an intriguing combination of a popular fragrance and... He sniffed as he kissed her cheek. Bubblegum?

"My, my, you look nice," she said, studying him with delight. "I know I've seen you in a coat and tie before, but that was your uniform. This looks so different."

"I like your dress." His voice came out hoarser than he'd expected.

"Do you? Denise and I went shopping on our lunch hour today, and I got it then." She twirled around, and he saw that the dress, perfectly demure in front, had a deep plunging V that left much of her back bare except for two narrow strips of fabric that crisscrossed over her shoulder blades.

His voice grew even hoarser. "Yeah, I do."

"Denise says that this restaurant is very nice, and since I'll be with the handsomest man there, I wanted to look my best." She suddenly seemed to run out of things to say. Self-consciously lacing her fingers together, she looked up at him from beneath her lashes, waiting for him to speak.

He sighed deeply. "Come in and sit down, Libby. I—I need to talk to you." Taking both of her hands, he led her into the living room and over to the couch. Even after they were seated, he continued to hold her hands. He needed that contact with her. "I planned this evening with Denise's help," he began hesitantly. "I wanted everything to be really special because I wanted—I wanted to ask you to marry me."

Seeing the bewildered look in her eyes at his use of the past tense, he hastily continued. "I still want to marry you, Libby, more than anything. I love you so damn much. But... before I ask you, before you decide, there's something you need to know."

She waited silently, her gaze on him, the look in her eyes trusting and full of love. It made his job even harder, and he handled it poorly by simply blurting it out.

"The 65th got orders this afternoon, Libby. We're going to Africa."

How was it possible, she wondered dazedly, that her entire world could change so quickly? That one minute she could be happier than she'd been in ages, and the next her future could literally disappear before her eyes?

We're going to Africa.

There had to be some sort of mistake. It was dangerous over there. They were preparing for *war* over there. Joe couldn't go. She simply couldn't allow it. She couldn't bear it.

But he *was* going, and he was going soon. He was going to leave her. He was going to go to a place he very well might not come back from. How could she endure that?

She didn't know she was crying until the first tears, hot and stinging, landed on her hands, still clenched in Joe's. She stared at them for a moment, two fat drops that left wet trails across her knuckles before dripping onto his thumb.

"When are you leaving?" she asked, sounding distant and calm and nothing like herself, and at the same time frantically, silently praying, *Let it be a month from now, God, two months or more.*

"In two weeks."

"No." She struggled against the tears, knowing they were ruining the makeup she had carefully put on and not caring. She tightened her fingers around his and said in a halting, anguished voice, "You can't go."

"Libby, I *have* to. I have to go, sweetheart, but I'll be back, I promise."

She jerked away from him then. "You *can't* make that promise! This isn't like getting orders to some other base and promising to come back when your assignment is up! We're talking about *war!*"

Joe grasped her arms and gave her a little shake. "It hasn't come to that yet, Libby, and it might not. We might go over and sit in the desert for six months, then come home."

"And you might go over there and get killed," she whispered harshly. She wiped away her tears, but they kept falling. "You can't go," she repeated. "Justin and I need you here."

"And the Army needs me there. It's my job, sweetheart. It's my duty. It's part of being a soldier."

"I didn't fall in love with a soldier," she reminded him, her voice breaking, her heart breaking. "I fell in love with *you.*"

"And that's what I am. A soldier."

Libby stood up and walked away, stopping in the bare spot where the Christmas tree had stood. For a long time she simply stared at the wall, hugging herself tightly and remembering the pain she'd felt the night Doug had left her. She had thought it was the most terrible pain a woman could ever feel, but it was nothing compared to this. Her heart was pounding as if it might burst from her chest, her lungs were barely functioning, and she was trembling so badly that she shook all over.

This wasn't just pain. It was fear—sickening, gut-wrenching fear. How-could-she-live-without-him fear. It made every part of her ache, made her stomach churn, made her heart hurt so badly. She wanted to give in to it, to just collapse into a huddled ball right there and sob hysterically, but she held herself together by sheer force of will.

"Libby?" Joe's voice came from close behind her, and an instant later he slid his arms around her, pulling her back against his chest.

"I'm sorry," she whispered, drying another tear with the back of her hand and smiling anyway. "I wouldn't make a very good Army wife, would I?"

"Why do you say that?" he murmured in her ear.

She turned in the circle of his arms and filled her hands with his jacket. "They're supposed to be strong, to be able to deal with any crisis, to be both mother and father to their children when necessary. They're supposed to be prepared for this sort of thing, for the possibility of losing the people they love."

"We're not talking about Superwoman," he said dryly, trying to tease a more believable smile out of her. When he failed, he stroked her cheek, ignoring the dampness that clung to his fingers. "You *are* strong, Libby, and you *can* deal with this. You've been both mother and father to Justin most of his life. You've made it through some bad times, and you'll make it through this. We both will."

"Aren't you afraid?"

He thought about it for a long time, trying to choose between being honest and minimizing the risk. Finally he went with honesty. "Yeah, I'm afraid. I've been in combat before. The only people who aren't afraid then are either fools or dead. But I'm more afraid for you. I know getting involved with me wasn't an easy decision for you, and I know you're probably regretting it about now. I'm afraid of losing you, Libby."

"How could I regret loving you?" she asked, her voice muffled against his chest.

But she didn't offer any reassurances that he wouldn't lose her, he noticed sadly. She didn't promise to continue loving him or to wait for him. She didn't say that someday she would marry him.

He held her for a long time. Occasionally a sob shuddered through her, but mostly she remained in control, even though it was costing her a great deal. He could feel the rigidity of her muscles, could see the strain in her face when she finally looked at him.

"I just need some time to get used to this," she said, her voice unsteady, her eyes dark with sorrow. "I ignored what was going on over there for so long because it frightened me, especially after I met you. Now I have to... I have to adjust to it. Please... give me a few days."

"You can have all the time you need, sweetheart."

She nodded gratefully, then used the tip of her finger to carefully dry around her eyes. "I must look awful," she said with a shaky laugh that ended in a hiccup. "Do you mind if we forget about going out?"

"Of course not. I'd rather be alone with you anyway." He kissed her forehead, then released her. "I need to cancel our reservations."

"I'll wash my face while you do that."

Picking up the phone, he watched her walk down the hall. "Libby? Don't take off that dress. I want to do it myself later."

With a tremulous smile she went into the bathroom. He called the restaurant, then touched the small velvet box in his pocket. He couldn't offer the ring to her now, couldn't expect her to take it until she'd decided whether she could cope with his deployment. And so it stayed in his pocket all through the long, quiet evening, through the heavy silences and Libby's occasional sniffles, through their soft, meaningless conversation and their gentle necking and gentler touching.

He didn't take it out until they went to bed, when he started to undress in the quiet of her room. Then he held it in his palm and faced her. "I'm not going to ask you for an answer, and I'm not going to ask you to wear this or even show it to you. But I want to leave it here so that when you decide...*if* you decide..." He trailed off and carried the box to the dresser. There he raised the lid on the wooden heart and set the jeweler's box inside. When he replaced the lid, he looked at her. "It'll be here."

It was the first time they'd slept together without making love. Lying awake early the next morning, unable to sleep, Libby thought it had been a terrible waste of time. They had so few nights left together—only thirteen. Then he would be gone.

She lay there on her back, Joe's body warm and hard against hers, and cried silent tears that ran down her face. She had asked for a few days to get used to the idea of his leaving, but in her heart she knew a few days would never be long enough. Even a few years couldn't prepare her for this. She had no experience with war. It had never touched her life in any way, and she wasn't prepared for the way it was touching her now.

It wasn't fair. As her mother had told her, as she occasionally told Justin, life *wasn't* fair, but damn it, this *really* wasn't fair. She'd waited all her life for Joe. It wasn't right that she had to give him up so soon after finding him.

Maybe he was right. Maybe there would be no war, and they would spend six months over there, as safe as they were here, then come home.

But it was more likely that he was wrong. The U.S. wouldn't have spent millions of dollars sending troops to East Africa unless there was a very good chance they would be used. With each passing day, that chance grew stronger. There had already been minor skirmishes on the border. Soldiers had already died. More would die.

Joe could die.

Unable to control her tears any longer, she slipped out of bed and pulled her robe on, then left the room. It was still dark outside, but she made her way into the living room without lights. There she sat on the sofa, her grandmother's quilt pulled tight around her, and gave the tears free rein.

She cried until she couldn't cry anymore, until her eyes were puffy and her head ached and her nose was stuffy. Then she lay back, tissues in hand, and watched the sky outside slowly lighten.

How quickly things changed. A week ago her biggest concern had been whether she could adjust once again to a transient life-style if she and Joe got married. Now she knew that had been a petty worry. She could live anywhere in the world if Joe was with her. She could move constantly, from now until they were feeble and gray, never having a home of her own, never staying put, as long as he was by her side.

What she couldn't do was live without him.

And that was precisely what she would have to do. The Army was taking him away from her. They were putting his life in danger. And he was ready to go, ready to put his life on the line, because it was his duty. She smiled even though it hurt.

"So you finally found something to smile about."

She saw him standing in the doorway, wearing his trousers and no shirt and looking too good to be true. "I was just thinking that my parents would adore you."

"Why is that?" He lifted her feet and sat down, then tucked the quilt more securely around her.

"My father places great value on patriotism, and my mother loves a man with honor."

"And what about you?"

"I also value patriotism, and I love an honorable man—" she smiled at the double meaning of that "—but I wish you were a farmer like your father and your brothers."

He grinned. "Can you imagine yourself as a farmer's wife?"

Better than being a soldier's widow, she wanted to retort, but she kept the words inside.

His grin gave way to solemnity. "I know you're afraid, Libby, but try to keep it in perspective. I'm going to Africa to do the job I've spent more than half my life training for. You were right last night when you said it's not the same as being sent to some other post for duty—but it's not the same as going into a combat zone, either. At this point we're just making our presence known—putting on a show of strength. I admit, that could change at any time. But don't anticipate the worst until it happens. You'll drive yourself crazy that way.''

She knew he was right, but how, she wondered in despair, did she stop the "worst" from barging uninvited into her thoughts? How could she focus on anything else when those fears were hovering right there, demanding her attention?

How in God's name could she face the possibility of losing him?

The next few days were undoubtedly the worst Libby had ever lived through. She couldn't concentrate at work, and all too often, regardless of where she was or what she was doing, she was suddenly gripped by paralyzing fear and an overwhelming urge to cry. She could hardly bear to be with Joe, because she kept counting the days until he left, yet she couldn't bear to be apart from him, either. She listened to every newscast, even though they fed her fear as the situation in Africa grew more intense. It was no longer, according to the experts, a question of *whether* there would be war, but rather *when*.

Justin had taken the news of Joe's deployment far better than she had. But the issue was much clearer for him. Going to war was something soldiers did, and Joe was a soldier. He would miss Joe, he'd said sadly, and had promised in his gravest voice to write him every day, but it wasn't devastating his life.

But it *had* devastated hers. She was terrified and anguished and sorrowful and angry. Frustrated, fearful and helpless. She had to regain control before it destroyed her, and she knew only one way to do it.

Six days after Joe broke the news to her, eight days before he was scheduled to ship out, she went into her bedroom and opened the wooden heart for the first time since that night. She removed the velvet case, wrapping her fingers tightly around it to avoid the temptation to open it and see what kind of ring he'd chosen for her.

Her heart thudding painfully, she went looking for him and found him in the living room, going through the Christmas pictures she had picked up this afternoon. He was smiling when he looked up at her, but the smile faded when he saw what she was carrying. It was gone completely by the time she set the small box on the coffee table in front of him.

Joe stared at it for a long time, then closed his eyes and still saw it. When was the last time he'd felt such a powerful need to cry? he wondered. When he'd been a little boy back on the farm? When he was fifteen and suffering his first heartache? When he was eighteen and in Vietnam and his best friend in the squad had died in his arms?

"So..." He had to clear his throat. "You made a decision."

"I'm sorry, Joe," she whispered. "But I can't live like this every day."

"And you think refusing to marry me is going to make it any easier?"

Clenching her hands together, she knelt beside the table. "I could handle moving. I could learn to adapt to new places. I could learn to adapt to the Army. But I can't accept a job that places you in danger. I can't handle knowing that you could die." She stopped her halting speech for a moment, visibly struggling to remain in control. "You *chose* the Army, Joe. *I* didn't. I knew all along that loving you was a bigger gamble than I could afford, but I couldn't stop."

"And now you can." He drew a deep breath, and it hurt. It hurt his chest and his lungs. It hurt his heart. "What's your reasoning this time, Libby? The sooner you get rid of me, the sooner you can start forgetting me? Get out now while you still can? Before you do something really foolish, like making a commitment?"

She wouldn't look at him—couldn't, he suspected, because he was right. She thought she could break up with him, could push him out of her life and make everything go back to normal again. She thought removing him would also remove the fear and the hurt and the awful sense of loss.

Maybe it would. Maybe he had misjudged her again. Maybe he had wanted so desperately to believe that she loved him the way he loved her that he'd fooled himself into feeling something that just wasn't there.

He carefully replaced the photographs in their envelope, then picked up the ring. "You're a coward, Libby," he said quietly, derisively. "You're so afraid that you would rather have nothing than something you might lose."

His movements tightly restrained, he rose from the couch and went to the coat closet, taking out his jacket. He had clothes down the hall in her bedroom and a shaving kit under the bathroom sink, but he couldn't stay here long enough to get them. He jerked his jacket on, then stopped in the living-room door. She was still kneeling there, her back to him. "When we first met, I thought you were a woman worth having. A woman worth fighting for. A woman worth loving. And you know what, Libby?" He didn't wait for her response. "I was wrong. But that's okay. I'll just look at it the way you do. The sooner I get away from you, the sooner I'll forget you. The sooner I'll quit loving you."

He started to leave, then turned back one last time. "I'm not losing Justin, too. *Not yet.* Tell Mrs. Franklin I'm picking him up after work tomorrow. I'm taking him over to spend the night at my apartment. I'll bring him home sometime Saturday."

He walked out, closing the door quietly behind him, then got into his car and drove away. He was cold and angry, but calm. In control. Then suddenly, a half-dozen blocks away, he swerved to the side of the street, screeched to a stop and leaned over the steering wheel. His breath came in great shudders as he fought back the anguish threatening to explode inside him.

Dear God, he couldn't endure this. He would follow his orders, would go to Africa and let everyone in the whole damn world take a shot at him if only he could know that Libby would be waiting for him when he came home. He wanted to go back and plead with her, wanted to beg her to reconsider. She didn't have to marry him before he left, didn't even have to say yes before then, as long as she didn't say no. As long as he knew that she loved him. As long as he knew they had a chance.

But Libby didn't take chances. She didn't know how, and she would rather spend the rest of her life lonely and alone than learn.

And that, he knew with dismal certainty, meant *he* would spend the rest of *his* life lonely and alone, too.

Four more days. At eleven o'clock Friday morning, the 65th Signal Battalion would leave Fort Gordon for an unspecified destination, from which they would depart for Africa. It had been on the television news and in the newspaper, and late this Monday evening, it was all Libby could think about. Four more days and Joe would be gone. Out of the state, out of the country, out of her life.

Physically he was already out of her life—had been since last Thursday evening. He'd been to the house several times to pick up or drop off Justin, but he hadn't come to the door. He'd chosen instead to wait in his car, a distant shadowy figure.

But emotionally... There was nothing distant or shadowy about his presence there. He filled her dreams and haunted her waking hours. Where was the relief she had sought in breaking up with him? she wondered desperately. When would the hurting stop? When would the healing begin?

She was afraid she knew the answers to those questions but was simply too big a coward to face the truth. Joe had certainly been right on that point. She had voluntarily given up the only person who mattered in her life besides Justin rather than risk losing him. What could possibly be more cowardly?

He'd been right about other things, too. Returning his ring hadn't made anything any easier. Neither had her refusal to commit herself fully, totally, to him. Neither had sacrificing her dreams of marrying him or giving up these precious last few days with him. The pain wasn't any more bearable. The fear wasn't any less devastating. Her life wasn't any less affected.

And her love hadn't diminished one bit.

She missed him.

She needed him.

She loved him.

That was the bottom line: she *loved* him. No matter what happened, whether they were separated by only a few miles or by thousands, whether they were a part of each other's lives or gave up trying, whether they were married or never saw each other again, whether they had fifty years or five, a few months or a few days, she loved him. That would never change.

What could be more cowardly than throwing away his love so that no one could take it from her?

Doing nothing to get it back.

There were a million things to do to get a unit the size of Charlie Company ready to ship out in three days, and it seemed to Joe that at least half of them fell on *his* shoulders. He didn't mind the heavy workload, though. It kept him too busy to think. It kept him too busy to feel.

Gear had to be properly packed for shipping. Immunizations had to be current, wills, powers of attorney and insurance policies updated. The single parents in the unit were scrambling to make suitable provisions for child care, as were those who were married to other service members. Families had to be prepared, too, so that the separation went as smooth as possible under the circumstances. Responsibility for much of that was his.

On the personal front, he had notified his own family—had spoken to his parents, his sister and each of his brothers. His mother had cried, reminding him all too painfully of the tears Libby had shed. He had given notice on his apartment, had canceled the utilities and scheduled a pickup for the rental furniture. He had packed one duffel bag to take with him, and everything else had gone into a half-dozen boxes that he would take over to Max Stanley's garage on Wednesday. His change of address had gone in to the post office, his will had been amended to include both Justin and Libby, and he'd made arrangements to store his car on post while he was gone.

He had only two things left to do: say goodbye to Justin...and dispose of the emerald ring. He had no safe place to keep it. More importantly, he had no desire to keep it.

The phones hadn't stopped ringing all afternoon, and the office had been like a zoo. The strain was starting to show on everyone he worked with, but, selfishly, he hoped it didn't let up until long after they were settled in the African desert. Then maybe he would be ready to slow down, to deal with what he'd lost, to accept what this damn war that wasn't even a war yet had cost him. Then maybe it wouldn't hurt so bad to think about Libby. Then maybe—

"Joe?"

He stopped in the act of sorting through the files to determine which ones had to go and which could stay behind. Maybe the strain was starting to show on *him*, because he would swear on his life that soft, hesitant voice had been Libby's, even though he knew it couldn't possibly be. She wouldn't come here. Why would she, when she'd made it clear that she wanted nothing more to do with him?

But when he slowly turned around, there she stood, pale and nervous and with a fragile air, as if the past few days had been as hard for her as they'd been for him. But in spite of that delicate look and the shadows beneath her eyes, in spite of the longing and the sadness and the weariness, he thought she looked more beautiful than ever.

Then his surprise at seeing her slowly gave way to wariness. Caution. Dull-edged anger. Last week she'd wanted to forget him, to stop loving him, so why was she here in his office now? Had she come to torment him a little more? To see if she could cause him just a little more pain before he left?

"I'm busy, Libby," he said curtly. "What do you want?"

Before she could answer, one of his soldiers barged into the office. "Hey, First Sergeant, do you have—sorry. I didn't realize you had a visitor."

"It's all right," Joe said coolly, holding her gaze for a long moment before turning his attention to the sergeant. "What do you need?"

He let her wait while he took care of business. When they were alone again, he gave her an impatient look. "Well?"

She slid her purse on the corner of his desk, then removed her gloves and dropped them beside it. Next she unbelted her coat and slipped it off, folding it neatly over the back of the extra chair. He watched and restrained the urge to tell her to hurry up, say what she wanted and get the hell out of his office. The longer he looked at her, the harder it was to forget he loved her and the more he wanted her.

Finally she raised her gaze to his once more; then, in a clear, steady voice, she spoke. "Joe...will you marry me?"

There was a surprised sound from the hall, and Libby slowly looked from Joe to the two soldiers, one a pretty young woman, standing there. Judging from the man's surprise and the woman's delighted smile, they'd overheard her question, but she didn't care. The only person who mattered was standing across the room from her, staring at her as if she'd just swept his feet out from under him—which she probably had, she admitted. This was probably the last thing in the world he'd expected from her.

"Marry you?" he echoed, sounding dazed and unsure.

"Yes."

"You mean when we get back...?"

She shook her head. "I mean before you go. There's no waiting period in Georgia. All we need for the license is a blood test."

He was getting his equilibrium back, but slowly. "And what if I don't come back?" he asked quietly.

Libby smiled, even though tears blurred her vision. "You will. You promised you would, and you always keep your promises." She blinked a couple of times, took a deep breath and continued. "I love you, Joe, whether you're here with me or off in some godforsaken desert doing your job. It doesn't matter where the Army sends you or what they send you to do. I'll still love you. I always will."

"You don't have to do this, Libby. We can wait until I get back. As long as I know you'll be here ..."

She shook her head. "I've waited long enough. I don't want to be your friend, Joe, or your girlfriend or your lover or whatever word people use today. I want to be your wife. I want that bond. I want that commitment."

Nervously she waited for his answer, waited for him— *prayed* for him—to say, "Yes, Libby, I'll marry you." But he didn't say anything right away. He just stared at his cluttered desktop. What was he thinking? she wondered. Had he changed his mind about marrying her? About loving her? Had he been more successful than she'd been at forgetting and moving on? Was he finding it impossible to forgive her cowardice, her foolishness?

Finally he set down the records he held and slowly started toward her. "Are you sure this is what you want, Libby? Are you positive?"

"Yes."

"You won't change your mind?"

She smiled uneasily as he slid his arm around her waist and used the leverage to pull her close. "Don't you think I've tried, Joe? But it didn't happen. I love you, and all the wars in the world aren't going to change that. I want to marry you, I want to have children with you, and I want you to be Justin's dad. I want to be the best damn Army wife ever. I want to spend the rest of my life with you ... but if that doesn't work out, I want to spend all the time we do have with you. Please, Joe, will you marry me?"

He kissed her gently, tenderly. "Yes, Libby. I would be honored." Then he kissed her again, this time with passion, with hunger and fire, turning her insides to mush, curling her toes, and he didn't stop until whistles, a few claps and one enthusiastic whoop from the hallway interrupted.

When he ended the kiss, they faced their audience outside the door. Libby remained warm and secure in his embrace as he focused his attention on one young man in an officer's uniform. ''Request Thursday morning off, sir,'' he said with his most mischievous grin. ''I'm getting married.''

It had been an unusual wedding day, Libby thought early Friday morning. The ceremony had taken place Thursday morning, performed by a chaplain in one of the post's chapels, and had been attended largely by soldiers in working uniforms. Joe had looked more handsome than ever, though, in his dress blue uniform, and she had felt beautiful in an ivory linen dress that was lavished with heavy lace.

After the vows there had been a cake, a toast and lots of best wishes; then Charlie Company had gone back to work, as had Denise, her only guest. Joe had changed to his Class A's, and they had spent the rest of the day taking care of business. There'd been a stop at the Military Personnel Center to get a military identification card for her, followed by another stop at the legal office for a power of attorney and a third one at the hospital to enter her and Justin into the military health care computer system and to get their medical cards. Joe had had to change the next-of-kin entries in his service record and amend his life insurance to make her and Justin his beneficiaries. Off post, he'd arranged to transfer the direct deposit of his paycheck from his bank to hers, then revised his Postal Service change of address from the battalion's Army Post Office to her house.

It had taken all day, and Justin had grown cranky and she had grown impatient, eager to spend some time alone with her new husband. But when Denise had offered to keep Justin overnight to give her the privacy she craved, she'd turned her down. Maybe last night had been her only night with her husband, but it had also been Justin's only night with his new dad. He'd needed the time as much as she had.

And now it was morning. Friday morning. The alarm had been set for five-thirty so Joe could take care of whatever last-minute details cropped up. The official send-off from the post was scheduled for nine-thirty; by eleven, the soldiers would be on board the buses that would transport them to their departure point.

By eleven, she and Justin would be alone.

Tears burned her eyes, but she held them back. She'd promised to be a good Army wife, and Army wives were strong and capable and didn't cry. They didn't plead for their husbands not to go, didn't beg or fall apart.

Dear Lord, she didn't want to be strong and capable. She wanted to beg. She wanted to fall apart. She wanted to keep him here safe beside her forever.

Joe stirred, then nuzzled closer to her. "Good morning, Mrs. Mathison." He chuckled softly. "I like the sound of that. Now you're *mine.*"

"I've been yours all along," she said. "This just makes it official."

He supported himself on one arm so he could study her in the dim light. "Did you get any sleep at all?"

"A few hours."

His voice dropped a few tones, deeper and softer and more tender. "Are you all right?"

"I love you," she whispered, emotion choking the words.

"Sweetheart, I love you, too." He settled back on the pillow and pulled her across so that she rested on him. "I've asked Reba Stanley to keep in touch with you. She can show you the ropes and tell you where to go if you have any problems. Some of the other wives will be calling, too. They'll get together and do things for the kids and for each other—sort of a support group. Don't feel that you *have* to get involved, but if you need them, they'll be there."

Her tears dripped onto his chest. She noticed with a wry smile that he ignored them, even though it had to tickle as they rolled across his ribs.

"My family's names and addresses and phone numbers are all in the notebook on the nightstand. They'll be getting in touch with you, too. They'll want to welcome you to the family." Finally, with a grin so strong that she could hear it in his voice, he asked, "Are you crying, sweetheart?"

"No," she lied, keeping her face hidden from him and drying the moisture from his skin with a corner of the sheet.

"Funny. I thought I felt something wet."

"Maybe it was this." She kissed his chest then, touching her tongue to his warm skin, bathing it, cooling it.

"I don't think so. That doesn't feel the same. Try something else."

She placed the next kiss a little higher. The third one landed on his nipple, and it puckered in immediate response.

Her tears slowly dried as she lost herself in his body, in the kissing, the stroking, the loving. When he sank deep inside her, everything else faded away, and when he filled her, the rest ceased to exist. All she needed was this. This man. This loving. This love.

The send-off was held at the reviewing stand at Barton Field, and for all its sadness, it was a solemn, impressive, proud ceremony. There were flags and bunting everywhere. The Fort Gordon band played, the chaplain offered prayers, and the post commanding general and the 65th's commander spoke briefly while the battalion stood in formation.

When it was over they had one last chance to say goodbye before the troops were loaded onto the buses. Joe lifted Justin into his arms, then gathered Libby, too. Her son was crying, Libby knew, and she was trying not to, but the tears kept slipping out anyway.

Then, all too soon, after a few whispered words, after last "I love you's," he released them. He was the last soldier to board his bus. The door closed behind him, and they drove away.

Libby clung to Justin the way she'd wanted to cling to Joe, and she felt that her heart must surely be breaking. Nothing else could possibly hurt this badly.

And then she looked around, and for the first time she began to feel that she might find a place for herself in the Army. She saw Reba Stanley and the other wives crying and holding their children, offering them comfort and taking it back in return. Army wives *were* strong and capable, and they *didn't* plead for their husbands to stay behind, and they *didn't* fall apart.

But they loved their husbands.

And they *did* cry.

Chapter 12

Dear Joe,

You've only been gone three days, but it already feels like a lifetime. I never knew it was possible to miss someone as much as I miss you. I don't know why I'm surprised, though. I never knew it was possible to love someone as much as I love you.

Justin has been moping around the house since you left. We framed one of the Christmas pictures of the two of you together, and he's taken to sleeping with it on the nightstand. I asked him if he had a message for you, but he said he would write to you himself.

Reba Stanley gave me the grand tour of the post Saturday. Yes, I know you showed us around, but she touched on the *important* things—the commissary, the exchange, the dental clinic, etc. She took us into the commissary and had to show me how to make out a check. I always thought having to show a credit card at the stores in town was a bit nosy, but heavens, the commissary wanted your name, rank, social security number, unit and phone number. I couldn't remember a thing and panicked about not knowing your social security number, but Reba informed me that it's on my ID. She insists that in no time at all I'll know *your* number from memory and have no idea whatsoever what mine is.

Justin really hit it off well with her twins. The three of them were holy terrors at lunch. I think it helped him to spend some time with kids who are in the same situation he is.

Colonel Davis's wife has arranged a support group meeting for this weekend. Reba says she might have some news for us about where you guys are and when we can expect to hear from you. Justin and I are planning to attend.

And your folks called Friday evening. Your mother, bless her heart, probably thinks you married some kind of idiot, because all I could do for the entire half hour we were on the phone was cry. She seems like a really nice lady. Your dad talked to Justin and cheered him up for a while. He's really looking forward to visiting the farm and meeting all of his new cousins. Maybe when you get back . . . ?

There's no news here . . . except that I miss you and love you and pray for you to come back. But you already knew that, didn't you?

Write to us when you can. We love you.

Libby

2030 hrs.
23 January

Libby,

I've never been much good at writing letters, as my family can—and probably *will*—tell you, but I promised I would write, so I'll give it a try.

We're getting settled in here in the Eastern African Republic, but I can't tell you where exactly, since that information's classified. I know it took a lot of hard work, but it amazes me that we could move so many people and so much gear and already be set up for business.

We're pretty close to the coast, so the humidity's higher here than inland. The nights are cold, but not too bad, and the days are pretty warm. That'll change in a few more months. According to the guys who've been here since last summer, this place gives new meaning to the term "hot spot." My wars—first the jungles of Vietnam and Panama, now the desert of the E.A.R. But better sweltering than freezing, right?

I'm looking forward to hearing from you and Justin. The mail's pretty slow—twelve to fourteen days on average for a letter, longer for packages. It'll be nice once I can finally call you. As I told you before, the Signal Corps handles all communications, including telephones, so maybe I can work something out soon.

Looking around this place, it's hard to see what the locals are fighting over. It's flat and sandy. The only thing visible in any direction is our camp. The wind hardly ever lets up, there's sand in everything from my clothes to my bunk to my food, and there are fleas in the sand.

Don't worry too much about me, Libby. I'll be all right, and you've got enough to take care of at home. I wish we could have done things differently—wish we'd had the time for a real wedding with our families, and a honeymoon. I wish I could have properly introduced you to Army life. I know the other wives will help you out, but I'd rather be there doing it myself.

This wasn't what I had in mind when I decided I wanted to marry you.

I'd better get some sleep while I can. We're working longer hours here than usual, but I like it that way. There's less time to be lonely.

Give Justin a kiss for me, and tell him I love him. And don't forget I love you, too.

                                                        Joe

                                                 January 24

Dear Joe,
Every night when Justin and I get home, it's a race to see

who makes it to the mailbox first. I know it's been less than a week. I know that realistically there's no way a letter could have made it here this quickly. But I'm still disappointed.

You'll probably think I'm foolishly sentimental, but happy one-week anniversary. I can't believe we've been married for seven days... and you've been gone six. I wonder if I'm the only Army wife whose ID picture was taken in her wedding dress on her wedding day...?

I got a call from Doug last night. He'd heard from some old friend that I'd gotten married and was hoping I'd chosen someone with enough money that I'd let him off the hook for the child support. Fat chance. I could hear his hopes fading from his voice when I told him that you were a soldier. He'd probably already spent the money in his mind on some little present for Barrie or himself. As usual, not a word from him for Justin and no apology for missing Christmas. But who cares? I reminded him to make the check out to Libby *Mathison* and hung up. As Denise so fondly reminds me, he's a bastard.

I got a card from your mother and one from your sister. Your mom included what she said was her favorite photograph of you. You're about Justin's age, barefoot and wearing overalls. How *cute*. When you get back, we'll have a half-dozen kids just like you.

Be careful, Joe. Came back to us.

                                                              Libby

P.S. Saturday—just got back from the support group meeting. *Fourteen* days or more to get a letter? That's *forever*. Didn't you say you people handle communications? Can't you get your hands on a telephone and *call me?*

                                                        January 30

Dear Joe,
I had to pull myself away from the television before I lost whatever control I have left. The President made the announcement that we were at war about eight o'clock tonight, but it had already been on the news. Denise came over

as soon as she heard. She got the job of answering all of Justin's questions, because I just couldn't think. I couldn't do anything but watch the news reports.

Are you all right? Are you safe? I feel so helpless not knowing, not having heard from you in nearly two weeks. I'm so afraid for you.

I knew it would come to this, but I wasn't prepared. War is awful enough when I don't know anyone involved. But when it's my husband, my friends' husbands, people I've met . . .

Don't worry about me. I'm finding out I'm a lot stronger than I thought, and there are a lot of people I can depend on.

A bit of happier news: my parents called, and I finally got to tell them that they have a new son-in-law. My father was most impressed by the fact that you're in the Army. My mother cried because they'd missed our wedding, and she scolded me for not telling her at Christmas that our relationship was *that* serious, and she's distressed that you got shipped out before they even had a chance to meet you. She says that as soon as you get back, we'll have to get married again for the families. I don't need another marriage ceremony—nothing could make me feel more married to you than I already do—but if this second wedding comes with a honeymoon . . . An entire week, all alone, just you and me. Sounds like my idea of heaven.

Libby

2300 hrs.
01 February

Libby,

I got your letter dated 21 January, along with Justin's, today. It's good to finally hear from you. I'd still rather be home with you, but at least this is something.

I borrowed an instant camera from one of the other NCOs and took some pictures of our camp. There's one or two in there of me. Give one to Justin, will you?

The fighting has been spreading, but it's still a long way from where we are. The start of the war has been both encouraging and sobering. Everyone wanted *something* to happen—either an end to the aggression or the beginning of the war—so we can do what we came for and go home. Of course, we wish that something hadn't been war, but neither the E.A.R. nor their neighbors were willing to give an inch.

I got a letter from my mom today, too. She doesn't think you're an idiot, sweetheart. She thinks you love her son very much. And she and Dad are both pleased that I've finally given them the grandchild they've waited so long for. They're going to love Justin.

I have to check on one of my men, then get to bed. He just found out this evening that his wife gave birth a few days ago—their first kid—and he's not handling missing it very well. I don't blame him. I think it would kill me to miss the birth of *our* first child.

I love you, Libby.

                                                              Joe

                                                    February 5

Dear Joe,
Two letters from you! Justin and I were both so thrilled that we could hardly stand it. And thank you, sweetheart, for remembering to print his so he could read it by himself. He was so excited. He called your father and read it to him over the phone.

We packed a small care box for you and sent it off yesterday. Since we really enjoyed the pictures you sent, there's a camera and plenty of film in there, along with a few other items, including some homemade chocolate chip cookies. Reba and I baked them here, along with help from the three kids. The recipe was huge, and we doubled it so we could have plenty for you and Max and the kids, but we wound up eating so much of the dough and so many of the fresh cookies that you and Max are only getting about a dozen each. Next time we'll know better.

Judging from the fit of my clothes, I think those might have been my last chocolate chips for a while. I never knew I had a tendency to eat when under stress, but that must be what I'm doing. My perpetual five extra pounds seems to have turned into ten. If I don't stop, you won't recognize—or want—me when you get home.

If there's anything you need, let me know and I'll send it to you in the next package.

Oh, yes, the small picture was taken by Denise, who sends her best. That's Justin and me standing on the porch beside our new flag. Yes, I know it's a little crooked, but I'd never hung a flag before. And the other is Justin's spring school picture. If you look closely, you'll see one of your soldiers peeking from his pocket. He carried it just for that occasion, so that you'd see it.

A few of the wives from Company A got to talk to their husbands last week. Any chance for us?

I love you, Joe.

Libby

0600 hrs.
15 February

Sweetheart,
Happy Valentine's Day. I never thought I'd be spending my first Valentine's Day as your husband half a world away from my bride of four weeks. If I were home, I'd give you flowers and candy and all the loving you could take. Not want you? Impossible. I will *always* want you, Libby.

The air war seems to be going well. At least it's kept the ground combat to a minimum so far. We see the fighters off the carriers fly over here every day and always hear them through the night.

The troops' morale seems okay, too. The letters and packages from home help a lot. Thanks for the camera and the cookies and everything else. Keep sending me pictures of you two, okay? I'm decorating my tent with them.

Sorry this is short, but I have to get to work.

Love you.

February 26

Dear Joe,

I always disliked starting letters "Dear" whoever, but in this case, it's most appropriate. You are a very dear man, and I love you more than words can express.

I got some news yesterday, but I wasn't sure whether I should tell you yet. I don't want to give you any further cause to worry about us. Heaven knows, you have enough on your mind over there. But... I never was good at keeping secrets, and Justin's even worse than I am, so... here goes.

Remember that five pounds I mentioned a few weeks back? It's more like seven now, but it's not all the chocolate chip cookies. I'm pregnant, Joe. Can you believe that? *Pregnant!* I went to the OB-Gyn clinic on post last week and had an exam and lab work because my cycle was late. Foolish me—I never even suspected that I might be pregnant. I thought it was just stress that had my whole system out of whack. But they told me yesterday that I am definitely pregnant—about two months.

All the times we made love I never once thought about birth control—or the lack thereof. I'm thirty-two years old and supposedly intelligent, but it never even occurred to me. Maybe it was because I wanted another baby so much. Maybe it was because I loved you so much.

I know this isn't the best time, and I know you'd like to be here, but we'll make the best of it. The doctor said I'm as healthy as can be, although he did warn me to watch my weight. So what's new? And I'm so thrilled at the prospect of having another child—having *your* child.

I haven't told anyone yet but Justin. He's excited, too, and talking to your parents or mine without spilling the beans is almost more than he can bear. But I wanted you to know before the rest of the family.

Be happy, Joe, and stay safe.

Libby

2245 hrs.
28 March

Sweetheart,
I just got off the phone with you twenty minutes ago but wanted to write you a short note. Phone calls are a mixed blessing. Talking to you and hearing your voice for the first time in more than two months was great, but now that the call's over, I miss you and Justin more than ever. It sends my homesickness level right off the charts. Every night I pray that you and Justin and the baby are okay, and that this will end soon so I can come home to you.

The baby... I love saying that. There were so many times when I thought that no matter how much I wanted kids, I would never be lucky enough to have any. Now I have Justin and the baby on the way. You've given me everything I ever wanted, Libby.

Take care of both of them and especially yourself. I love you.

Joe

April 22

Dear Joe,
Remember how your parents kept inviting us to visit them in Kentucky, and I kept turning them down? As much as I wanted to meet them, I know this sounds silly, but I felt that I shouldn't leave North Augusta. This is where you left us, and I wanted us to stay here until you get back.

So *they* came *here*. I just opened the door last Tuesday evening, and there they stood. They stayed five days, and we had a wonderful time.

I would have known your father anywhere. He's a handsome man—you look just like him. They're special people—no wonder you turned out so perfect. They treated Justin exactly like my parents do. You'd never know from watching them together that he's not really their grandson.

And they're really happy about the baby, too. Neither of them said a word about the timing—although I did see your nother counting the weeks. I promised them that as soon as you get home, we'd all visit them in Kentucky. I'd like to see where we're going to live someday.

And then, only a few hours after they left, my mom and dad got home. I wasn't expecting them for another couple of weeks, but they'd decided they'd been on the road long enough. I wish they'd made it here in time to meet your folks. Maybe next time.

Oh, Joe, I'd been caught up so much in you and the war that I'd forgotten how much I'd missed Mom and Dad. It's been so good having them here. They had a wonderful time and have *boxes* of photographs and souvenirs from all the places they saw. Justin could hardly wait to see what they brought for *him*.

All my clothes have gotten snug—I'm going to have to start shopping for maternity clothes soon—but the doctor says everything's fine. I do wish you could be here. Soon I'll have Denise take a picture of me, and you can see what you're missing.

Watch out for yourself, First Sergeant. I want you home.

Libby

May 28

Dear Joe,

School is out this week, and Justin is literally bouncing off the walls. Mom and Dad are going to watch him during the day and give Mrs. Franklin a well-deserved rest. Dad's been talking about taking him up to visit your folks for a few days. He rather liked traveling—Mom was the one with the yearning to come home—and he'd like to see your family's farm. I told you, didn't I, that he grew up on a farm himself?

I had my five-month checkup this week and had to see a new doctor, because mine's been transferred to fill in for some doctor who got sent over there. The new guy's nice, but he doesn't inspire a lot of confidence. He's so *young*. I swear, he hasn't begun to shave yet. As usual, everything's fine—physically, at least. You know how being pregnant is

supposed to make you moody? Not me. My moods are fine
it's my hormones that are going nuts. I think about makin
love with you far more often than is proper for a married
pregnant lady. I fantasize about you during the day an
dream about you at night. I feel positively wicked some
times!

They told us at the wives' meeting over the weekend tha
you guys had moved. Now that the ground war is really hot
they said we probably won't be able to hear from you as of
ten. I guess that's why I haven't gotten any letters lately.

Please be careful, Joe. You've got three people countin
on you back here. I miss you. I love you.

                                                                                          Libby

                                                                                  July 1

I want you to come home, Joe. *Now.* I've tried to be stron
and cheerful and all the things I'm supposed to be, bu
damn it, enough is enough. I want you *here. This* is where
you belong. You're my husband, we've been married nearl
six months, I'm more than six months pregnant, and we've
spent *one night* together. That's just not acceptable.

Oh, Joe, I'm so sorry, but I don't think I can endure thi
anymore. I know you're the one who has it hard, living i
the desert with the heat and the insects, and with the war, the
missiles, the danger and everything else. I know I have n
right to be complaining when I'm living comfortably here i
North Augusta, but I can't take this any longer.

Is it so awful to want my husband here when I'm preg
nant? To know that you'll be with me when our baby i
born? To be able to count on you to take care of things whe
I'm tired and need to rest?

Is it so awful to want to go through my childbirth classe
when they start with you instead of Denise? (Yes, Denise.
My mother's too squeamish—when she gave birth, it wa
still customary to sedate the mother into unconscious
ness—and it would be too difficult for Reba because of the
twins.)

I'm sorry, Joe. Maybe I should tear this up and start again. But I don't think I will. I think you know me well enough to know how I really feel—and how I feel is quite simple. I *hate* this war. I hate the Africans for starting it, I hate the United States for getting into it, I hate the Army for sending you to fight it. I hate *everyone*... except you.

As you've probably guessed by now, I haven't had the greatest of days. It's been so hot and humid, and I feel as big as a whale, and I haven't had a letter from you in weeks. I went to the doctor this morning and waited more than an hour for a ten-minute exam. I don't know if they were testing my patience or my endurance, but whichever it was, they won.

Then I went to the commissary for groceries, bought lots of frozen and refrigerated foods, started home and had a flat at the bottom of the hill outside Gate One. I had to unload the groceries to get to the spare tire, and I was driving your car, and I couldn't get the lug bolts off. I must have made quite a picture, almost seven months pregnant, struggling with the stupid wrench and surrounded by melting, thawing and spoiling groceries in hundred-degree heat. Fortunately a young MP came along and changed the tire for me and loaded everything back into the car. He was sweet—he even pretended not to notice that I was crying. (Pay no attention to the tearstains on this letter. I thought I was all cried out, but apparently not. But I'm okay. Really, darling, I am.)

Please, Joe, come home. I don't want to sleep alone anymore. I don't want to communicate by letters anymore. I don't want to raise Justin by myself, and I certainly don't want to give birth without you.

Please, Joe. I'm so afraid without you.

I'm so lost without you.

                                                              Libby

                                                         1800 hrs.
                                                         08 August

Sweetheart,
If I've given you any reason to believe that you have to put

on a cheerful act for me, I'm sorry. If you have problems at home, believe me, I want to know about them. I don't know if I can do much to help, but at least give me the chance.

Libby, I would come home this instant if I could. I know you know that. If it had been up to me, I never would have left you. And I give you my word that if it's at all possible, I'll be there when the baby's born.

We're still in a relatively secure area. The only threat to us here are the missiles. It's impossible to get a full night's sleep, between the sirens, the jets and the explosions. Between the enemy's incoming missiles and our own antimissile missiles, it reminds me of a giant-scale, billion-dollar video game, like something Justin might have ... only this isn't a game, and the casualties are real. Charlie Company's been lucky. Our only injuries so far have been minor. Pray that it stays that way.

I know things haven't been easy for you, Libby. You never imagined getting married one day and undergoing an enforced separation the next, and you certainly never intended to be pregnant alone. You have every right to complain. This war has been tough for everyone—not just the people over here, but also for the families left behind. Just hold on, sweetheart. It won't last forever. One day the war will end, and I will come home, and I swear, I will never leave you again.

Joe

September 14

Dear Joe,
Justin has been back in school for several weeks, things are quieting down around here, and I do believe the temperature dropped a few degrees below ninety today. Fall is on its way.

Well, we're entering the homestretch. The baby-faced doctor says your son—or daughter—should make an appearance sometime around September 24th. Hmm ...

memories of Christmas past. What a precious gift you've given me. Have I remembered to tell you thanks?

I'm still working, but next Friday is my last day. It's been a long time since I could afford the luxury of staying home, and I'm looking forward to it. No more struggling into panty hose every morning or trying to find shoes that fit when my feet are swollen and also when they're not or wedging myself behind the steering wheel of the car. I haven't been able to drive the Mustang for quite some time now for just that reason. I think I'll lie on the sofa all day and wear nothing but nightgowns and fuzzy slippers and be incredibly lazy.

Justin brought something up last night that I want to discuss with you. We were discussing names for the baby—if it's a boy, do you have anything against Joseph, Jr.?—and he asked what last name the baby will have. It bothers him that you, the baby and I will all be Mathisons, while he's still a Harper.

Anyway, he asked if I thought there was any chance that you might want to adopt him, so he could be a Mathison, too. I told him that it was more complicated than that and that his father would have to agree, and he seemed to forget about it. But now that he's brought it up, I can't just forget it, Joe.

I honestly don't know if changing his name would be a good idea—it would mean cutting his last ties to his father's family, but what good is the name when that's *all* his father has given him? But on the matter of adoption... if anything happened to me, I'd want you to raise Justin, but as things stand now, Doug would gain custody. Of course, he would probably be willing to give him up, but if he wasn't... I don't think I could bear knowing that he was raising my son.

Think about it, will you? If you're interested, I really do think that, in order to get out of his child support payments, Doug would agree to it. When you get back, we'll discuss it, okay?

I'd better close and get to bed. I wish you were here to rub my back...but considering the way I look, maybe it's a good thing that you're not. As much as I miss sleeping beside you, we couldn't even snuggle very well now. I doubt you could even get your arms around me!

Happy eighth-month anniversary. Here's looking forward to many, many more.

I love you.

                                                                Libby

                                                   1037 hrs.
                                                   25 September

Libby,

When my plane landed at Bush Field an hour ago, I was so anxious to see you that I hurt inside. And when I came through the gate and found only Justin and Denise—how can I say *only* Justin about the person I love second best in the entire world?—my heart almost stopped. Before I even finished hugging him, he told me that he and Denise had dropped you off here at the hospital so you could get his baby brother or sister. Denise said that you'd been in labor practically all night. We didn't even bother to get my duffel but came straight here. Denise and Justin have gone back to the airport to pick it up for me.

I expected to come into this room and find you—I don't know, doing whatever women do when they're in labor. Suffering. Enduring. But instead here you are asleep, looking so utterly beautiful and precious and lovely. I knew all along that you were exaggerating in your letters, but now I can see just how much. Your body is beautiful, Libby. As soon as the nurse left us alone, as soon as I'd kissed you, I pulled the blankets down so I could look at you. I touched your stomach, and I felt our baby move. I'd never felt that before, you know? Of course you've been experiencing it for months now, so it's nothing new, but for me it was...awesome. Wondrous. You and I created this tiny person, this entire other life, and I felt him *move*.

My leave is only for fourteen days, and the colonel, the captain and I had to pull a lot of strings to get even that. I wish I didn't have to go back. I wish I could stay with you forever. But at least I can help you bring this little guy into the world. At least I can share the first two weeks of his life.

And I *will* be back, Libby. The war's winding down. There's not a man alive in East Africa who doesn't know by now that the allies are the best equipped, best trained, best motivated fighting forces in the world. It's just a matter of time before a cease-fire is declared, and then we'll be home. For good. Forever.

I thought when I started this letter that I could let you sleep, that I could sit here quietly, and look at you and touch you and not disturb you, but I'm not that strong, sweetheart. It's been eight months since I've seen you. Eight months since I've kissed you—*really* kissed you. Eight months since I've held you. I'm going to close now and wake you. I'm going to hold you. I'm going to love you.

My life, my love, my Libby.

Joe

26 September

Company C
65th Signal Battalion
15th Signal Brigade
Eastern African Republic
Charlie Company:

It's a girl. Born at 1307 on 25 September. Nine pounds, eight ounces and as pretty as her mother. Daughter fine, mother perfect, father ecstatic.

Take care of yourselves until I get back. See you in two weeks.

1SG J. Mathison

* * * * *

From the popular author of the bestselling title
DUNCAN'S BRIDE (Intimate Moments #349)
comes the

LINDA HOWARD

COLLECTION

Two exquisite collector's editions that contain four of
Linda Howard's early passionate love stories. To add
these special volumes to your own library, be sure
to look for:

VOLUME ONE: *Midnight Rainbow*
Diamond Bay
(Available in March)

VOLUME TWO: *Heartbreaker*
White Lies
(Available in April)

 Silhouette Books®

SLH92

OFFICIAL RULES • MILLION DOLLAR ZODIAC SWEEPSTAKES
NO PURCHASE OR OBLIGATION NECESSARY TO ENTER

To enter, follow the directions published. If the Personal Zodiac Chart is missing, hand-print your name and address on a 3″ ×5″ card and mail to: Silhouette Zodiac, 3010 Walden Ave., P.O. Box 1867, Buffalo, NY 14269-1867, and we will assign your Sweepstakes numbers (Limit: one entry per envelope). For eligibility, entries must be received no later than March 31, 1994 and be sent via 1st-class mail. No liability is assumed for printing errors or lost, late or misdirected entries.

To determine winners, the sweepstakes numbers on submitted entries will be compared against a list of randomly, pre-selected prizewinning numbers. In the event all prizes are not claimed via the return of prizewinning numbers, random drawings will be held from among all other entries received to award unclaimed prizes.

Prizewinners will be determined no later than May 30, 1994. Selection of winning numbers and random drawings are under the supervision of D.L. Blair, Inc., an independent judging organization whose decisions are final. One prize to a family or organization. No substitution will be made for any prize, except as offered. Taxes and duties on all prizes are the sole responsibility of winners. Winners will be notified by mail. Chances of winning are determined by the number of entries distributed and received.

Sweepstakes open to persons 18 years of age or older, except employees and immediate family members of Torstar Corporation, D.L. Blair, Inc., their affiliates, subsidiaries and all other agencies, entities and persons connected with the use, marketing or conduct of this sweepstakes. All applicable laws and regulations apply. Sweepstakes offer void wherever prohibited by law. Any litigation within the province of Quebec respecting the conduct and awarding of a prize in this sweepstakes must be submitted to the Régies des Loteries et Courses du Quebec. In order to win a prize, residents of Canada will be required to correctly answer a time-limited arithmetical skill-testing question. Values of all prizes are in U.S. currency.

Winners of major prizes will be obligated to sign and return an affidavit of eligibility and release of liability within 30 days of notification. In the event of non-compliance within this time period, prize may be awarded to an alternate winner. Any prize or prize notification returned as undeliverable will result in the awarding of the prize to an alternate winner. By acceptance of their prize, winners consent to use of their names, photographs or other likenesses for purposes of advertising, trade and promotion on behalf of Torstar Corporation without further compensation, unless prohibited by law.

This sweepstakes is presented by Torstar Corporation, its subsidiaries and affiliates in conjunction with book, merchandise and/or product offerings. Prizes are as follows: Grand Prize—$1,000,000 (payable at $33,333.33 a year for 30 years). First through Sixth Prizes may be presented in different creative executions, each with the following approximate values: First Prize—$35,000; Second Prize—$10,000; 2 Third Prizes—$5,000 each; 5 Fourth Prizes—$1,000 each; 10 Fifth Prizes—$250 each; 1,000 Sixth Prizes—$100 each. Prizewinners will have the opportunity of selecting any prize offered for that level. A travel-prize option if offered and selected by winner, must be completed within 12 months of selection and is subject to hotel and flight accommodations availability. Torstar Corporation may present this sweepstakes utilizing names other than Million Dollar Sweepstakes. For a current list of all prize options offered within prize levels and all names the sweepstakes may utilize, send a self-addressed stamped envelope (WA residents need not affix return postage) to: Million Dollar Sweepstakes Prize Options/Names, P.O. Box 7410, Blair, NE 68009.

For a list of prizewinners (available after July 31, 1994) send a separate, stamped self-addressed envelope to: Million Dollar Sweepstakes Winners, P.O. Box 4728, Blair, NE 68009.

ZDS492

NORA ROBERTS

Love has a language all its own, and for centuries, flowers have symbolized love's finest expression. Discover the language of flowers—and love—in this romantic collection of 48 favorite books by bestselling author Nora Roberts.

Starting in February, two titles will be available each month at your favorite retail outlet.

In March, look for:

Irish Rose, **Volume #3**
Storm Warning, **Volume #4**

In April, look for:

First Impressions, **Volume #5**
Reflections, **Volume #6**

Collect all 48 titles and become fluent in

THE LANGUAGE of LOVE

LOL392